Appointment with a Smile

I0664868

SCARLET CLOVER PUBLISHING, L.L.C.

This book is a publication of Scarlet Clover Publishers, L.L.C.

Red Clover comes in three varieties: Scarlet - the most intense, crimson and pink.

Fields of Scarlet Clover are not bashful!

Dedicated to all those who smile, and especially to those who make me smile: my family and friends. And in the memory of Jay Conti.

ALSO WRITTEN BY KIERAN YORK:

COMING SOON FROM KIERAN YORK:

Appointment with a Smile

A SCARLET CLOVER PUBLISHING BOOK

By

Kieran York

This is a work of fiction. All characters, locales and events are either products of the author's imagination or are used fictitiously.

APPOINTMENT WITH A SMILE

Copyright © 2012 by Kieran York
First Edition: Published March 2012
Second Edition: Published January, 2015

This is a work of fiction. All characters, locales and events are either products of the author's imagination or are used fictitiously.

Cover design by Ann Phillips
Second Edition Formatting by Karen D. Badger

Published by Scarlet Clover Publishers, L.L.C.
www.kieranyork.com
P.O Box 621002
Littleton, Colorado 80162

And www.scarletcloverpublishers.com

ISBN-13: 978-0692285411
ISBN-10: 0692285415

Printed in the United States of America and in the United Kingdom

Acknowledgements

First Edition: I want to thank the extraordinary women at Blue Feather Books for publishing *Appointment with a Smile*. Publisher Em Reed, Jane Vollbrecht, Editor Chris Paynter, Line Editor Nann Dunne, and Artist Ann Phillips. They became friends, and we were family, and I'll remember with love and gratitude – each one.

I am profoundly appreciative for Blue Feather Books. It took courage to publish a book by, about, and for the Sapphic golden woman. A romance! That romance, by a relatively unknown author became a 2013 Lambda Literary Society Award Finalist in the romance category. I'm also appreciative for the chance they gave the controversial *Careful Flowers*. Many publishers would have rejected it. They didn't. Thank you, Blue Feather Women!

Second Edition: I want to thank the extraordinary women working to make Scarlet Clover Publishers happen. Beth Mitchum – mentor, artistic and technical director, and friend. Karen D. Badger worked her magic to reinstate *Appointment with a Smile* and *Careful Flowers* into print, and onto e-book. I thank my friend Karen, for riding to my rescue. A shout out to my favorite radio host, Shawn Marie Bryan – I thank her for building my website www.scarletcolverpublishers.com. Words can never express my gratitude that these women are all part of my life.

I am so very blessed with the friendships that publishing made possible. We are book-loving women!

I thank all of my friends, and my family. Their encouragement makes it worth the doing.

And I thank the Scarlet Clover CEO and Centerfold, Clover York. Keep on barking, my schnauzer friend.

Chapter 1

Sometime in the center of autumn, a lilting laugh from the past rose from a side street.

I saw her smile. She was watching two street entertainers with their band of marionettes. The puppets appeared to be zoo characters, wildly lurching. As was my heart.

Nearly thirty years had passed since she'd missed our appointment. Now we were an ocean and half a continent away from where we were to have met back then. Three decades ago I was in Denver, Colorado, standing in front of a ticket counter awaiting her arrival. She'd called and told me she'd return to me and to our home. That was not to be.

It appeared the thirty intermittent years had treated her with kindness. She remained lovely. Her face was fuller and gently formed with creased laugh lines. Her eyes were still bright and tender. I wondered how similar she was now to back then. When we approach thirty, the future seems so unclear.

Was that because we never connected those true dots of tomorrow, thinking we wouldn't live such a very long time? I'll be sixty in December, and she turned sixty last month. I remembered her birth date. I remembered everything about her from the eight years we spent together.

Not knowing if I should speak or if she would recognize me, I lingered a moment. I slid my sunglasses back over my eyes to filter the rare brightness of London's October sun. As she moved toward the central street market, my heart began beating rapidly. I felt flushed, and my hands were sweating.

She seemed to be alone. Carrying one shopping bag, she moved gingerly, yet with all the grace she possessed years ago. So many years, I mused. I swallowed the lump in my throat. No, she was always with me.

Muted street sounds, smells, motions surrounded me, but all I could see was her beautifully matured face with piercing bronze eyes and lovely olive complexion, surrounded by dark hair streaked with silver highlights. Her hair, shorter than it was when we were together, fell against her neck. She'd swept it back, as she often had when she finished a shower.

She looked comfortable in her clothing. The confident style remained. Tan slacks and a blouse with tan, blue, and coral embellishment. I only saw splashes of color. Matching stylish dress sandals, sans socks, and a huge handbag looked expensive. Her medium-tall frame still reflected a casual carriage. As always, she carried herself with a proud air.

As if watching a motion picture play out, my gaze followed her. She picked up a book in front of a bookstall and flipped pages. I paid little attention to the book; instead, I focused on her face. Amused for a moment, she slid the book back into its proper place. Suddenly, her hand reached up to her face, and her eyes clamped shut for several moments. When they opened, they reflected enormous pain.

My chest thumped as if I'd experienced the same pain. I wanted to take her in my arms and comfort her, but that would not only be inappropriate, it would be embarrassing.

Those eight years we shared with one another taught me her signals. Within a minute, I knew she would again be smiling. And she was. From the opposite side of the street, I followed her. She stopped in front of a knickknack stall and glanced at her watch. Lifting a miniature blue and white teacup and saucer, she allowed a smile, too true to be fraudulent.

She was rarely bogus about anything or anyone. But on certain occasions she told someone they looked nice, when they were a wreck. She praised my aunt's hair color and my grandfather's lemon-gin drink. And for years, I believed that she loved me.

Perhaps in her way she had loved me, but I was doubtful.

Thirty years ago, when she didn't arrive at the Denver airport, I was heartsick. Standing alone, more alone than I had ever been, perusing the Jetway, whirling around to examine the terminal, I gasped for air.

I waited three hours at the airport with an inconsolable longing for her. With tears in my eyes that eventually rolled down my cheeks, I drove to the rented townhouse we had shared. I entered and saw her belongings that she'd left behind. I was living my worst moment because I believed I would never see her again.

Now, as I walked toward her, she turned. With a look of amazement, she said, "Danielle, is it really you?"

"Yes. When I first saw you, I wasn't certain you'd recognize me."

"Of course, I'd always recognize you. You look wonderful."

"You, too, Molly. You haven't changed."

She laughed. "Still flattering?"

"No, I mean it." After a slight hesitation, I asked, "What are you doing in London?"

"I'm visiting London with my daughter, Samantha, and her family."

I stalled momentarily. "You're married?"

"No. My partner's child, actually. You remember Pamela?"

How could I forget her, I wanted to say. "Pamela Meade. I didn't realize she had a child."

"That was one of the many things I should have mentioned and didn't. Her little girl was five when we got together."

"I guess that would make her thirty-five." I tried to keep venom out of my voice.

"And you? What are you doing in England? I remember you saying that you'd never leave Colorado."

"I haven't. I still live there. I bought my home out in the suburbs of Littleton a few months after you left. Foothills, Jefferson County. After my grandparents' estate was settled, I had enough for a small down payment." Wanting to extricate myself from her possible pity, I added, "The townhouse's rent went up, so I decided to leave the place we shared."

"You always wanted to live in those glorious Rocky Mountain foothills."

"Yes, although where I live now has grown enormously. Are you still teaching?"

"Retired now. Made it to a professorship a few years after I left Colorado. Are you still painting?" she asked.

"I am. I'm exhibiting here now, in fact."

"I suppose I should have Googled you. But…"

"I know. There would have been no reason for you to look me up."

"I would have liked to know that you'd succeeded with your art career."

"It's a very minor showing," I said. "I wish I could tell you that I'm renowned." I smiled at her, as always a little self-conscious about my slightly crooked teeth. "Do you have time for a cupper, as they say here?"

"I wish I did, but Samantha made plans. Maybe later in the week?"

"I'm staying at the Marshall Hotel."

"I'll phone," she said. "I'll look up the number in the book."

I was about to give her my cell phone number, but she turned away from me and moved toward an arriving cab. I stood alone again. My best bet was that I'd never hear from her. And that meant I'd never again see Molly's smile.

Chapter 2

"Skies are pissing rain. Might keep the attendance down," Fiona Revere said.

About thirty people milled around the deluxe, upscale art gallery.

"I almost wished they'd all go home so I could return to the hotel and rest," I said to her, my devoted agent of twenty years.

"You worked hard all day getting this exhibit ready for tonight's opening. Maybe you overdid it." Fiona's cadence with a slight accent was the same as one might hear from an Eastern Ivy League college woman. She had exaggerated airs. With her bright kiwi-green eyes, her thick cosmetically enhanced lips, and stylish strawberry blonde hair, she might have been going to a very elite cocktail party. She'd arched her thin eyebrows with the precision of a painter. Framed, those glowing eyes always hinted at a secret that she promised yet would never give up.

She'd had her slightly aquiline nose fixed once. Although she playfully denied it, she'd also had work done on her eyes and around her lips. She often joked she'd not look her fifty-five years, no matter what it cost. She'd selected a brightly splashed sheath dress of oranges, bronzes, and lime-greens. Her trim figure stood five-feet-eight inches, and she walked with an elegant, sensual gait: quick, yet smoke-like. Perhaps I used that description because she allowed the smoke from her cigarette to float behind her.

"I didn't sleep well last night. It was more like I didn't sleep at all. Maybe a couple of hours." Seeing Molly had troubled me. "I think I'm running on adrenaline."

"Shows are stressful. Last month one of my artists had a Cincinnati showing and very nearly went to the dirt hotel. Stroke. My first thought was that he was allergic to Cincinnati. Understandable."

"You haven't booked me for Cincinnati yet, have you?"

"Naw," she said. "I'm saving that horror show for when you're anesthetized. Or pissed off at me. But at least you're smiling."

"The coffee I had earlier might be helping. And it wasn't stress over the show."

She nudged me. "The couple looking at *Magic Guardians* seems interested. I'll check." She moved a step away and then turned. "You might join me in a moment or two and tell them it's your favorite work."

Fiona's quick grin and wink were part of the reason I had been in her stable of artists for so long. She got me. She understood my inability to promote myself. She attempted to prod me toward marketing my work, but I resisted. The painting wasn't my favorite, or it wouldn't be for sale. My favorite painting was, and perhaps always would be, *Twilight with Molly*.

Fiona and I were polar opposites. Although we were about the same height, the similarity of our looks ended there. Her coiffure was neatly sleek and trimmed to perfection, and my own short, graying blonde hair curled around my face. My eyes were hazel-colored; my lips were thin, just as my light-complexioned face was thin; all making me ordinary looking. Fiona wore designer clothes, while my clothing was whatever I found, wherever I located different come-together looks. She wore heavy, expensive perfume. I smelled only of soap. Her nails were long and perfectly manicured. Their color changed with her outfits. My nails were trimmed short enough for a nailbrush to keep the paint cleaned out from under them.

Also, Fiona was accustomed to extravagant, luxury living in New York. I lived in the center of America in less than opulent surroundings. With the help of surgeons, she looked younger than her age. I was a couple of months short of sixty and had allowed the aging process to have its way with me. She scratched her way up to fortune from the mean streets of New York City. I'd only painted and hadn't come far at all. She was completely straight and chased mainly younger men. I was Sapphic and chased no one in particular.

We did have a few similarities. We both could be arrogant. She was the best artist's agent on the continent where I lived and the one I was currently visiting with my exhibit. While I'd only had minimal success in the art world, I felt as though I was one of the best contemporary portraitists. Critics had called me a modern American realist. Although some of my subjects were not paintings of people, most were.

The exhibit gallery had started to fill. That would please Fiona. I hoped it would be enough for her so that I wouldn't have to flit around making small talk with prospective buyers. She knew my philosophy: I'd gone through the agony and ecstasy to paint each canvas. Why was I also obliged to sell them?

She also knew the worst thing I could hear from a potential purchaser was how much I expected my work to appreciate. Appreciating monetary gains had never been high on my list of concerns. I hated discussing money. And secondly, I despised it when someone announced they'd purchased my work because it matched their décor. A time or two, for that very reason, I'd refused to sell my work.

Fiona pointed at her diamond-studded watch. She once stated in total sincerity that I'd helped pay for it. Although we'd laughed, I didn't doubt for an instant that a percentage of at least one of my paintings had picked up a portion of the tab.

She led me to the small back office, lit up a cigarette, and blew smoke out of the side of her mouth.

"Nearly ten o'clock. I'm sure *Magic Guardian* is sold," she whispered as though it were confidential. "Three others went early. And *Myths and Memories* just sold. It has been a very good night. Very promising, as well. Oh, and I sold two by e-mailing photos to a buyer in Ireland. Who knew the Irish are big Danielle O'Hara enthusiasts?"

"Think it might be my last name?"

She answered with amusement in her voice, "I wouldn't be surprised. At any rate, seven sales make it a very lucrative night. Keep circulating. I'll finalize *Magic Guardian*." She motioned toward the door. "Let's go shift some paintings."

I smiled briefly. "You can keep the cheese; just let me out of the trap."

"Come on, you sweet Saph, work your crowd magic. Let's strike while the fire seems to be heating up. After all these years you've been painting, you ought to know that art is a very shy blood sport."

"I think this *Saph* would just like to remain unknown."

From the corner of my eye, I saw Max Parker approaching. "Going damned fine," the gallery owner reported. He made a swipe at his thick black hair. He was well-groomed and dapperly dressed. Shorter than I, he stood as erect and tall as he could. He was equally as arrogant as Fiona—perhaps a bit more so than I. "Some of them haven't heard of you and are falling in love with you."

Fiona glibly agreed. "Yes. Max, I've told you for years that you really need to explore Danielle O'Hara's work."

"I thought you were hiding her from me." He appeared delighted when he turned to me. "This has been a wonderful exhibit. I want to represent you exclusively in Europe."

"Everyone will soon want that," Fiona said in a teasing way. "Your public awaits, Danielle." She looped her arm around my waist. "Go on out there and show yourself."

The gallery representatives were attempting to finalize acquisitions. The time to close the doors had nearly arrived. Certainly gallery employees wanted to go home. Exhausted, I was more than eager to return to the hotel.

"I just purchased *Myths and Memories*," a voice behind me said.

Turning, I saw a woman who looked to be in her thirties. She was a few inches over five-feet tall and slightly stocky, yet in an athletic way. Stylish, long, raven black hair pulled back to frame her round face. Rosy cheeks complemented her soft brown eyes.

"It's one of my favorites," I said. I could have easily cleared a polygraph test. The portrait was of Molly.

"I hate to bother you, but I was curious about what you were thinking when you painted it." Her face was expressive with a trustful beauty about it.

"You're not bothering me. I painted it last year around my birthday. I was slightly depressed over the thought that my next birthday, my sixtieth, would be one of those bookmark years. I painted a recollection of a woman important in my past."

"Someone in your past?"

"Yes, thirty-plus years ago. Someone extraordinarily special in my life. Perhaps when a person ages, memories are allowed to become myths. Or perhaps the myths magically become memories."

"Interesting concept," she said softly. "Memories can be very painful. I can't imagine attempting to capture the emotion on canvas."

My joy dwindled. "I can't imagine not capturing my remembrances of emotions on canvas. I sometimes wonder if it isn't a way of reliving them—soothing the raw ends of those embattled nerves that time produces when unresolved."

She studied me intently. "You're called a contemporary realist. Agree with that description?"

"Pretty much, I do. Although I experiment, I always find realism more to my liking."

"I see something unique in your work. Is there any singular aspect with which you approach a painting?"

Her pointed questions caught me off guard, but I felt compelled to answer. "I believe our sensory skills need to be inclusive within a work. Just to give an example. On a hot day, if you fan your face, each sensor within each portion of your skin feels the breeze. It's the same with sight. When you first see a canvas in its entirety, you should be able to sense each part of it. It should be that alive for you, the viewer. I also never want to paint a stale work of art. I want it to be fresh for me so it will never be trite for you."

"You very much do just that. I read your bio. You haven't done much self-promoting in the past. But your genius for showing your subject's soul is amazing."

"Genius is a very large word. Admittedly, I haven't attempted to promote my work as much as I should have or as much as my agent would have preferred."

"I can tell from the subjects in your paintings that it's a labor of love," she said. "What other artists have inspired your work?"

"So many. The artist inspiring me most is Cecilia Beaux. She was an American society portraitist. Not so well known, but I believe her to be one of the finest."

"What are you working on now?"

"Just doing some sketching. I'll later convert a few of them to oil, and I'll shove some in a huge trunk. I call it my scribble dumpster."

"What are the themes of your latest sketches?" she asked.

"You conduct a very in-depth interview," I said lightly. "I never know what I'll be interested in capturing. It could be an emotional moment, something from my past, a street scene that reminds me of something. Last night I made sketches of a street market. A place where I spent a portion of yesterday afternoon."

"London is an interesting city."

"Do you live here?"

"I'm in London with my husband and mother. We spend vacation time each year in England. Some of my husband's family lives here. And I love England."

Fiona materialized by my side. She was now slightly infused with wine, as was her custom at showings. "I see you've met Mrs. Wesley. She purchased *Myths and Memories*. She was asking questions about it. I pointed her in your direction."

With a self-conscious smile, I said, "Mine's a simple secret. I attempt to paint who people are, rather than just what they look like."

"Ms. O'Hara was kind enough to give me some insight about the painting," Mrs. Wesley told Fiona. "It looks as if it's closing time. Thank you for your commentary on the painting."

"Thank you for your interest," I said. "I hope you'll enjoy *Myths and Memories*."

"I purchased it as gift for my mother."

"If it isn't to her taste, I'll be happy to have it exchanged for any of my other work. Your mother might not like this portrait."

"I rather think she will. She might have been the model."

A sudden and very icy chill darted through my body. I found my voice. "Are you Samantha?"

Chapter 3

When the show closed for the evening, Samantha Meade Wesley and I walked to a small, all-night coffee shop called Crumpets and Brew that I had passed yesterday. Although the rain had ceased, remnants of a misty fog lingered.

The smells of various roasts wafted up as we opened the door. Walls were forest green with a mahogany coffee bar. Small round tables, placed systematically in a rectangular space, completed the décor. Their gold-flecked plastic tops flickered as light hit them.

The menu offered sandwiches and a wide array of pastries. I was certain the cinnamon buns, drenched in frosting, could cause a sugar coma in three bites.

The bleakness from outside had followed us, but our conversation was pleasant.

"Thank you for agreeing to talk with me," she said nearly timidly as we sat at a table. "And for answering my questions."

I frowned. "And I have questions for you. Did Molly know you were attending my exhibit?"

"No, I didn't tell her. In my defense, I wasn't certain I would go. I walked by the gallery several times before I summoned the courage to enter. Through the window, I saw the painting and knew immediately it was she. I had to purchase it."

"She had told you about me?"

"Yes. Mostly my biological mother, Pamela, mentioned you over the years."

"I've never met your mother. I spoke with her on the telephone only once. As you might imagine, the conversation was very brief."

"I gathered the two of you never met. I look very much like Pamela. Or so I'm told."

"And did she mention the circumstances…"

"Oh, yes. Your name came up quite a few times when she and my true mother, Molly, fought. At least when I was a child. Later they fought in, or maybe with, silence."

"They must have cared. They've been together for thirty years."

"Pamela died ten years ago. They were together a little over twenty years. I thought, romantically speaking, it had been a nineteen-year sleepwalk. It seemed meaningless. Even as a child, and later a young adult, I felt their lack of love. It wasn't how my husband and I feel toward one another."

"I'm sorry. Love rarely comes with a warning label. We sometimes make mistakes when selecting. I have."

Samantha sighed and nodded with compassion as if she knew I was still in pain. "Everyone has their own marathon, I suppose. We stand, we run, we fall."

"A very astute observation."

"Both Mother and Pamela were philosophy professors and exposed me to constant wisdom. As far as marriage was concerned, I was prepared for imperfection. It amazes me that I married a man with so few imperfections."

"Pamela..." I had to stop as I practically spat out her name. "Pamela was once an enemy. I harbored a hatred against her."

"In truth... she wasn't easy to live with," Samantha said. "But my life hasn't been entirely sad, thanks to Jeffery, my husband, and my mother Molly." She exuded a mellow harmony, and her face reflected an arbitrator's introspection.

"Molly told you about our meeting yesterday? She didn't have time for a chat."

"She was extremely shaken. It took her until late last night to tell me about seeing you. And yes, Mom was to meet up with Jeffery and me. Jeffery and I looked on the Internet gallery to view your work. He's also impressed. Being somewhat of an art connoisseur, he believes that a painting should become the mind's home. And the longer one stays in that home, the better the work of art. He observed your cyber gallery."

I smiled. "I like his belief a great deal. When I do a portrait, it's as if I want to introduce the person to the viewer. When I'm painting, if I'm unable to catch glimpses of my subject's emotion, it's similar to painting only a halftone."

"I see that in your work. I'm very impressed."

"Yet you came to my opening, and Molly didn't." I was curious but also wounded. Molly hadn't called the hotel, nor had she taken the time to find me at the gallery. Even for old time's sake. Her daughter had taken the trouble.

Finding out Pamela Meade died ten years ago confirmed that Molly was no longer thinking of me. She hadn't attempted to contact me. She hadn't merely run to Pamela all those years ago. She'd run away from me.

"Forgive me, but this is a shock." I blinked back the tears that were welling in my eyes. "I feel a bit overwhelmed. Maybe I've put in too many hours uncrating and hanging my exhibit. I like hands-on when it comes to placement. Guess that makes me a temperamental artist."

"Your work is absolutely wonderful. I'm so glad I got to see it and to meet you."

I drank the last of my coffee and stood. "I've enjoyed meeting you as well. It's been a hectic couple of days, and it's getting late. I should go."

She rose and embraced me. "Danielle, would you like my telephone number? I'm sure Mom would enjoy hearing from you."

Returning her hug, I replied, "I'm not certain. As much as I wish to see her, I don't believe she's interested, and I'll accept that."

Choosing not to take a cab, I walked the few blocks back to my hotel. Fresh air, I believed, cures a foggy brain. At this point, my brain seemed nearly soggy, as well.

I passed by the gallery on my way to the hotel and saw Fiona and her assistant, Spencer Murphy, inside talking with Max. I rapped on the glass.

Max opened the door and gestured me inside. "The star of our show," he gushed. "Have you come for your share of the takings?"

We laughed. "I think I can wait until tomorrow."

Fiona pulled a chair toward me as I entered the office. "Glad you stopped by. We sold two more paintings since you left."

"I was concerned that we might not even sell one in total."

Spencer sniggered. "I figured at least three. They are extraordinary." His boyish looks made him seem younger than his mid-twenties. Yet he had somehow become Fiona's go-to assistant. He worked diligently on the many details in running one of the most successful agencies in the art world. He traveled with Fiona, kept her notes, and in general, kept her somewhat sober. Although romantically she liked younger men, he was not her lover. I strongly suspected he was gay.

"Spencer," I said, "we were both wrong. I may be a hit after all."

Fiona gave me a hug. I could tell she was somewhat inebriated. "The fools are coming to their senses. Now the collectors are like old lions with a piece of meat." She cackled as she took another huge gulp of wine. "Want a sip? You haven't done much celebrating, and it's time you did. Past time."

"Thanks, but I'd rather just go back to my hotel to sleep." I stood, made my way to the door, and turned to see them toasting a night of success. For me, this was more than another great night—it was monumental. It marked the first night Fiona had sold so many of my paintings.

I was grateful for the triumphant evening in many ways. I also felt enriched that I'd met someone who'd played such an important part in Molly's life. Although not biologically connected to Molly, Samantha had assimilated Molly's kind and tender ways.

As to the future, I had but one guess. Molly wasn't interested in meeting with me again, and I had to accept it finally. Or at least attempt to accept it.

Chapter 4

I waited for my best friend of forty-plus years, Esther Lilly, to arrive from Colorado. When I called her yesterday, she recognized that my seeing Molly again had upset me and said she'd join me in London today at noon. We were meeting for lunch. I suggested Clouds, a small, exclusive, as well as expensive, café with an outdoor area located near the hotel. I asked the hostess to seat us outside under one of the parasol-style umbrellas.

As I sipped wine, my thoughts drifted back to leaving my home a couple of days before. I missed both my residence and Clover, my sweet little seven-year-old schnauzer. With light-silver, nearly platinum-colored, hair, she had lovely eyes with heavy, long lashes. A local art student, Roxie Tate, was watching my home and Clover. Clover and I adored Roxie. She e-mailed me the happenings of each day and did so with a great deal of style and zest. Each morning, and most evenings, I checked for her messages on my compact notebook. She referred to Clover as "Lashes," and hadn't told me how she referred to me. Roxie would also be taking care of Esther's dogs.

Esther and I became fast friends in college and remained best friends over the years. She had recently retired from her career as an astrobiology professor. She once told me that one teaspoon of a neutron star weighed one-hundred-million tons. Esther was the queen of minutia.

Just slightly over five feet, Esther was a force. Her curly, shoulder-length, blonde-grey hair surrounded an angular face. Piercing blue eyes gleamed as if she was constantly scrutinizing.

I'd just been seated and had ordered one of our favorite wines for each of us. I was sipping mine as she arrived and slowly approached. I gave her a wave to get her attention.

"And?" she said. She dropped her shoulder bag luggage next to her chair and pitched her oversized traveler's handbag on the table. "Has Molly called your hotel yet?"

"No. But her daughter, Samantha, showed up at my opening."

"Let me get this straight. Samantha attends, Molly is missing in action, and no call?"

"It's a very strange situation, Esther. Surreal. My brain has been in a blender all morning. I can't figure it out. Samantha not only attends but purchases *Myths and Memories.* Tells me it's a gift for her mother. Then she alludes to the fact that the woman in the painting might very well be Molly. She knew damned well it was."

Esther gave a low whistle. "*Myths* is one of your priciest works."

"She put thirty grand on her charge card as if it were thirty bucks. Then when we had coffee together, she tells me her biological mother, Pamela, died ten years ago. Suddenly, it occurs to me that the woman I was in love with—"

"Are in love with," Esther said. "And don't bother denying it. I know you too well. When you saw Molly, it all came rushing back to you. She's always been close to your heart."

"Of course I was excited to see her, but it seems I've not remained close to *her* heart. What's puzzling me is she says she'll call and doesn't. That was a clue to her not giving a flip about me. Add to that, if she were interested, she could have contacted me ten years ago after Pamela's demise."

"Danielle, all these years you've pined for her. You'll be upset more if you don't make an attempt to contact her. Resolve it."

"I've carried on with my life."

"No, you haven't. You've done some sporadic dating. You've never fallen in love or even come near to falling in love. And your encounter with Molly has stirred the dreams that you've held inside. Call her."

"Even if I wanted to, I don't have her phone number."

"You said Samantha charged the painting. Maybe there's a record."

"They don't give information out on a charge card."

"So unless she contacts you by calling the hotel or the gallery, you have no way of contacting her?"

"No. Her daughter offered me her number, and I declined."

Esther threw her hands up in the air. "Danielle, you are hopeless."

"If she'd wanted to contact me, she would have. I refuse to chase her." I swirled my glass of pinot Chardonnay and took a reverential sip. "Fiona wanted me to stay around this week. You know, drop in the gallery a few times. But if I want, I can go back to Denver anytime."

"I didn't just fly over the pond so I can leave before this jetlag finishes kicking me in the rear. Let's rent a car and drive up to Scotland for a couple days. Maybe Ireland."

"Fiona said someone in Ireland purchased two of my paintings. She isn't certain who it was. It's very strange. Everything's seemed strange since I arrived."

"Can't you hear the pain in your voice? It's especially obvious when you're attempting to change the subject by talking about Ireland and someone else purchasing your paintings. You're miserable."

"I don't need to hear the pain. I feel it, see it, and taste it. All I want to do is barricade myself in a cave and paint. If only she would've called to catch up. We spent eight years waking in one another's arms. A quick call. Anything. It's as if she ran away again as quickly as she could."

"Maybe she'll relent. Maybe she's been busy with Samantha. Maybe she feels badly about dumping you thirty years ago. Maybe she couldn't face you because she's too ashamed. But you can't run off, in case she gets it together and calls."

I stared at Esther in disbelief. "Why are you so enthusiastic about my seeing Molly? You don't even like her."

"I don't like what she did to you. There's a difference. But that was thirty years ago, and you haven't moved on. Let's have a great lunch, walk, see the gallery, and then go back to the hotel. You need to paint, and I need to nap."

The waiter arrived and we ordered divinely intricate salads and fancy burgers. Along with another glass of wine—we agreed we needed it.

"It was a long trip," Esther said. "I should have had him bring an entire bottle. Or, better yet, a damned case. I have a feeling you're not in the same frame of realism as I am."

"As a realistic painter, I'm trained to search details. My brain feels rotted out by searching."

"Molly has always exacted that reaction in you." She took a sip of wine. "Seeing her again might release you from the pain."

"I'm uncertain how seeing Molly again would be a cure-all. Esther, thanks for coming over. I appreciate it." I touched the top of her hand and squeezed. "Have you got a room yet?"

"Directly beneath yours. So if your tears seep through and flood the room, I can be at your side in two minutes." She smiled knowingly.

I tipped my head back at her. "Remember when you introduced me to Molly?"

"Ten seconds later you began your eternal pilgrimage to her. I remember. I had just met her in an education class. Thought of you immediately. It worked eight years."

"I thought it would work forever," I said in a wistful tone.

"Any good astrobiologist will tell you that 'forever' is probably not in the cards."

"And some probabilities are much less probable than others," I added with complete agreement.

"Talk about sad probabilities. Take a look at your wardrobe. You just peddled a thirty grand painting, and you look as if you're out of a dumpster."

I glared. "I don't peddle my paintings." Then I stole a look down at my clothing, which was, what they call in the trade, pulled together. You definitely couldn't find these clothes in a fashion magazine. "They're clean and cover what needs to be covered."

Observing closely, Esther shook her head and mumbled, "A few of those bucks need to be spent with a nice clothier while we're here in London."

A quick scan of her outfit told me she was right. Her hyacinth-blue crinkle jacket with three-quarter sleeves covered a striped blouse that matched the blue. She wore fashion denim jeans and elegant denim-replicated shoes.

My own attire was, as usual, somewhere between eclectic and thrift store. I wore pewter-colored slacks. Stodgy, but comfortable, black loafers. An oversized sterling gray blouse and a moss-green, shard-print crewneck T-shirt completed my hodgepodge ensemble.

How many times over the years had she given me fashion commentaries? I often wondered if she considered my closet her lifetime's work.

Esther continued her rant by saying, "Fashion defines you. Be more innovative." She paused to scrutinize my attire. "What message does your fashion statement evoke?"

"Point taken," I said, never more thrilled to have a waiter arrive with our orders. "These salads are a meal themselves."

Chapter 5

The Marshall Hotel, a grand old lodging from the past, sat proudly in a historic, trendy area. Not the most luxurious hotel, it had undergone updates and remodeling multiple times. Certainly it was more elaborate than the squalid little motel rooms I'd once occupied in my early days of painting.

My deceased grandparents had been middleclass and very thrifty. They held claim to the idea that the richest person wasn't the one who had the most but the one who needed the least. A motto Fiona found ridiculous. And she certainly hadn't minded pointing out the error of that economic misinformation multiple times over the years.

At any rate, I'd decided to return to the Marshall to paint.

Glancing around the Queen Anne style small suite, I observed tranquility in progress. It consisted of a sitting room and bedroom. The bedroom housed a walnut sleigh bed with rosette inlay on the scrolled headboard and footboard. A bedspread of flaxen color and powder blue matched the walls and décor. A lowboy and wardrobe held my clothing and incidentals.

The ivory sitting room displayed richly decorative woodwork. Within were a sofa; wing chairs in floral reds, violets, and greens; a table; a liquor cabinet; and a drop-lid desk with a pull-out arm. All furniture had cabriole legs and matching woods. The suite's atmosphere was an excellent environment for my painting. When light was available from the London skies, it poured in through tall windows. And the suite was comfortable, which was most important for my soul's serenity.

I had scrutinized my sketches before selecting one. One time I traveled without my supplies when I wanted to clear my head of art and felt actual pain when I had nothing with which to work when I needed it. So I always made it a point to bring my case of acrylic paints, supplies, and two or three 24x36 inch canvases with me.

After I primed the canvas, I began touching it softly with the brush. Raw outlines twisted and bent with the subject. Boldly, I transferred the market scene from sketch to canvas. Soon there was enough paint to resemble Molly's face. Only a premature sketch, but she was looking at me.

My mind whirled as I remembered Molly's seeming indifference. And I relived the memories. We were at the Denver Botanical Garden. She touched the petal of a flame-orange begonia with the same gentle touch that she caressed me. She had such generosity and love in her spirit. When she left, I believed that generosity had snarled, and her touch faded.

When I saw her in the market, I realized she was the same person. And she still had the ability to transport me to a place of loving her. As I continued painting her image, tears pooled in my eyes. I stopped to dab them away with a paper towel I kept to wipe my brushes and clean minor drippings.

I most enjoyed capturing the human spirit in my art. Life told a story. In every story, there was tension. Each face held intensity, passion, and a rare exactitude of its own power.

When I looked into my own mirror-reflected face, although I seldom did self-portraits, I saw the power of abandonment. Desertion by my parents and the woman I loved had left an obvious imprint on my soul.

Perhaps this brought about the edginess within my work. Each canvas emitted a levitating unanswered question. I had never done this with purpose. I didn't paint jagged edges or any semblance of disorder and disharmony. The tension was my way of viewing life and channeling creativity. Nothing more, I had come to believe.

As I worked, I recalled the many paintings I'd done of Molly in past years. Her face of today was a bit fuller, with tiny lines edging her eyes. The frames of aged eyes sagged a bit, but the sheen within hadn't fled with the years. Her body was slightly wider, her hair at the temples streaked with a lush silver.

Wanting the colors to be just right, I clamped my eyes shut, remembering. Color was so integral to seasoning and texturing a work. I often inspected the world's hues to study how to best mix the exact match. How would I replicate grass stains, the undersides of clouds, and glass's reflection?

My first memories were of coloring moonlight. For my fourth birthday, I'd received a coloring book and crayons. I'd crawled from my bed and attempted to recreate the moon's brilliance. It took many sheets of scrap paper and countless canvases to begin to understand color.

For the next three hours, I decorated the space of the canvas, composing more with each stroke of the brush. Globs of lifeless paint began to breathe, to blink, and to exist. I felt the tenderness of Molly's face as if she'd sprung to life on my canvas, just as she had at that market. I saw her bewilderment at seeing me, but I also recognized love. Or perhaps I wanted to recognize love within her eyes.

On my iPod were my favorite songs from ABBA's greatest hits, along with many of my other favorite CDs. I did not expect to hear ABBA as my brush lightly pressed the canvas. When "I Have a Dream" began playing, I placed my brush down. ABBA had released the song about the time Molly was leaving me.

With Molly gone, romance also seemed to have left my life. I'd doom any attempt at romance by warning each woman I dated that I was still in love with my first love. Some took it as a peculiar challenge. As Esther had aptly put it, others dropped me like a ton of turds. Smiling, I wondered how many times over the years she'd pulled out that line. Each time I tried to fall in love, it simply wouldn't work.

I picked up a small brush and daubed a slight bit of black on the tip. I usually didn't bother putting much of the color black on my palette. Known for vibrant colors, I used umber, sienna, or sometimes just a darker version of the color I'd shaded. Adding black to color dulled a picture's life. And my life once again felt the darkness as I dulled it down to black.

Chapter 6

Fiona stared at my latest work. It rested on the cabinet in the gallery's back room where they framed the canvases. "You painted this in one afternoon?" she asked with a frown.

"Yes, this afternoon. Alla prima. Done in one sitting. It seems a bit unfinished when comparing it to my usually precise work. But it is finished."

"A new style for you. And it's extremely precise. The eyes are lovely. Perfectly executed." She stood back, squinting. "Yes, maybe the best rendering of eyes I've ever seen."

"Perhaps that's all I truly wanted to be seen."

"After those sales last night, did you phone Roxie about sending additional paintings as I asked you to do?" She gave a tug on the hemline of her glitzy turquoise- and tangerine-colored overblouse. With a swirling feather pattern, it seemed to compete with her makeup. She wore black stiletto pants, with matching stiletto shoes.

"Yes. She shipped them this morning, the few that I recommended."

Fiona arranged for shipping companies to crate and convey artwork to any destination as quickly as possible. I was never certain if she achieved exactly what she wanted through threats, cajoling, large quantities of money, or her charm. But she always triumphed.

"Do thank Roxie. And please assure her I'll put it right with her for the bother. A few sent today will be a start. You want to put this one in?" Fiona asked with her most encouraging voice. "We may sell out in a week. And I can't expect a painting a day from you, although it would be nice."

"I'll do my best as far as productivity goes." I usually spent a great deal more time on one painting. The notion of rapidly completing a work was a stranger to me.

"It's raining money, and it's past time you got drenched, my dear. Have a chat with your muse. This London trip is taking you to new places. Paint and let it rain!"

"You could use a few raindrops as well," I joked.

"Me in particular. So don't worry about showing up at the gallery and putting in time. Besides, you're a piss-poor rep of your work. You're in the midst of a glorious first solo exhibit of this magnitude. And you're creating. I love it. This is an art odyssey. Paint," she repeated.

"What about Max?" I asked. "I don't want him to feel as though I'm letting the gallery down."

"As much as I adore him, he's a fool. But I can convince him we'll make more money in the end. That's his objective. And once he sees this painting, he'll agree. He runs the gallery. I run the artists." She gave a husky laugh before puffing heartily on her cigarette.

"Art is its own secret," I said. "Value is no one's secret."

"And art is no secret from you, is it, you sweet Saph?" she asked as Spencer approached. "Look at this, Spence."

"Whoa!" He stepped back. "This is absolutely *absolute.*"

"Thanks." I greeted him with a slight wave. He looked particularly haggard. "Had a rough night?"

"No. Just studying some of your work on the Internet that we have at the gallery back home. I got a message that sales have picked up. Did some price restructuring. Looks like we have a rising star. Do me a favor." He threw his arm around me. "Don't go establishment."

Fiona snickered. "Fuck the establishment."

"That can be our battle cry," he said.

Fiona looked at me. "You've always been my favorite artist, Danielle. Always. You never give me headaches. Some of those goddamn babies want their balls scratched. If there's an accident, they expect me to be everyone between the first responder and the coroner. The fools."

"And you're not a promoter-slash-profiteer?" Spencer playfully kidded. For whatever reason, he was her only employee who could tease her and keep his job.

"You can get by with anything," I told him. "So what do you have on her?"

They both gave a few conspiratorial giggles. Fiona said, "Danielle, it's taken you awhile, but you're in the winner's circle now."

"Maybe if I'd had a higher education, stayed in college, and got more art training, I might've been here sooner."

Fiona waved her hand dismissively. "You've always had the basics down by heart. I don't think art school would have done much. Other than teach you to be like everyone else. And you're not like everyone else. Just look at this painting. Extraordinary. Is this painting part of the dream of a reunion with your Molly?"

I shrugged. "I'm not sure."

"Can we include it in the exhibit?" Fiona wouldn't let up.

"You can put it in the show, just like it is. I want a hundred thousand for it, though. So it isn't likely to sell."

"Realistically, no. And what is the title?"

"I'm calling it *Farewell to Molly.*"

Chapter 7

After spending time at the gallery, I met Esther for a late dinner. We stopped in at the adorable Lindsay's Tea House. Small and sweet and serving traditional fare, its vintage glamour and elegance seemed right for us.

I ordered an herb-encrusted cod dish that included a salad and side of roasted vegetables and naturally, Lindsay's specially blended tea. Esther decided on roast beef, salad, and veggies, along with orange-spiced tea.

She looked as relaxed as I was, but she had her daily planner in hand. She'd probably planned a thousand tours, so I immediately began distracting her with my normal diversionary question.

"How are things in the heavens today?" I asked. She didn't disappoint me.

"Hydrothermal vents are able to support bacteria on earth and may support it in outer space. It is extremophile bacteria and could be in other parts of the cosmos even as we speak."

I nodded as if I understood. "I was wondering what had become of all extremophile bacteria."

"I'll tell you this, we don't know all the chemical formulations. I wish you'd taken a course in chemistry," she said with some exasperation. "Or at least passed a course in chemistry if you ever took one. There's the theory of panspermia that relates how life may have come from a distant planet. Or even an asteroid, or interstellar space. Life might've been carried here on the backs of distant debris."

"I'd rather believe I'm whittled from a monkey's sperm. Distant debris is too much like catching a dumpster ride across the cosmos in a garbage bag."

"See, I can't really talk with you about the origin of life. My field. I can't."

"Sorry. Guess it's like when Molly and I were together. I never felt bright enough to be a part of her life. As a philosophy student, all her friends were a true part of academia. At least they pretended to be preeminent intellectuals. I never got the nuances of philosophy. And I was little more than an isolated soul wearing paint-smudged shirts and possessing a well-nourished imagination."

Esther frowned at me. "Calm down and dry off, for God sakes, Danielle. Stop with the inferiority crapola. You've kept up with your reading. You're certainly not the gatekeeper of astrobiology, but I've tried to keep you up to speed in the sciences. Pain blocks the view of ourselves. Your parents ignored you. Molly dumped you. But you're too damned sensitive. Think about how great your grandparents were."

"They were wonderful." I had lost my beloved grandfather while I was in college. And my sweet and kind grandmother died right before Molly left. I was in a constant state of mourning when she died and often wondered if that contributed to Molly's leaving. But looking back now, it probably wasn't the case.

"I also loved them," Esther said quietly. "They were better than most parents. That's for sure."

"My acrimony with my parents has softened over the years. They were too young to raise a family. The old saying about if you're going to have a baby, you can't be the baby, in their case was absolutely true. That might be why my mother turned to illegal additives and some legal ones that pour into a shot glass."

"Additives and not illegal drugs," Esther repeated with a sharp cackle. "At least you still have a sense of humor. When your mother died she couldn't have been over forty."

"Forty-two. Died alone in a creepy, rat-infested hotel in Kansas. And my father died in Texas. His new family hadn't even contacted my brother and me. I heard it long after the fact from an aunt." I blinked a few times to prevent the tears from falling. "But we survived. We've lit the candle inside our joy and made a party. Like now."

She toasted with her teacup. "To us."

"To us," I repeated.

"Now then." She straightened and flapped open her daily planner. "What would you think about a day or two visiting the Isle of Wight? Maybe we could decide on Scotland or Ireland. Or be extraordinarily bold and see Paris. You've always loved visiting the Louvre."

"Beginning with a smaller agenda and then moving up to the continent?" I laughed and pushed my dessert plate back. The blueberry cobbler was delicious but very rich. "Not only that, you're enticing me with promises of viewing magnificent art."

Esther chuckled loudly. "Busted. You could never turn down those full-figured seventeenth century nudes."

"They have them here in London. But Fiona wants me to work. You know, I've had my pieces exhibited with other artists in group showings. But until now, my work hasn't been impressive enough to have my own exhibition. I've even been invited to lecture but didn't want to travel." I took a sip of my tea. "Maybe we can take a daytrip. Stratford on Avon, or like you suggested, maybe a day on the Isle of Wight. It's lovely there."

"That's an improvement over sitting in your hotel room all week. I really think getting out a bit would regenerate your spirit. If you're not really interested in sightseeing, I'll go shopping and check out the women."

"You're going to chase the Brits?"

"Brits are fine women. And I'll allow them to chase me. I enjoy that more. What do you say? Shall we rush through London on a damsel hunt?"

"I'd be hard-pressed to do much rushing."

"You're in great shape for an old broad," she teased. "But if you're not up to it, I'm still going to scout out the action."

"So spread your net and snag one of those darlings. An English rose might be a great adventure for you. I'm afraid Fiona's expecting more painting from me. I'm putting the painting I did this afternoon in the show."

"You finished a painting?"

"Yes. Acrylic paints dry quickly. It's a picture from the street market sketches. And Molly."

"I thought as much. She was in those street market sketches. Amazing that you finished so quickly. You usually agonize a couple weeks."

"This was completed in *its* time, not mine. Fiona is framing it when she's certain it's dry enough. Good thing I don't slather paints on too thickly. And before you ask, I've titled it *Farewell to Molly*."

Esther tossed her napkin on the table and sat back. "That's a dramatic enough statement. You really don't think she'll contact you?"

"No. I'm pretty sure that isn't going to happen. I've instructed the hotel and the gallery to either get her number or give her my cell phone number if she calls. So I wouldn't have missed it, if she had called by now. She's had enough time, even for an extraordinarily busy person." I glanced away, not wanting to see Esther's caustic, scolding expression. She knew me too well.

She must have decided to let the lecture be because she said, "Danielle, I can't wait to see your painting. Is it for sale or just showing?"

"It's for sale. The price is firmly set at a hundred grand."

Esther's head snapped up. "That's really hitting the ceiling."

"I'm pretty sure it will be making its way back to Denver with me. You know what Gertrude Stein says. 'There is art and there is official art, there always has been and always will be.' That pretty much sums it up."

A moment of silence allowed me to consider the under-painting of my soul. I must have believed I was a fine artist. Why else would I have devoted the past forty-plus years to my art?

"Gert Stein." Esther gave a sigh. "We really should go over and find her grave in France. Tour her burial site. She's interred in Paris. In the Lachaise cemetery, I believe. You know, we could spread a few flowers on her grave or something. She helped sisters and also the art world."

"I wonder if she would've liked my work."

Esther debated a moment. "Not in a million years."

"You're right. I would hope she might like it at least as much as she liked Matisse."

"She liked soiled toilet paper more than she liked most of Matisse's art. She might have appreciated your effort. She was a pretty insightful old broad. And you're cute as a button. Not beautiful, but cute. She'd probably have risked the great Toklas's jealousy and ire."

Laughing, I choked on my tea. After I got my breath, I said, "I would have been safer with Picasso chasing me. And being chased by him was by no means a safe prospect." We chuckled a moment, then I smiled at her across the dim-lit table. "In spite of everything, this has been a marvelous day." I held up my teacup to toast. "Ladybugs Rock!" This was the traditional toast of our group of friends back in Colorado.

She lifted her cup and clinked it against mine. "Ladybugs Rock! And I'm going to try to rock. We need to find women and settle down. But I'm somewhere between a work in progress and a bitter disappointment where relationships are concerned," Esther confessed. "And you're slightly worse."

"Maybe we need to begin getting contracts and giving retainer fees."

"We need to get ourselves out there, and you need to wake up. You're living back in Mollyland. You need to find a new love."

"You go out and chase women, Esther. Be as adventuresome as possible. Then save your stories to tell me. I'll live my sexual fantasies vicariously through you. You little planet hunter, you."

"Keep thinking only of Molly, and that might be as much as you can hope for. But remember, we're not getting younger."

"Yes, but I might have forgotten the erotic parts of romance. It's easy to settle in and forget the world outside."

"If you're not careful, you're going to end up with a clinical depression. You're in need of companionship, Danielle."

I motioned for our checks. "Let's get out of here. I'm tired of your crappy diagnosis of me. I need to ward off my clinical depression with another painting."

"You are one hardwired artist."

I pondered that and nodded. "Guilty as charged."

Chapter 8

In the morning, before Esther had a chance to complain about spending her first full day in London alone, I offered to go shopping with her. She was more than fine with that, and I needed a break from painting.

We spent the day sightseeing as we browsed and chatted. In the early evening, we stopped for dinner. As the taxi drove us to the restaurant, I called Fiona and asked what frame she'd selected for *Farewell to Molly*. To my astonishment, she said an undisclosed buyer purchased the painting almost immediately after she'd placed it on the gallery's website. Fiona had no idea who the buyer might be.

My first suspicion was that Samantha Meade Wesley had purchased it, but she'd already openly purchased a painting. It made no sense at all for her to have purchased *Farewell to Molly* anonymously.

Fiona's first guess was that it might be an art speculator who'd heard that my show was doing extraordinarily well and had then acquired *Farewell*. Successful art speculators keep their finds under wraps.

While the driver took us to one of London's fancier dining rows, I told Esther about the purchase.

"Sold for one-hundred grand," she said, her voice rising with each word. "A single painting. I seriously doubt you've made that much in the last two years for all your work."

"And more than I ever thought I'd be making."

"The dinner tab is all yours," she muttered dryly.

I gazed out the window at the choice of restaurants. "How about a bit of pub grub?"

"I'm too overdressed for pub grub." She gave my wardrobe a second look. "Even your attire is too elaborate. Amazingly enough."

I wore tobacco-colored gabardine casual slacks, an ecru crewneck tee, and a bronze-colored quilted jacket. "Actually I'm rather dressed in between. Up market or casual."

Esther snorted. "It's called thrift shop or garage sale. Or as they say here, and accurate to our conversation, jumble sale. If you're ever interested in becoming a chick-magnet, don't be. You're as invisible as dark matter. As for the restaurant, let's try something other than pub food."

"Okay, you pick anywhere at all. We'll make it a festive treat. I'll be happy to snag the check. Just appreciate the fact that I'm a good sport about being ridiculed."

She chose a highly acclaimed restaurant called Toddy's. Although it was a weeknight, we thought it would be impossible to get a reservation. I placed a call, while the cab driver redirected his drive to Toddy's. For the second time that day, fortune smiled. We were able to get a table due to a cancellation. Our cabbie made better than average time, and he delivered us to the doors of Toddy's with a few moments to spare.

As we waited for the hostess to seat us, I went to the restroom to freshen up. My hands were still damp from washing them, when my cell phone rang. I quickly dried them.

"Hello?"

"Fiona here. Danielle, I checked out the name Jeffery Wesley. A hundred-thousand dollars would be chump change to him. He is primary owner, president, and CEO of Wesley Aeronautics located in Los Angeles," she said with evident excitement. "Married to Samantha Meade and they have two children, ages seven and eight, both boys. Jeffery has a law and business degree from Harvard, graduate business degree from Harvard also. An avid pilot. Art collector. Worth multiple millions. It says a more realistic estimate measured their personal wealth at a billion. Their business is worth multi-billions. If he bought his wife a painting for one tenth of a million, it would be chump change. Are you still there?"

We continued talking as I walked back into the dining area and stood beside Esther. "Yes, and thanks for checking it out. So they can afford it. But that doesn't mean they actually bought it."

"No. But they're both art collectors. When I talked with Samantha, she seemed very well-versed on art."

"How so?"

"She told me your work was a composite of many women artists yet unlike anyone else's work. She pointed out the treatment of the flowers in your *Pale Daffodils and Their Gardener* as being reminiscent of O'Keeffe's *Two Jimson Weeds*. And she thought some of your work has similar brushstrokes to your portrait goddess, Beaux."

"If she and her husband are mega collectors, it seems reasonable she would have studied various other artists. Thanks, Fiona. Esther and I are just being shown to our table, so I'll call you later."

"Where are you dining?"

"I'm splurging. Toddy's."

"Paint another picture like *Farewell to Molly*, and I'll take you to a truly plush joint," she promised.

"I'll hold you to that."

"Seriously. We must plan a dinner while we're here. I'll treat both of you."

"Sounds great. It will be good talking art rather than stars and extraterrestrials," I said, loudly enough for Esther to hear.

"Have a good time at dinner. Congrats again on the sale. Word of advice—don't order shellfish. I had it there a couple of nights ago, and it didn't set well at all. Either that or I hadn't had enough martinis. Oh, and don't let your paints dry out."

Toddy's was indeed elegant. Walls were emerald-colored with huge bas-relief in glittering gold. Conical overhead lighting reflected on the same bright gold columns that surrounded the main dining room. Our tablecloth and napkins also exhibited the opulence of the restaurant. Orchids and greenery, as well as candles, completed the gorgeous décor.

I tucked my cell phone back in my pocket. I had placed it on loud and vibrating mode, just in case. I still held out hope Molly might call.

Esther perused the menu. "It all looks delicious."

"Fiona warned not to order shellfish."

Esther flipped her menu shut to look at the cover. "The filet here looks luscious."

"Sometimes photos aren't accurate."

"Is your latest painting of Molly accurate?"

"She did look great. We've all aged, but she's aged in a wonderful way."

"Big stars have relatively short lifetimes, and small stars provide little heat. You need to approach this in moderation. Meeting in the middle is probably best. Right now you're once again red-hot for Molly." She took a drink of her water with a smug expression.

"Esther, you've spent too many years searching for space aliens. Haven't been able to confirm their existence, so you're now peering into my psychological discrepancies. I'm fine. I think I've been handling this like a trouper."

"Not so. I'll bet you've got your cell phone on high volume and with the vibrating mechanism powerful enough to provide ten dozen orgasms. You don't have me fooled, Danielle."

Ignoring her comment, I closed the menu. "I'm going to have lobster."

"You said Fiona nixed the seafood."

"Fiona probably had picked up a very young man and wasn't paying a bit of attention to the meal's quality."

Esther was tickled. "What makes you think she likes younger men?"

"What makes you think she's a food critic?"

Chapter 9

I returned to the Marshall Hotel. My suite seemed lonely except for the corner where my easel and paint case rested. Of course, I'd find solace in painting. I needed it after an evening with Esther. The night seemed to have vanished with talks of women, art, and her wonderland of galaxies. After talking with her, I always felt it necessary to sit and do an internal geography of my soul.

I inventoried our conversation. It contained the usual humor, wisdom, and a sloughing off of yesterday's old skin. Esther had mentioned a recently discovered planet named WASP-17. In a retrograde orbit, it had been involved in a collision with another planet. With a slingshot effect, it flung into a backward orbit. She used this analogy to tell me that I was a great deal like a backward planet. Artists often are out of orbit with the world, she said.

After I poured a glass of wine, I changed into a pair of denims and a large, sloppy, plaid shirt, both splashed with a myriad of colors from yesterday's work. Carefully, I placed the drop cloth down, set up my easel, and began squishing paint from the tubes.

I took a small taste of the pinot grigio and clamped my eyes shut as I mentally primed my canvas. When I blinked my eyes open, I saw the emptiness on the canvas. But my vision of what would occupy the space had already taken shape.

I continued filling the disposable palette sheet with what I needed for the initial background. Having never considered "properly" building an arranged palette, I pressed various small pillows of acrylic paint out as I believed they would be used.

This practice had ended my college career. My art professor insisted that I place complementary colors facing complementary, with each color slotted in a precise spot. If we didn't follow his instructions, we wouldn't receive a passing grade. I had noted that some of the worst, least-talented artists in the class had perfect palettes.

In a fit of defiance, I had lifted my palette and pressed it against the empty canvas. When I pulled it back, multiple splotches dotted against white. I wildly pitched the tubes of paint into my case, slammed it shut, picked up my dotted canvas, and left the classroom. Perhaps Esther was right—I *was* a planet whirling the wrong way.

And now, my palette's personalized plate was speckled with paint colors used in my portraitures. Carefully, I mixed several of them with my pallet knife. I picked up a large, wide, sable brush and loaded it with color for Molly's cheeks. I sketched the memory of her smile with wide sweeps. This portrait would show the entirety of her face, and all else would be underexposed background.

By midnight, I'd created a likeness but not truly Molly. My cell phone rang. Frustrated, I answered it somewhat tersely. "O'Hara."

"It's Fiona. The gallery closed, I dined, and then I remembered one of the gallery associates said a woman called several times for you. She thought it was the same woman."

"Get a number?" After one additional swipe of the chisel edge of my brush, I set it down.

"No. She asked, but the woman refused to leave a number. I thought you might want to know."

"Thanks, yes. Think they have a caller ID number?"

"I'll ask her. How was Toddy's, by the way?"

"I had lobster. It was excellent. I told Esther that you were probably concentrating on your youthful date and thus weren't cognizant of how superb the shellfish really was."

She roared with laughter. "My man of the hour is also superb and certainly not much over thirty."

"Cougar."

"Well, you should talk. You're tied up in knots over a woman you had thirty years ago. Now, my darling Danielle, you want your prodigal ex back again. Hell, I'd say you're trying to become a romantic double-dipper."

"Very funny for such a late hour," I said with a mild chuckle. "Fiona, thanks for making me laugh when I need to laugh."

"Painting?"

"Yes. Could you tell?"

"Always when there's a faraway sound in your voice. That's how I know you need a little humor. And your subject?"

"Molly. Who else? But there's a chance I may end up painting over it with a seascape."

"Not in a million years, you crazy Saph. When you're finished, bring it by. I'll be at the gallery most of the day. I'm having lunch with one of my fellow agents. Had an affair with him years ago. Now we're friends. Nice when relationships end like that. I'll ask him about Jeffery Wesley."

"I wish I could at least have that much of a relationship with Molly."

"Don't go getting an exaggerated sense of optimism, but someone is calling you. It might be Molly."

"Thanks for checking for me. I'll keep painting, and if it's any good, I'll bring it by. I'll probably be stopping by anyway so the gallery doesn't think I'm disinterested."

"Don't worry about anything except bringing your work to the table, Danielle. You're on a roll. I know you're not interested in finances, but money often translates into value. Value is a way to show that you're being noticed."

"I do want my work to be noticed."

"Critics are saying that you don't just reproduce a subject's looks, but you capture their spirit. Your work is well-executed, yes, but a camera can come up with an exact image. Your magic elixir is revealing the soul. An art dealer I met tonight stated your interpretation is unlike other portraitists. And he's right. But he also mentioned that you must be a fine judge of character. I didn't respond to his theory."

"You've got to admit, I've surrounded myself with fine people. Esther, Roxie, the Colorado band of merry women. And especially you, Fiona."

"I selected you, O'Hara," she reminded me.

"Maybe. But I've been smart enough to hang on to you."

"I wish I could have done more earlier. I swear I tried. But now it *is* happening. I see it. The critics are getting you. A little late, but your time's arrived."

"Perhaps late appreciation has saved me from the booze, drugs, and insanity of Caravaggio, Modigliani, and Van Gogh."

"You missed a few of the bonkers boys and babes," she said with amusement.

"I don't have all night to name them all."

"You'll be fine, Danielle. Now, continue on your marathon."

"Most artists are marathon painters."

"Yes, but your muse has reappeared after thirty years."

"She's not exactly chasing me."

"Seduction is overrated. You loved her in your youth. We savor love with an adolescent narcissism. And youth has a significant effect on later life. You're a living example of that right now."

When we ended the call, I wondered if painting others was how I warded off the loneliness that cordoned me from humanity. I felt drained, but sleep was irrelevant. Even if I attempted sleep, my mind would continue painting long after I'd left the canvas.

The contents on the canvas remained inanimate. Molly's face hadn't awakened. I worked on Molly's expression at the very second she glanced my way. I needed to replicate her smile and capture that millisecond when her eyes glinted with recognition. I'd call it *Reunion's First Glimpse.*

As I feverishly filled the canvas with that immortal moment of Molly, I suddenly felt invincible.

Chapter 10

I had finished the painting with the final touches of my blender brush. After signing my name with the strip liner in burnt umber, a sigh rushed through my entire body. I was happy but also apprehensive.

Applying varnish had been an afterthought. Then I succumbed to a couple of hours of midmorning sleep.

After I showered and dressed, I touched the canvas to see if the varnish had dried. It had. I was again appreciative that I didn't subscribe to the impasto method of heavily slathering paints.

I examined the painting to ensure there were no minuscule errors. Then I backed up once more to peer into the face. It was Molly.

By the time I was ready to loosely wrap it and leave my hotel room, I was satisfied. Gingerly carrying the canvas by wrapped edges, I set off for the gallery.

While I was walking, my stomach growled as a reminder that I hadn't eaten since last night. I was about to pass a nearby Tasty's Fish-and-Chips Shop when fumes of grease and malt vinegar hit me. I made a U-turn into the shop. A wonderful Brit meal would be my treat for having worked so diligently last night and into the morning. That concept, I hoped, would appease my guilt for having ordered fish-and-chips. I normally ate healthy.

I topped off my meal with an English ale then lifted the canvas to my side and struck off for the gallery. At nearly two in the afternoon, I arrived at my destination.

After greeting Fiona and Max, I unwrapped the painting. I watched the faces of Max Parker, two of his employees, and Fiona. Fiona gasped. Everyone seemed transfixed.

Uncomfortable with their silence, I asked, "Comments? Is it awful or awfully good?"

In unison, they answered it was terrific. The manager and his small crew took photos on their phones and then made a dash for the office. Fiona quietly continued staring at it.

I finally broke my own silence. "What's wrong? If they're disappointed and trying to be nice about it..." I paused to gather words. "Well, which is it?"

"What the hell are you talking about?" Fiona incredulously glanced back at me. "This is the most brilliant work you've ever done. It's the genius I've always believed in. You were so near to creating masterpieces. And now you have."

"All my life's work has been rubbish until now?"

"No, of course not. They're all extraordinary. I wouldn't handle you if you weren't magnificent. You know enough art history to know that not all Renoir's, Rembrandt's, Cassatt's, Van Gogh's, and Picasso's works are masterpieces. This painting, what is it titled?"

"*Reunion's First Glimpse.*"

"Naturally, you realize how remarkably phenomenal my client list is. Once in a rare while, a painting makes me shiver. I like to think I can pick a true masterpiece. I could be standing nude in the Arctic and not experience this goddamn shiver, Danielle. Better than any of the others. Yes."

"You're putting me in some pretty grandiose company."

"Only time makes masterpieces, so who is to say? But your *Reunion* has everything. I was shocked when you painted *Farewell*. I thought it might be the best work you'd ever produce. But this? This is even better."

"Do you think maybe I'm moving into a different period of work?"

"Most definitely. And if you're judged on only the last two you've painted, you'll have written a new phase for the modern art world of portraiture. It's that good. I can't believe you didn't work with a live model."

"My heart memorized Molly. Her smile of recognition. Last night, my hands recreated that memory. Her contemplative eyes spoke in verse."

"What were you considering as to price? This is one of those blessed times when you *truly* can name your price."

"It isn't for sale."

"You just sold *Farewell* for a hundred-thousand dollars. Galleries and museums, along with private collectors are interested.

Max told me publications are sending reporters. A TV crew wants to set up an interview with you. You can ask any price."

"Fiona, answer me this honestly. If I asked a million for it, do you think it would sell for that?"

"I honestly do believe it might."

"Then it isn't for sale. Not at any price, if you believe it will sell." I bowed my head so I wouldn't look into her eyes. I knew they would be pleading with me.

"Danielle, please think this over. If we get an offer with status to secure your entry into the world of the finest museums, you'll need to reconsider. Will you at least think about working with me on this?" I felt her staring hard at me.

"Let's just show it and see if there are offers." I stepped away, not taking my gaze from *Reunion*. I didn't believe I could part with it. Anymore than I could bear to part with Molly. In her case, the choice wasn't mine. With the painting, it was to be my own determination. No one could look into that painting without believing they had located part of Molly's soul. Perhaps they would simply come to love her as I did.

I turned away from the painting as my eyes began to well with tears.

Chapter 11

For over an hour, I made myself available to speak with several of the gallery's patrons. Then I escaped the public relations side of the art world.

Once on the sidewalk, I rummaged in my oversized bag for my cell phone. Esther hadn't called, and I was wondering what my doppelganger had been up to all day. Strongly suspecting she'd done a daytrip, I glanced at my wristwatch. She would probably be back by now, I supposed, so I called. She answered and agreed to meet me for a snack. I needed to tell her the latest.

I arrived at Crumpets and Brew coffee shop before Esther and ordered for both of us. The cappuccinos and pastry brought the word "divine" to a new level.

"This sounded urgent," Esther said as she sat down.

"Did you happen to drop by the gallery?"

"Yes. I thought you'd be there, but I just missed you."

"Must have nearly crashed into one another. Did you see the painting?"

"The minute I arrived. The entire staff had gathered around it, and Fiona is very high on *Reunion*. I'm an absolute flop at judging art, but I loved it. I'm with Fiona. It's even better than *Farewell*. And I was nuts about that one."

"I know she wants to sell it for some wild, off-the-charts price. She might have her chance at really making some money with me, but I haven't been cooperating. I don't want to be banned from her stable of artists."

"I think she understands why you've got a 'not for sale' ticket on it. She didn't say anything negative to me. She gushed on and on about the painting. Which is not to say she won't try to encourage you to sell it. I agree with her. You need to strike while the fire is flaming."

I changed the subject. "So what mischief did you get into today?"

Esther carefully spooned a big dollop of foamy milk from the cappuccino's bonnet in a not-so-subtle stall tactic. "Not a lot," she finally answered.

"Before I forget, Roxie e-mailed me about Aggie becoming the alpha dog."

Esther agreed. "She is the alpha in our home. Sadie and I are her true followers." Esther had rescued Sadie, a lovely German Shepherd and Keeshond mix, several years ago from a shelter. She had been a stray found in a field where heartless youths had been using her as target practice. Obviously guarded about trusting human beings, she immediately bonded with Esther. The shelter's staff was amazed. And naturally, Sadie and Esther left the shelter together and remained together. From the same shelter, Esther rescued Aggie, an adorable Miniature Pinscher-Dachshund mix.

"Clover rules in my home," I said. "But she now defers to Aggie. Seems Sadie and Clover have been enchanted by Aggie. Roxie is getting a kick out of it. All is well, she said to tell you. Sadie and Aggie are eating and pooping on schedule."

"Great. The alpha dog thing bothers me. You need all the alpha in your life you can get. You lead a hermetic life. Clover is a help by being alpha commander. Heck, you probably need a bossy woman to help Clover out with you."

We shared a laugh and sipped the foam from our cappuccinos.

I thought for a moment. "Admittedly, I am a homebody. I'm missing the late harvest from my garden. The squash, pumpkin, and other autumn remnants are extraordinary. Some of the herbs are still hanging in there. Roxie said she took a couple of pots inside and covered the rest with tarps when it got cold last night. She loves herbs. That girl can paint and cook."

"No wonder Sadie and Aggie haven't missed me," Esther said. "What else did Roxie say?"

"Clover has been attentive to the beagle next door. His name is Buddy, and she flirts with him constantly."

"Eyelashes aren't the only thing Clover and Fiona have in common. Any other news from back home?"

"Only that Roxie's been regularly visiting the gallery's website and approves of my latest work." I took a bite of the delicate, flakey, peach Danish. "Delicious."

"Absolutely. I taste a light hint of rum." After a brief pause, Esther exhaled loudly. With a breezy formality, she murmured, "Met a woman."

"Met a woman!" The cappuccino spilled over the cup's edge as I lifted it to my lips. I grabbed my napkin and wiped it up. "Where did you meet a woman?"

"They do make up half the population," she said with her typical sarcasm.

"I can't wait to hear this."

"I was at a feminist bookstore. Got to talking with her, and we instantly hit it off. She said she'd show me London's lesbian nightlife. Her name is Carrie. The bookstore people seemed to know her and like her."

"What does she do for a living?"

"She didn't mention an occupation. We talked mainly about books."

"What do you know about books?" I furrowed my brow. "Other than astronomy ad nauseam?"

"Contrary to what you think, you *can* find a date in a bookstore. And I wasn't even in the astronomy stacks. We both enjoy love poetry." Esther smiled with a wistful expression.

"You don't enjoy love poetry or any other poetry."

"I do. I just never spout it around you."

"Ode to Gertrude Stein?"

"Danielle, come on, pretend you're correct, and I'm not a bleeping poetry expert. But I do know enough poetry to impress a woman who loves poetry. Okay?"

"Okay. What does she look like?"

"Taller than I am. Thinner than I am. Younger than I am."

"Younger?"

"She's about forty or so. Reddish, longish hair. Brown eyes. Great smile. Smart dresser."

I laughed. "Fiona isn't the only cougar in London."

"So Carrie's younger. I always say youth may know what to do, just not always *why* they're doing it."

"Let's hear what you know about her so far."

"She claims to be at the helm of a firm called Insults Incorporated. Kidding, of course. She reminds me of a British version of Roxie. Rox is always calling people pork heads and numb nuts. Well, Carrie is like that."

"If that's the case, keep my name out of her mouth." I made a circular motion with my hand. "Go on."

"She has these names she comes up with for people around her. She does them in a cockney accent and it's hilarious. Her actual speech is cultured English. For example, I heard her call one guy a fritter goon. She called me wonder bum. When I turned her down by saying I was too old, she called me Daisy Doom."

"Glad she speaks interstellar."

"Right. And she argued that all of her friends are over fifty."

"So did you tell her you're well over fifty?"

"Why would I start telling the truth about my age now? If you look a decade or two younger, lie. Then people will think you look your age or slightly older. And they will credit you with having had a difficult, arduous life. That's my theory at least."

"Why wouldn't it be? You're entire career is the study of billions of years clustered up in the skies. What's a decade or two?"

"Precisely," she said. "After all, we're in London a few more days. Might as well enjoy the lovely women while we're here."

"You wanted to meet someone and have. I think it's great, Esther."

"Sure, it's junior high school revisited. But what's wrong with flowers, chocolate, and sweet greeting cards? I like romance."

"I'm certain she's never heard of a high school sock hop. Where are you going on the date?"

"We're having dinner. She knows some *women's* clubs. I haven't been to a gay bar for years. Why not?"

"Not a reason I can think of."

Esther tapped the table, which was one of her ploys to change topics. "And I take it there's been no call from Molly?"

"I doubt if she'll call," I said with a sigh. "She's not interested. It's abundantly clear to me. But to stop loving her is a different matter."

"Are you going to be painting another picture of her tonight?" She saw my reaction. "I don't mean it that way. I know you still love her, call or no. And I know the next portrait you paint will be of her."

"I hope I'm going to be sleeping early tonight. I'll order room service and then crash. If not, I certainly might paint another picture. I have no idea about the subject. I do know that I'm about out of canvases, so now would be the time for this painting frenzy to stop. Or I should pop over to an artist's supply shop and pick up a few things. I not only need canvases, I should replace some paint as well." I glanced at my watch. "If I leave now, I might be able to make it before the shop closes."

"I can tell by your mood that you're not ready to stop painting. You'll be swinging your brush again."

I laughed. "I think you'll be swinging much more than I shall."

Chapter 12

An amazing art supply store was located only a fifteen-minute cab ride away. The canvases I'd brought with me were small, a manageable 24x36. I'd already used two and had one remaining. But I wanted a larger, wider format to paint the street market. I wanted to capture the look of wonder when Molly lifted the book. Maybe that was the quality I fell in love with from the start. I also wished to capture her nostalgic expression when she'd picked up the miniature cup and saucer set. It seemed simplicity pleased her as much today as it had so many years ago.

I'd buy the canvases and supplies first and have them delivered to the hotel. I'd then go by the market and take a few photos with my camera phone. A couple of days ago, my focus had only been on Molly. But now I wanted to recreate the scene. I would call this work *A Scene from Our Story*.

Long title, and I planned to use a long canvas: 44x56, or perhaps a 40x60, or maybe even a 48x60. Once I was at the shop, I prudently decided to buy all three sizes. I would know which size when I was ready. Just as I seemed to know colors when I mixed the proper combination of pigments for the work. I would pick up the proper brush. My intention was realized in art but certainly not in areas of my romantic life.

There was very little I appreciated more than sauntering through an artist's supply shop. After selecting canvases, I placed them at the counter. With shopping basket under my arm, I roamed the aisles of supplies and picked up the paints I needed to replace, as well as a dozen brushes. Looking down at the basket, I thought about the mystical conversion creation offered. These paints would become an image of my love of England and my love of Molly. Alone with my imagination, I would seek sanctuary from a heartache through the placement of these colors.

After I made my purchase, I gave instructions for the store to deliver the canvases to my hotel lobby's check-in counter within the hour.

My next stop was to be the street market where I had seen Molly. I snapped a multitude of photos for later reference. I needed to make sure I had a feel for the recessive light. I wished desperately that Molly had been there smiling at me. And she wasn't. Thirty years ago I would watch her smile carefully, believing if I blinked it might vanish. And then one day it had.

As I was finishing my shopping, Esther called from her cab on the way to her date. She was more than slightly nervous. I told her to find out if Carrie was single and available. I chided her about the old saying that when the cat ate out of the dog's bowl, the cat could expect to get its whiskers bit off. She laughed and said she missed Sadie and Aggie.

Since the dog's bowl story hadn't eased her nerves, I asked, "What did you decide to wear?"

Bingo, I thought, as she started in on an inventory of her wardrobe. "My nutmeg taffeta twill jacket. I liked the matching blouse but decided on the tangerine one. And cinnamon slacks."

"Hmm. Am I picking up on a citrus and spice theme?"

We giggled.

"Well, have a great time, Esther."

"Are you're going to stay holed up in your hotel suite all night? Painting?"

"Blissfully, yes. So don't become ratty just because I'm staying out of trouble and doing what I want."

"Who's being ratty now?"

"Esther, romance is a cumbersome chronicler of human expression."

She added, "Remember batteries not included."

"You're terrible. Someday a flipping black hole is going to swallow you."

"Speaking of which, you know how powerful black holes are. Those concentrated fields of gravity don't even allow light to escape from them. One intermediate class of black holes could explain how super-massive, light-sucking monsters develop in the heart of galaxies."

"Light-sucking monsters? If I were you I wouldn't try to impress this poor Carrie with any astro-chat. And stay away from alien munchkins, too."

"Listen, the restaurant is a couple of blocks away. Got to smear my lips and apply some powder to my cheeks. Have a terrific night painting your memories."

"Have fun, and don't let your whiskers get bitten off," I said as I heard the click of the phone.

I took two more photos then ambled away from the market. Merchants were beginning to pack up their wares. The shadows of early evening fell, and I watched the rhythms of the traffic. I turned back for one more glimpse of the place where Molly and I had briefly reunited.

I wondered what she might be doing now.

Chapter 13

Esther had left an early morning voice mail saying she would return to the hotel midafternoon, and we would have a gabfest then. She sounded elated. I spent the remainder of the day attempting to finish my latest painting. After quick calls to Roxie on the home front and Fiona stationed at the gallery, I poured my soul into my work.

By two in the afternoon, I needed a break and hoped that Esther might be on her way back to the hotel. Curiosity was running at an all-time high. I called her. She was on her way and said she wanted to do a little shopping before returning to the hotel.

I jumped right in to glean as much information as I could. "Are you going to give me the latest space info report? How is that light-sucking monster of a black hole? Or are you going to tell me what happened on your date?"

"Iron emissions reveal that a black hole is spinning rapidly and chomping matter quickly."

"Good, we've got the space narration out of the way. Let's cut to the chase. Get to the human interest portion of your story, Esther."

"Okay. And before you ask. Forty-two."

I laughed. "Would that be her bust measurement or her license plate number?"

"Danielle, sometimes you can be a real turd. It's her age. So she is well beyond the age of consent."

"Just not as well beyond as we are." Before my tittering became a source of annoyance, I stopped. "I'm truly thrilled for you. Nothing like a vacation romance. I assume the stay-over with Carrie went well. Any more details you want to offer?"

"Her full name is Carrie VonHuber. She owns a travel agency. Has a lovely, immaculate apartment with a roommate she wants you to meet."

"Let's retrace our steps. Travel agent. Did she take you on a trip around the world?"

"You are rotten. Are you taunting me to amuse yourself or as a method for diverting the question of going out with her roommate?"

"Is her roommate over the legal age? I'm not interested in being charged with degeneracy by dating a teenager."

"You're hardly reprobate material," Esther said dryly. "Her roommate is a gorgeous, classy lady of fifty-four. I think you can handle that. You can be so damned boring, Danielle."

"I'm not interested in meeting anyone, even if she is of age. But thanks for the offer."

"I'll put it another way. Her name is Bethany Cortland. She's a manager with a major airline. Prior to that, she was a flight attendant. Hair like Joan Baez—sort of salt-and-pepper on top and darker sides, same trim. And we're meeting them for dinner tonight after they get off work."

"Esther, I need to paint."

"You need to get out with a charming woman. As far as that goes, you need to get laid by any available woman. And I take it Molly hasn't bothered to call."

"Not a word."

"There. That settles it. You need to get out. I've always maintained if your sexual appetite is sustained, your painting improves."

"Quite the opposite. My creative endeavors seem to detract from desire. I direct my sexual energy toward my work. Sorry, I'm not available right now."

"What did you do last night? Another painting?"

"Nearly. I'm finishing up even as we speak."

"If it has 'Molly' in the title, I'm going to scream."

"It's called *A Scene from Our Story*."

"Another picture of Molly?"

I didn't answer.

"Your silence is telling me I'm right. Face facts, Danielle. She hasn't called. And you're pouring your heart out painting pictures of her. You're getting myth mixed up with history."

"This painting is different. I'm trying to capture a look of hers as she shopped. It was unlike any I've ever seen."

"And you remember all her expressions for the eight years you were together?"

Pain gripped my heart. "I think I may well remember them all."

"To me, it seems she's ignoring you. She knows where you're staying. She knows where your work is being shown. Damn it, Danielle, she can call if she's interested and she hasn't called."

"I'm well aware of that," I shot back.

"Bethany Cortland is a sublime woman. She is *hot* and smart."

"What about your sweetie? Why were you checking out this Bethany?"

"I have wonderful peripheral vision. I noticed Bethany, but I notice all lovely women. She's about your height, a little slighter maybe. You're both skinny broads."

"Why don't you take both Carrie and Bethany out tonight? I have to finish this painting. And stop heckling me about my weight."

"Consider the painting finished. Get fixed up and let's party. Only one night. I'm sure she couldn't put up with you on a second date. Even if you feigned charm."

I rolled my eyes. "It could be a mutual rejection, you know."

"Nope. She's adorable. She's articulate. Lovely. She's trim. Harp-string muscles."

"Harp-string muscles. Is that British for saying she's extremely masculine?"

"Oh, no. Trust me. She's all woman. When I commented on her athletic body, she corrected me, saying she's well-trained. Toned and feminine. And she abhors competitive sports. See, you've got a commonality right there. Come on, Danielle, stop being catatonic. End celibacy. It might not even be a resounding success, but do try. You're hardly the lascivious type, but you could attempt to be a wanton, brazen bitch for one night."

"I'm not searching for a torrid affair."

"Contrary to what you think, sex isn't on the protected species list. While you still have a full range of motion and some energy, give it a go."

"Absolutely not."

"Here's how it's going down. I'm going shopping for a new pair of shoes. I'll be back at the hotel by four or so. I'll get ready. Then we can go to the restaurant together where we'll meet our dates. Come on. I flew all the way over here for you." Now she'd resorted to whining.

I paused and reviewed my options. "Okay, I'll go."

"That's my girl. As the Brits say, do try to make an effort. A little makeup might not hurt your chances. Don't be timid. Glam up a tad. And be friendlier."

"Is Carrie all for this double-date junk?"

"Yes. She mentioned she hoped you weren't going to be a storm cake."

"Storm cake," I repeated. "Storm cake?"

"I told you Carrie is a total and complete hoot and has a full vocabulary of these British sayings. You'll enjoy yourself. And maybe you'll enjoy Bethany."

"Esther, I'm not all that good with age differences."

"Five years is nothing. And come to think of it, twenty-plus years is marvelous. Now, cheer yourself up."

"Have you ever been accused of being a control freak?" I asked.

"Not to my face. No one would dare." A moment later she muttered, "I have been called a general before, though."

I laughed. "So, what time are we leaving?"

"Five. We're meeting them at six. But I want extra time to scrutinize your outfit and make sure you're presentable. If you're not, it might take an extra half hour to do something with you."

"What could you ever imagine doing with me that would only take half an hour to render me resplendently gorgeous?"

"You're right. Meet me now and let's begin with a new shoe wardrobe. Then we'll go to an adorable little boutique and get you fitted out in something that meets with my approval. A hair salon. After that—"

I cut her off. "I'll be ready at half past five. I'll give a quick perusal in my mirror. That should be enough."

I'm sure most of London heard her groan. "Danielle, I beg of you, do make an effort."

"I'm not out to chase women. I'm trying to finish a painting. When I know the time is right for me, I'll make an effort."

"Here they call it pulling a bird."

I was certain she could feel the glare through the phone. "From Ovid's *The Art of Love*, there's this quote that mousetraps don't run after mice." There was a pause. "Well?"

"The Brits pull birds. Nothing at all to do with mice. Just be ready." She hung up.

A few curse words tumbled from my lips. The dread settled into my psyche. Strangers made me uneasy.

Chapter 14

Returning to my canvas, I glanced at my wristwatch. I wanted the time to approach *A Scene* with empathy. I needed to achieve what seemed to be an impossible balance. As I painted, I thought about those glances of Molly's. At the stall, as she thumbed through the book, there was recognition, suddenly a sliver of pathos, and then abject sorrow. She held the book to her bosom as she lowered her head.

Perhaps Molly was recalling Pamela and the two decades they'd shared. She had obviously loved Pamela. Or at least felt something. At any rate, for a brief moment she seemed completely vulnerable. I wanted to recount and preserve that split second. I wanted to understand the years of thought that bunched up within a human soul. The exploration of memories compounded. And I wanted them recorded via art.

The knock on the door proved an intermission. Spencer had come to check on how I was doing and if I needed anything.

He stared at the painting. "I adore *A Scene*," he said with a note of awe. "Aren't you ever going to take a break?"

Spencer had become my personal liaison—my champion and my moaning post. "I'm finishing up this work, and then I'll socialize. A date of sorts."

"The newest releases are posted on the web page, so maybe they will do the work of a dozen personal appearances."

"I'm sure Fiona buys into that."

"Her raison d'être is selling, not buying."

I gave him a playful shove. "Spence, you're the best. And you do like the newest painting, so I am saved. You've been under Fiona's tutelage for long enough to get her astute observations when it comes to art."

"I've been raised on art, actually. A complete tutelary."

"I'm finishing up the painting. Then I'll get showered and dressed, go out and party, while wishing I were back here with brush in hand."

"Social butterfly." His grin was contagious. "Go out, fuel up, and pretend to be having fun."

"Pretend is so much like lying."

"Danielle, you're empowered by understanding the difference. Maybe that's what helps you paint. On the other hand, exploiting the use of pretence isn't your greatest attribute. You're personable, but your social skills…" He scrunched his face as if searching for the right words. "Well, not so much."

"I'd have to say I agree, Spence."

Although I enjoyed his company, I was glad when he left. I wanted to finish working on the stretched canvas. While there was a celebration of the heart when I completed a painting, getting to that point always produced tension. I always felt a flicker of fear that I might have taken it too far, or incorrectly. Although I was certain it wasn't rational, I could see the parallel between creating and loving.

Risk was involved in allowing the passion needed for each of these wonders. And it took the exact requirement. The contrast—chiaroscuro—could be in varying intensities. Words, caresses, brushstrokes, they all needed to be forged with such care and precision. I had only learned this with years of experience.

After applying additional paint, making corrections, and carefully examining the painting, I showed my approval by giving it a thumbs-up gesture. I signed it, feeling great satisfaction and fulfillment.

Glancing at the brushes, springy pallet knives, and splattered palette paper pad, I considered the cleanup. As I'd done what seemed to be a million times before, I took the implements of my trade to the sink, carefully cleaned them, and wiped them down completely. I pressed them back into the storage case. I glanced at the painting. Yes, I thought, it was what I wanted. I crushed the messy paper I'd torn from the palette pad and tossed it away.

As I shed my clothing and stepped into the shower, I turned to look in the mirror. I'd been blessed with health and much happiness in my life. But age was a great leveler of self-expectation. We all wanted age to evolve us gently and with human grace. Yet there was always an awkwardness about age. Nature automatically deconstructed us. In various increments, we lost what we had been.

My limbs were good, and I'd not allowed many rolls or cellulose. I exercised and attempted to maintain a dietary plan that met with my doctor's recommendations. My face was lined, and I had no desire to "touch" it up. Just as in my paintings, I had enjoyed creating those facial road maps.

The image of me at sixty had become a woman with an ever-so-slight girth around my thin frame, graying hair, and lines upon my thin face. My face was more haggard than it once was. The coloring not as pink with youth's luminosity. It could be worse, I thought with a pause before turning the shower's handle. The water hit my body in sheets and splashed downward. My body sagged very little, everything remained in working order. And I still smiled freely. So yes, it could have been far worse.

After suds and water had thoroughly doused my body, I patted myself dry. I had laid out my cloth armor on the bed. I layered a vibrant crimson turtleneck over lace lingerie and slipped into a pair of tawny-colored slacks. I wished my creativity included fashion design. I wrestled my arms into a matching lightweight jacket. Finally, I stepped into shoes. I'd never taken the time to coordinate fashion colors as I did with oils and acrylics. Esther would say more was the pity on that one.

I put on a multicolored, multi-stone gold necklace. Somewhat splashy, with spots of crimson, purple, and many shades in between, the main stones were agate. My dangling earrings matched the necklace. As an afterthought, I slipped on an oval ring.

I hadn't come to London to date, nor to involve myself in a fashion show. Regardless, if I had, I wouldn't have been a frou-frou woman. This was an outfit for galleries, going to dinner, and not impressing anyone with anything other than pointing to my artwork.

Looking out the window, I thought about all the chic and trendy people walking below. Londoners had a certain tailored sense of fashion. I probably wouldn't be mistaken for a Brit, although that would have been nice.

I wondered about the interior dressings of my timeworn body—my soul enshrined inside. Youth often provides exuberance, passion, and exploration. Age can provide wisdom, experience, and knowledge. But any one of those attributes might be traded off. Well-seasoned souls needn't be ancient. Conversely, well-aged bodies could be energetic, inquisitive, and fervent.

Age proved such a quandary. And no cross-references seemed available as one moved across its charts.

Chapter 15

Bethany Cortland's laugh was jubilant. We were in the midst of a wonderfully lingering dinner at an exquisite restaurant called Chantilly Park. High-end and tucked away in its own enclave, it was perfect and intimate. We sat in a private dining room with yards and yards of lace curtains and delicate antique dining furniture. The walls were alabaster and the feel was light and airy with tints of baby blue and bamboo-colored décor.

Bethany was indeed as lovely as Esther had described. At first glance, she was chic, trim, and gregarious. The way she carried herself was spirited and self-assured. Her dress was a grade above casual. She wore a pastel purple silk overtop that was neat and trendy, taken in by a golden coin belt. Black wool slacks and matching pump shoes were definitely stylish. Her attire seemed expensive, with what looked to be pricey jewelry. She wore layered gold chains around her neck, and on her left finger, she sported a large, oval diamond cluster ring. Fashionable, yet not ostentatious.

I imagined painting her portrait. Her eyes, the brightest cerulean blue I'd ever seen, much less painted, glowed like translucent sapphires held up to the light. Her short, elegantly clipped hair was salt-and-pepper with side waves in dark brown. The bridge of her nose, cheekbones, and jawline were slim and nicely formed. With her rosy complexion, I would paint her flesh tones lightly and with a hint of alizarin crimson. Most extraordinary was her mouth. Her teeth had a lustrously white look of being recently polished.

More than anything, her joyful love of life and positive outlook on the world enchanted me. While Esther and Carrie chatted, I told her she seemed to be at home with herself.

"Why not?" she said. "I've traveled the world over many, many times. So I guess it's second nature to be at home wherever I am. Do you like travel?"

"Not so much. I do love London," I said. "I've been to Europe several times but concentrated mainly on art. I've been a part of group exhibitions. And all my wanderings took me to museums and galleries to see the magnificent art."

"Not even a day off to check the tourist areas?"

"Naturally, I've seen some. To be truthful, I discourage any form of travel when there's an exhibit opening. Unless it's in London. I'm not a polyglot. What French and Spanish I know is sparse, and my French is mainly art related. My agent's job isn't easy. I'm probably her biggest problem. She usually wins any disputes, and I spend a day or two in a city where I'm totally not at ease. I prefer my own home. It's a place where my life's perfect. Everywhere else is strange, I suppose."

"Your home sounds completely comfortable for you, Danielle. And Esther said you have a dog."

"Clover. Yes." I took out my phone and pulled up her photo.

"She's adorable," Bethany said with a smile. "Look at those eyelashes."

Esther must have been eavesdropping, because she chimed in. "Clover is sweet. It's Danielle who's the terrier. I'm also the mutt in my home, compared to Sadie and Aggie." She looked at the picture. "I just noticed Clover's lashes are even longer than Fiona's."

"The woman at the gallery?" Bethany asked.

"Yes. My agent," I said. "She's a tad bit showbiz, but she's a lovely person. And a great agent."

Esther joked, "Is 'showbiz' a comparable term for garish?"

"That, too, but she's been my rock of security."

"You like the security of home, of art, and all?" Bethany said.

"Yes, I do. And you?"

"Of course. I like being settled with someone mostly. But I also like the adventure travel offers." The next photo that came up was my home. Bethany looked at it. "Very nice."

"Thanks. It's pretty much an average home by U.S. standards. Bi-level, with a huge backyard. Two acres. Apple trees, a locust tree, and crab apples. Also, a large garden, and some sheds where I keep gardening equipment. There's a double-garage-sized art studio on the side of the house."

"It sounds lovely."

"Thank you."

The waiter appeared, and we ordered. Carrie continued to keep us entertained and seemed very smitten with Esther.

The cuisine was modern European. The aromas in the warm, intimate setting were extraordinary. I ordered cottage pie, and Bethany ordered stuffed trout in wine sauce. We then split them so we could sample. Both were delicious, and the accompanying pinot grigio was excellent.

In between bites, Bethany said, "May I ask why it is you prefer staying only in Colorado?"

"I strongly suspect it's from my childhood."

She leaned nearer with a look of interest. "Why is that?"

"I spent my childhood traveling from one parent to the other. They were divorced when I was four. I went from Texas with my father to Kansas with my mother, and the wonderful interludes between were spent with my grandparents in Colorado. I attended college in Colorado and decided to live there."

"Esther told us you live in a suburb of Denver, the foothills."

"My maternal grandparents resided in Littleton, Colorado. I stayed with them so much as a child that I came to love the area. My brother and I went to school there. After Molly left, I moved from Denver to my current home."

Bethany raised her eyebrows. "Molly? The woman Esther says you're still intrigued with?"

"She's the one. And Esther has a big mouth." I spoke loudly enough to get Esther's attention.

Esther bristled and said in a mocking tone, "That's right. I told her every little boring detail of your life."

"Esther, what crawled up your trouser leg?" Carrie asked.

"I knew Danielle would complain."

Carrie was an attractive woman with exaggerated gestures and a loud, showy exterior. But one sensed that down deep she was extremely sensitive. She dressed with a youthful, urban look. She wore a pale jade top with an exotic print. Gold-tone designer embellishments studded her cognac-colored skirt. Gold bangles lined her arm and jangled when she lifted them while she talked.

In short, she was larger than life. Her rust-colored, stylishly trimmed hair rested on her shoulders. Her eyes were blazing and sorrel. Her makeup was perfect for her light complexion. And she was as funny as Esther had advertised.

Carrie shrugged at Esther. "There are times I'd like to send Esther on an all-expense vacation to the ASBO."

"ASBO?" I asked.

"Anti-Social Behavior Order. It is not a good thing."

Both Carrie and Bethany chuckled at the comment.

"Sounds perfect for Esther," I agreed.

"That's why I love the travel industry," Carrie said. "I can send the doolally arses on their way. The farther the better at times." She patted Esther's shoulder. "You, my little sunbeam, are hard work in the best of times."

I looked at the smiling faces around the table and found that, much to my surprise, I was very much enjoying the evening.

"Molly looks like a lovely woman," Bethany told me.

"How do you know?"

"Esther told us about your exhibit. I dropped by the gallery on the way here. I noticed a couple of paintings of a woman. One was titled *Reunion's First Glimpse*." Her gaze followed my every move, as if she were closely scrutinizing my reaction. "And I'm guessing that would be Molly."

I sipped my wine. "Yes."

"You painted it with immense love."

"Certainly it's painted with immense something." My voice trembled a little.

"Your eyes show how wounded you are."

I couldn't deny her guess. I glanced away and took a quick bite. "This cottage pie is delicious. Are cottage pie and shepherd's pie the same thing?" I'm sure it was painfully obvious I was moving the conversation to safer ground, and Bethany let it go.

"Cottage pie has beef in it, and shepherd's pie is from lamb."

"I love the Brits for their precision with the language," I said.

"I'm in hopes you also love Canadians. I'm from Canada originally." Bethany handed me a dessert menu. She recommended we sample the various desserts, and all four of us agreed. We would order the chocolate orange soufflé, lemon geranium ice cream, redcurrant cheesecake, and a chocolate cake lathered in raspberry and rum sauce.

With desserts, Bethany had also ordered an array of after-dinner drinks that perfectly paired with and complemented each dessert. As we sampled dessert, we sipped drinks. At one point Bethany lifted her glass and tipped it toward my lips.

"Yum." I gazed into her eyes. "You know your way around good dining."

"Lots of travel. And good taste." When I didn't respond, Bethany asked, "Aren't you going to question why I think I have good taste?"

"Okay. Why?"

"Because I'm going to ask you out tomorrow night."

Laughing, I replied, "And my taste is exemplary as well. Because I plan on accepting."

"As soon as we finish up here, I'd like to introduce you to a special club called Sophie's. It's comfortable, easy listening music, and homey. Dancing if you like. If not, we can sit in a booth and get to know one another better. Sophie's Hideaway is terribly British."

"I've heard of Sophie's but have never been there. It's highly recommended. Not your standard pickup joint."

With a hint of her magnificent smile, Bethany whispered, "Rest assured, I won't behave badly. That doesn't mean I wouldn't like to hold you throughout the night and try to heal your hurt."

When the bill arrived, Carrie immediately snatched it. Although I attempted to retrieve it, she was insistent. "You're our guests. And besides, I'm well-minted. And well-comped."

"She is," Bethany said. "She is indeed toffee-nosed. And also owns a travel agency where she gets complimentary passes to everything imaginable. So, it's on the house. Quite literally."

"Freebies are my big draw with women." We all joined in Carrie's howling laughter. "There's truth to that statement."

We'd called for a cab. While we waited, Bethany said with a smirk, "After a couple of drinks, Carrie likes to snog in the backseat of the cab. Just warning." She took my hand in a nonchalant gesture. "Act like we don't know them."

"Snog?" I asked as we entered the cab.

"Make out," Esther answered. "Interchangeable with canoodling."

"Well, let's canoodle our way to Sophie's," Carrie said.

The short trip by cab was riotous, exciting, and agreeable.

"Love a slap-up meal, then a little dancing," Bethany said as we entered the club.

Sophie's Hideaway was dim-lit and filled with women of our persuasion. The dance floor was surrounded by tables, and a wraparound bar ran along two sides.

Esther maneuvered herself beside me. "What are you thinking?"

"This is terrific."

She gave a nod in Bethany's direction. "And?"

"And she's nice."

"Nice? Carrie calls women like you custard brain. Bethany is beautiful, in case you haven't noticed."

"Oh, I've noticed. And quit calling me custard brain."

"Well, what am I supposed to say when it seems you're not getting the picture? Amazingly, she seems to be impressed by you and seems to find you somewhat agreeable. I'm very proud of you, Danielle. So try not to botch it."

As Bethany approached, she asked, "What are you two plotting? An early escape?"

"Absolutely not," I said, although the thought had crossed my mind. I wasn't sure how I wanted the night to end. She put her arm around my waist as we walked toward a table. "I'm truly enjoying the evening."

I realized I hadn't honestly given anyone a chance because I'd been waiting for Molly. Bethany had so many qualities I admired. She was jovial, and yet I imagined could be formidable. She had a strong confidence, a humor, and she was more than attractive. Esther was right. Bethany was indeed a catch.

After two more glasses of wine, I agreed to a dance. When we entered one another's embrace, our eyes locked for a moment. I was the first to break from our gaze. Bethany's touch was warm and tender. We moved well together with the music.

Esther and Carrie danced, cavorted, and laughed. I was happy to see Esther so enthralled. We stayed long enough to close down the bar and then found a cab. Carrie suggested we go to their apartment.

Bethany glanced my way for approval.

"I'd really rather get back to my hotel, if you don't mind."

"Make the first stop the Marshall Hotel," Bethany told the driver.

"Sorry."

She patted my hand. "It's okay. I don't have expectations. Maybe hopes of a goodnight kiss. But if you'd care to save that for"—she looked at her watch—"tonight's date. That's fine."

"I didn't say I wanted to be alone in my hotel suite."

Staring down at my mouth, she caressed my chin. She guided my lips toward hers. And toward our first kiss. She whispered into my ear, "Danielle, may I accompany you to your hotel?"

"I'd like that very much." Our lips gently met again. Her kiss was soft and sensuous. "Very much."

Chapter 16

Although Bethany came to the hotel with me under the ruse of continuing our conversation, we both knew there would be more. She enticed me by saying she gave the best backrub in the world. It was divine, as was her prescribed remedy for my happiness. She said I needed to be held in her arms.

Of course, it didn't end there. We made love. No promises, no commitments, and no other incarcerating words were spoken, nor were needed. We talked afterward into the early morning hours, sharing bits and pieces of our lives. It was simply a night we both wanted to share. And had.

Now, as I stood near the bed and watched her waking, I thought it had been one of the most divine adventures of my life. Although sex was better understood with age, it was nearly as confusing as when I was younger. The novelty of sexual encounters had gone, but its mystery endured. It had been an amazing exchange of tenderness and passion. It had also been, as promised, medicinal.

I had awakened with happiness. Or perhaps I awoke beside happiness. For Bethany's upbeat demeanor had an impact on my previous gloom. Even her smile as she was waking told me of her blissful spirit. So much of a person was written on their face, I mused. Bethany's morning face was lovely. Her sensitive nature, her humor, and grace made her shine.

"Good morning," she said softly. "Nice celebration."

"Very nice." I returned to the bed and kissed her forehead. "I was about to call room service for breakfast. What are you hungry for?"

Her laugh was low and sexy. "Would you like to make that order specific to brekky?"

"Coffee or tea? And breakfast?" I asked with a smile of satisfaction.

"Coffee. Ham, eggs over easy, and wheat toast."

I ordered breakfast and sat near her on the bed. "Last night was wonderful."

"Yes, it was. Danielle, I hope you haven't gotten the wrong idea. To be honest, I don't sleep around. I've had to know someone extremely well before. I've never shared love with anyone after first meeting them."

"I thought I had retired from Sapphism altogether." I ducked my head, suddenly feeling a little shy. "Before what I believed to be retirement, I had only slept with someone I'd just met once. And that was Molly."

Bethany raised my chin with a touch. "I suppose that means I'm in good company. But for what it's worth, I didn't view you as a stranger from the moment Esther introduced us. I've told you so much about myself, and learned so much about you, that it's difficult to think we're in any way foreign to one another."

I nodded. "It's as if I really know you. You told me about your parents and your siblings. Your life in Canada and moving to London. And your degree from Oxford University. How impressive." I leaned over and kissed her. "Lucky for me, you stayed on in London, or we never would've met."

She returned the kiss with a little more ardor. "And you told me about your brother, Dylan. About how we share the love of art, our other likes and dislikes. I think if we'd signed up for a dating service, we'd have been paired together, don't you?" She noticed one of the sketches on the bedside table and reached for it. I'd drawn the sketches of her before she awakened. "It's me. How did you capture me so quickly?" She flipped through the other drawings.

They were striking resemblances of her while we were at the club last night.

"I'm fortunate. For whatever reason, it's as if my mind takes a photograph of people and things I'd like to paint. Moments captured in time. This morning, I did some drawings of you from our date. Especially your smile."

"Amazing. They're lovely."

"I first realized I could memorize what I saw when I was staying with my mother in Kansas. There was a bison reserve not far from her apartment. I would trek to the reserve and sketch. I tried to picture the bison so I could paint them. I can close my eyes, even now, and see them clearly. I think all people can recall images. See in the mind's eye. My visual recollection seems to be very accurate."

Bethany closed her eyes. "I can see my family. Not well enough to paint them though."

"You don't object to my sketching you, do you?"

"Not at all. As long as I'm fully dressed, I'm honored," she joked. "Lovely."

"You're lovely." Glancing at the few sketches, I picked one out. "You can have the others if you'll allow me to use this one to paint your portrait."

"You mean do a painting of me?" she asked with a note of wonder in her voice.

"If you don't object. You would need to sign an artist's release form that Fiona makes me present with my work. I even made Molly sign one years ago when I was still in college. We were together, so it was a joke. One of my art instructors had told me my portraits were too realistic for me not to always make certain I had a release. Molly signed it as a lark. I'm fortunate that she did."

I took a preprinted form from my art case. Bethany signed, adding a happy face at the end of her name. "I'll bet your other models didn't draw you a happy face."

"No. And not one of my other models has made my face as happy as you have in one night." I gathered my courage. "Perhaps it's presumptive of me, but since you have the day off, would you like to do something? Spend it with me?" I proceeded with a rush of words. "I know we have a date for this evening, but you'd had a couple glasses of wine, and I won't hold you to it. But all day and night would be a luxury."

"I'd love it, Danielle. I'll call Carrie and ask her if she'll pack a change of clothing for me. I'm guessing Esther is probably still at our apartment, and maybe she can bring my overnight bag with her when she returns here."

"Maybe Carrie and Esther would like to meet up for a late lunch. Well, very late lunch since we're about to eat breakfast."

We called them, and they quickly agreed to the plan. Room service arrived, and we went into the sitting area to eat. Afterward, for the remainder of the morning, Bethany and I lounged, laughed, and enjoyed one another's company. When I heard a knock on the door, for a moment I experienced a pang of disappointment. Time was so easily spent with Bethany.

"Got your clothes, luv," Carrie said as she greeted Bethany. "And you"—she gave me a hug—"are a dark horse."

Esther was behind Carrie sputtering and giggling like a schoolgirl.

"Can't we just call me a paisley filly?" I asked with a laugh.

"Look at the drawings!" Carrie approached the table. "Bethany, you're a model."

"Danielle might paint my portrait."

Esther looked over Carrie's shoulder. "It's Danielle's ploy to woo women. Paint their portrait. Nudes when they're agreeable."

"I've painted very few nudes. Your ploy is to enchant women with talk of the stars. Or of a search for extraterrestrial intelligence."

"I actually search for extremophiles. You know, organisms able to survive in extreme environments." Esther made crawly motions with her fingers.

"Like London?" Carrie teased.

"Well, a tad more extreme," Esther said. "We just don't know what the universe is capable of coding."

Carrie added, "I don't want E.T.s roaming around. We have enough scum creatures posing as wind-up dolls." She continued to examine my drawings. "These are superb. Do you always draw and paint people?"

"I've done very few that aren't. I love the diversity of the human face and form."

"And for some reason, most of her work seems to be pictures of women," Esther said with a wink.

Bethany left the room, carrying her overnight bag, to shower and change into fresh clothing.

Carrie pointed to the chair and waited for me to sit down. "Listen, Danielle, you take care not to hurt Bethany."

I glanced over at Esther for support. There was none. "Pardon?"

"Bethany is an extraordinarily special, kind woman. I don't want to see her hurt."

I gave a quick nervous laugh. "Carrie, I care for Bethany. She's a wonderful, bright, affectionate person. But we had a talk before… Well, before…" I felt my face flush. "No strings attached. We both agreed."

"You just bedded her, luv," Carrie said and glared at me.

"I… I…" I stammered.

She and Esther burst into laughter.

Esther was holding her sides and had to catch her breath. "Gotcha!"

I covered my eyes with my hand. "I'm going to need a midday toddy after that."

"I have a comp for that, too," Carrie said.

"I'll bet," I told her.

Carrie sat down on the nearby sofa. "Speaking of comps, let's plan on Clouds. We can have a chin-wag, and they have the most luscious crab cakes with avocado sauce on the planet." She pointed at Esther. "No comment about interplanetary cuisine from you, please."

"I'll leave the two of you to skirmish about other worlds." I stood. "I'm going to grab a shower and dress. I hope you two get a grip by the time I return."

"If you're planning to shower with Bethany, we might have a long wait," Esther said. While I glared at her, the two of them howled with laughter. I nearly danced into the bedroom in my attempt to escape.

Chapter 17

Between moments of being hassled unmercifully, I had checked voice mail. Fiona wanted a confab. Roxie said that Sadie, Clover, and Aggie were playing hard together and enjoying autumn camp. It did my heart good to know the three dogs were managing without us.

Esther, Carrie, Bethany, and I went to lunch at Clouds. Carrie was right. The crab cakes were the best I'd ever had. We then returned to my suite, and I did a quick sketch of Carrie and gave it to her. She was enormously pleased and promised not to call me a bossy boots, git, scruff, wally, or twit. Without any success, I also offered the same deal to Esther. She told me she had enough of my drawings, thank you very much.

Esther and Carrie broke away, opting to go on an afternoon shopping spree. Since I needed to stop by the gallery, Bethany suggested I give her a guided tour of my exhibit. She wanted to see the paintings through my eyes.

Entering the gallery with Bethany was so different from entering alone. She showed enormous enthusiasm for each picture, which made me feel special. I was impressed with her knowledge of classical art. When we arrived at the last painting I'd done, she was enthralled with it. *A Scene* had an impact on us both. I liked the larger format. I planned at that moment to use one of the two remaining large canvases for my painting of Bethany.

"Danielle," Fiona called to me. "Can I borrow you for a moment?"

I followed her to the office where she shut the door. "What is it?"

"One. The owners want you to stay on another week. Two. They would like you to put a price on your last paintings."

"*Reunion* and *Scene*?"

"They've had a great deal of interest in them."

"*Scene* only went up yesterday afternoon."

66

"Work with me on this, Danielle. They also have a TV interview scheduled for later this afternoon. The media is sending a production team over here."

"I'll stay an extra week. I've never left Clover so long, though." I chewed on my lower lip, thinking about my sweet schnauzer. "But Roxie should be able to manage another week."

"You know Roxie is great with the dogs. And you've said yourself that Clover loves her."

"I'll do the interview, of course. As for selling the paintings..."

Fiona sighed. "The gallery isn't in business to *show* your paintings. They're here in this fancy area with high overhead and luxury décor so they can *sell* your work."

"I'm aware of that. But they have a couple dozen other paintings to sell. A few more that Roxie's sending should be here this afternoon."

"Danielle, please don't be difficult. This is important. I heard that a museum in Amsterdam and one in Paris might be after *Reunion*. Come on, you are on the threshold. Don't turn diva on me now. Getting you here has been a struggle."

"Don't get me wrong, Fiona, I appreciate everything you've done for me."

"One of the things," Fiona said, "that separates the Sunday painter from the true artist is the ability to understand that none of your work belongs to you. Not if your talent is truly priceless. It belongs to generations beyond." She kept pushing. "You're late in coming to the party. You don't have time to fuck around. Great museums chronicle art history. Give your works a good home so you can be placed within the hierarchy of history. I'll give you an enlarged studio photograph of each of them. Have the duplicate photos to hang anywhere you like. But get your work into museums."

"Are you talking as my friend or my fifteen-percent agent?"

Fiona gently squeezed my shoulder. "You may not agree with me. But trust my professional decisions. You must know why I represent you by now. One thing I have always done as long as I've been your agent, and I'll continue doing it. I look out for your best interest. As your friend *and* agent. Don't become too attached to your work."

"As my friend, can you understand how I feel?"

"Danielle, you're a true artist. You aren't some self-proclaimed exhibitionist interested in the spectacle, celebrity, and money. I do know your art matters to you. Critics are pushing you now. A reviewer compared you to a master chef who has the knack to perfect a sumptuous dinner. They say you implement all the qualities of advancing and retreating colors and your gradation of color is brilliant. Please think this over carefully. I worked with enough self-delusional imitators when I started this business. I tried not to market some of the fools. They were money-hungry frauds. They aren't like you. You're my prize. I've always believed in your talent."

"I don't understand why these paintings are so important to you."

"Where you're represented is vital. Museums and collections pave the way to greatness. They are critically important. I want you to sell those paintings for astronomical sums because they're worth it. Prices value you. I want your work in the most prestigious museums and shows in the world. Because these painting will elevate you to where you belong. These two paintings are that great. But if you fiddle fart around, the train will leave without you."

"Give me a moment. I want to look at them." I went out to the floor and stood in front of each painting for many minutes, allowing myself the time to let them go. Fiona had followed and stood behind me. "I do trust you, Fiona. I do. Okay. You put a price on them."

"Four-hundred thousand for *Reunion* and six for *Scene*."

My mouth dropped open. "You can't be serious!"

"I can be and I am. After all, *Goodbye* sold for one-hundred thousand. Right now, there's a rush to collect your art. We've advanced pricing on all of your work. Ones you painted years ago have more than quadrupled. And I expect them to be appreciating daily. Especially those two latest works. I give you my word. If they don't bring my price, I won't sell them. It's nonnegotiable."

I nodded. "Fine." Tears filled my eyes. "Fiona, it's probably for the best. I'm not sure I could look at either of them day in and day out. It might break my heart entirely."

"Just because Molly hasn't contacted you might not mean she doesn't care."

"It's a pretty damned good imitation of not caring," I said as I swiped at my wet cheek. "I do wonder why I read love in her smile."

"We all have our ways of caring. Maybe you don't know the entire story."

"For the first time in thirty years, maybe I do know."

"That reminds me. Samantha Wesley called." Fiona retrieved a slip of paper out of her breast pocket. "She's been trying to reach you. Mystery solved. She's the one who's been calling but didn't want to bother you at your hotel when you're working. At least see what she wants."

I took the slip of paper. Without looking at the number, I pressed it into my handbag. "What time would you like me back here for the interview?"

"Half past three. Four at the latest. And give me a promise you'll call Samantha Wesley."

"Of course I'm going call her. I want to ask her if she knows who purchased *Farewell.*"

"Would it help you to know?"

"I like knowing where my paintings are living. If they're going to be well taken care of." I waved my hand at her. "I can't explain it."

"You have the right to know where it is. When the gallery signed the purchase order and authenticity papers, there was a confidentiality clause. The identity of the buyer must remain classified. Off the record, don't bother asking Molly's daughter. The Franklin-Lewis Institute of Art purchased it. They're enormously high on your work. They also have two others. One of their directors in Ireland acquired those."

"Ah, another mystery solved. The online purchases. I promise not to mention it until they release the information."

"Right. We like foundations to make their own announcements. Any more overnight paintings to show me?"

"I was busy last night. Gallivanting. And then busy."

Fiona smiled her mystical, flickering smile that lit up her face when she had information. Or presumed information. "I don't doubt that for an instant. Gives you incentive. Maybe a little inspiration. I guess you'll paint again as soon as you stop gallivanting."

I leaned back against the counter. "Fiona, I know you think my need to paint emanates from some elevated muse. But for me painting is an attempt to document my vision. And yes, admittedly, to replicate an emotion."

"It's nice you're able to replicate by recharging your emotional reserve with..." She let her words trail off as she chuckled. She pointed toward Bethany. "What did you say her name is?"

"Bethany. Come on, I'll introduce you. She's fifty-four. Way too old for you, and at this time I've got to add, way too old for Esther."

Fiona issued a mock gasp. "Surely not. Esther is a cougar now?"

"It would appear so. She hasn't given me one of her astro-reports for two days. I haven't a clue what quadrant of the sky Venus is in."

"Obviously, Venus is directly over you." She gave me a sly grin. "Wouldn't you say?"

Chapter 18

The television interview seemed to meet with Fiona's approval. I was thrilled when it finally ended. Bethany had watched patiently in the wings. From the corner of my eye, I would catch a glimpse of her from time to time. Her smile warmed me. Encouraged me.

We bid Fiona farewell, then Bethany and I went to a small Italian restaurant Fiona had highly recommended. We laughed and shared stories over a sampler platter for two containing small portions of Portobello ravioli, sausage lasagna, mussels fra diavolo, and chicken saltimbacca. For dessert, we split a tiramisu. Agreeing we overdid it on the caloric intake, we promised we would order salads for at least the next ten years.

Once we were back in my hotel suite, I made multiple sketches of Bethany. I felt happier than I had in perhaps thirty years but didn't try to analyze the reason. We continued our conversation about our lives as I started the painting using the 44x56 canvas. My arm seemed to circle the canvas as I traced the outlines of Bethany. Her smile was entrancing, and I tried to capture it in my painting. After I began to form facial features, I stood away from the canvas a moment. Bethany got up from the sofa where she'd been sitting and looked at the painting. She glanced at me, her lips turned upward. She took her thumb and wiped paint from my cheek. Then she kissed the side of my mouth and went back to her pose on the sofa. "A perfect likeness, Danielle."

"Give it time," I joked. "I think I can get a little more realism."

"But you do get mussed up, luv."

"I wear as much paint as I put on the canvas."

Painting her was an enchanting experience. Touching her was the same, and I shivered with memories of my fingertips on her skin. When I concluded for the night, I put down my brushes.

With the same ritual of the previous evening, we undressed, showered, went to bed, and made love. Afterward, we fell into a deep, satiated, and peaceful sleep.

Morning arrived early since Bethany needed to get up at six for work. She was conscientious about her job, and I fully appreciated that. She had told me that, for the past decades, she'd been on call, worked round the clock, and often went two or three weeks without days off.

I didn't want her leaving my side. Our kiss goodbye lingered. She promised to call me later. I hoped she would.

To keep my mind occupied, I began painting immediately after she left. A couple hours later, I closed my eyes for a moment then opened them. Her image was beginning to appear, and my heart felt a rush. As I set down my brush, I glanced over at my purse and remembered the slip of paper Fiona had given me with Samantha's number. Now was as good a time as any to call her.

She answered immediately. "Danielle, I'm so happy to hear from you."

"I wasn't sure why you were calling. Is Molly okay?"

"She isn't aware I'm phoning. Could we get together for lunch today? I realize it's short notice."

"It's fine. I'm available."

"Let's meet at Razzmatazz at noon. I'll book us a table."

"I'll be there." Somewhere deep within me was a hope that Molly would accompany Samantha. But Samantha had stressed Molly wasn't aware of her call. I reined in my hope. "Noon at Razzmatazz," I said before hanging up.

Glancing at the clock, I saw I had a couple of hours to paint before getting ready for lunch. I began daubing colors gently. Then I heard a rap at the door.

"Danielle, it's Esther."

I pulled back the door. "Come in. Just dragging yourself back to the hotel at midmorning?" I teased. "British women will be calling you their Yankee crumpet."

"At least one woman is referring to you as that. I saw Bethany this morning. She scurried in, got ready for work, and announced you are wonderful. Then she scampered off to work. Wonderful, Danielle. Shocked me."

"Wonderful?" I said as I poured Esther a strong cup of coffee. "This java is probably a little cool from when I had brekky earlier this morning."

"It's fine. Anything that will wake me up." Esther sat across from the table and sipped. "That portrait is really good. Bethany makes a nice model."

"I've just begun actually. It'll probably need a couple of days' work before it's where I want it. I'd like to have had Bethany continue sitting for me, but she had to go to work."

"She was so excited that you're painting her portrait. You do realize she thinks you're special?"

"We're very compatible, and I'm comfortable being with her. Oh, I meant to tell you I'm staying on an extra week. Fiona says the gallery is going to extend my show." I added more paint to the canvas. "So, any chance you'll stay on until the exhibit is over?"

"Let me check my retiree calendar." She unfolded the air and turned imaginary pages. "Ah yes, I'm open and certainly it would be great to remain here. My retiree travel budget will be shot for a while, but oh well."

"You can move up here with me. The gallery is splurging for my suite."

"If I bunk with anyone, it really should be with my squeeze. In fact, Carrie asked this morning about my staying with her. It would be more convenient if I were there. But I think I'll manage where I am. Independence, you know?"

"Yes, I do know you." I added a stroke to the canvas. "Samantha called. I'm meeting with her today."

"Samantha?" Esther bolted upright. "Can't Molly do her own bidding?"

"Molly isn't aware of the meeting. I took it Samantha would prefer she didn't know about it. Maybe Samantha wants to talk about art. Fiona said she's well-versed in the art world. I agreed to meet her at noon. Razzmatazz."

"Upscale restaurant. Carrie would say posh."

"Carrie is fun. I like her. And so do you."

"And do you like Bethany as much as she likes you?"

I couldn't help smiling. "We're sharing time and enjoying it. Then I'm going back to Colorado, and she'll continue to be a Londoner."

"Danielle, she has feelings for you. I can tell."

"If you're implying she's smitten, you're wrong. She's well aware I'll be leaving. I do hope we can continue our friendship from across the pond."

Esther leaned forward, her expression earnest. "She's allowing you to forget Molly."

"No one allows me to forget Molly," I said with irritation. "If I haven't forgotten Molly in thirty years, I rather doubt my mind is going to cancel her out now." I threw down the paintbrush and crossed my arms. "Love isn't a self-dissolving emotion."

Esther raised her hands in supplication. "Okay, don't get upset about it."

"The time I'm spending with Bethany is wonderful. Molly is still in my heart. Even if she wasn't, Bethany loves London and loves her profession. She's been with the airline forever, and at only mid-fifty, she's hardly likely to leave it."

"With thirty years' service, she's eligible to retire. I remember her mentioning it at dinner."

"Were you listening to our conversation?" I asked, my anger now gone. "Goodness, but you are a little busybody. So what's going on with Mercury right now?"

"Mercury is somewhere over Denver. There's probably a meteor shower pounding down trying to locate you. The goddesses wish to tell you how stubborn you are."

"Or maybe they're searching for you to tell you how daft you are."

"You're still holding out hope for a reunion with Molly." She wasn't asking a question.

"Esther, I'm not certain what I'm doing right now. Other than painting a portrait."

She stood up and examined it closely. "It looks exactly like Bethany. Are you planning to convert it into another Molly masterpiece?"

I glared at her. "You'll stay the extra week?"

"Sure, but after that, I should return. Poor Sadie and Aggie."

"Aggie is having the time of her alpha life. Sadie will be fine. They're very well-adjusted dogs. Like I say, the offer remains if you want to bunk with me."

Esther wrinkled her nose as she sat down again. "I do love you, my friend. But I can only take you in small doses." She smirked as I gave her a harshly reproving look. "Come on, O'Hara, lighten up. A little joke is not the end of the universe as we know it."

"You can be very snitty. I certainly have no idea about the end of the universe. I just know life seems a little out of control right now."

"This has been a lot to process in a short time," she said. "Just seeing Molly would have been emotional. Or just meeting Bethany. The fates are ganging up on you."

"Fates," I repeated. "Esther, it's surreal. My sudden success, meeting a woman I could fall in love with. Seeing the woman I'm still in love with. In some ways I wish I'd never set foot in England. Never left Colorado."

"The way you're acting, I'll bet London women also wish you'd never set foot off of Colorado soil."

"You know, Ms. Lilly, if I drop-kicked you from here, you probably could set foot on some nearby galaxy's major supernova's soil."

Our laughter came in gales for several moments.

"Think of me up there with all that gas and dust. All those ultraviolet and X-rays. Out there searching for the light of life. In my element."

"What?"

"Ah, yes. Homochirality!"

Frowning, I said, "And it gets worse."

"It's a good thing as an artist you don't need to do research. Try doing a little scrutiny of past visuals."

I glanced at my wristwatch. "I've got to get ready. And I'd like to do it without any banter."

Esther finished her coffee and stood. "What do you think you'll be discussing when you meet with Samantha?"

"She simply wants to talk with me. I agreed. I like her very much. I won't even ask about Molly. Will that make you happy?" My anger returned, burning my face. "I'm completely without the ability to do anything concerning Molly. That inability has been with me every day for the past thirty years. For God sakes, I'm trying to hold myself together. Molly is here in this city, and I can't do one damned thing for her love."

"Danielle, don't get your hopes up. This isn't necessarily a signal you're getting back together with Molly."

"It doesn't mean we couldn't."

She took my hand in hers. "Don't set yourself up."

"No. At least I'll try not to hope."

I was glad when Esther said goodbye and left me alone with my thoughts.

Chapter 19

The Razzmatazz sat on the corner of the block in an elite area. As I entered, I made note of the luxurious recreation of a Jazz Age bistro. Walls were ruby with gold sconces and décor. Brightly styled furniture displayed aqua, roan, and ivory colors. Poster-sized, black-and-white photographs of Jazz Age celebrities lined the walls, with at least one above every table.

The restaurant was filling up rapidly. Samantha sat near an F. Scott Fitzgerald photo. I spotted her as she waved in my direction.

As I joined her, I noticed she'd already ordered a bottle of wine and filled two glasses. I smiled. "How have you been?"

"Life seems to speed by so rapidly, and I never get anything done," she complained with good humor. "But I'm taking priorities first. It's important that I speak with you about Mother."

"Maybe she'd rather you not." I was curious, and when interrupted by the server, I was slightly impatient. We ordered quickly. Thankfully, Samantha continued where she'd left off.

"Danielle, there are things you might not understand."

"The facts I see indicate Molly doesn't want any part of me. If she wanted me in her life, she would've contacted me ten years ago. And certainly after we met at the market. I told her where I'm staying. She also could have easily looked me up at the gallery, just as you did."

"She's still in love with you."

I sat back and allowed Samantha's words to resonate with me. "She's ignored me for all these years because she's still in love with me?" I laughed harshly. "I think not."

"I realize it's difficult to believe. But I've always known she loves you."

"Then why didn't she contact me? She knew I would have taken her back without questions."

"Her life with Pamela was complicated. My biological mother was brilliant, beautiful, and certainly manipulative. Pamela wrote books about philosophy. She lectured in the most prestigious universities. Molly was her acolyte when they first met. The older, famous, author-slash-professor swept her student, Molly, away. Molly was seduced. Then after they were together, it was too late to leave Pamela."

Frowning, I took a sip of my wine. "She falls for her gorgeous, celebrated, rich professor, and I'm not a raging beauty. Leaves me after an eight-year relationship. I've been scraping by for years. Until the last few years, no one has even known my name. She picked the woman she wanted and stayed with her for twenty years. End of story."

"She didn't stay because of Pamela. I'm the reason she stayed." Samantha stared down at the table.

"I don't understand." Our lunches were placed before us. Although they looked and smelled delicious, I had lost my appetite. So many questions beleaguered me.

"Danielle, the reason I'm trying to make things right now is because if it hadn't been for me, she would've gone back to you. I know she's in love with you, and I know from your painting you're in love with her. But it's complicated."

Now I was intrigued, and I allowed some of my bitterness to slip away. "I'm listening."

"After a year or so, Pamela's drinking problem began to increase. My biological mother was an alcoholic. She was careful not to show her drinking to Molly at first. I strongly suspect when the affair began, Molly had let her guard down because she had been, as they say, plied with alcohol."

"Did Molly say that was the reason?"

"She implied it once when they were fighting. Yes."

"Molly wasn't even a drinker."

"I know. I'm sure after Pamela seduced her, Molly felt guilty she'd succumbed. Then, after terminating your relationship and relocating, she understood her mistake when confronted with Pamela's rages and tantrums. Molly realized she'd be leaving me behind to take the brunt of Pamela's cruelty. She wouldn't leave a child behind to be mistreated. I was only a few years old, but I knew what was happening. The only happiness in my life was Molly. She knew I relied on her."

It was starting to make sense. "She couldn't ask the courts to make her the custodial parent. Biological mother would win that one. Especially thirty years ago."

"Exactly. Pamela saw what an immediate and strong bond I had with Molly. She was aware Molly would never leave her because it meant leaving me with a cruel alcoholic. I feel responsible for Molly staying. Pamela would often scream that Molly would never see me again if she left. So now I would like to see the woman I consider my true mother happy."

"Molly was your link to safety, wasn't she?"

"She protected me from Pamela's vicious temper." Samantha held my gaze. "You're right, she was my only lifeline. I adored Molly's kindness. I was a child, but I knew I was in jeopardy."

"Staying was Molly's decision. You can't take responsibility for her staying with Pamela." I paused and regrouped my thoughts. "That explains away twenty years. But after Pamela died, why didn't Molly contact me? When you became of age, why didn't she contact me then?"

"I asked her that not too long after Pamela died. She said she would have been embarrassed after the way she treated you. She didn't want to mess your life up again by allowing you to care for her. She also believed you had probably found happiness with someone else."

"I'm so sorry you had such a troubled childhood. An alcoholic or a parent with a drug addiction is a treacherous minefield to get through." I had my grandparents. Samantha had Molly.

"Molly sacrificed so much in making my childhood good, as well as safe. And now I'd like to do what I can to reunite the two of you."

"What did she say when you gave her the painting?"

"*Myths and Memories.* She loved it. She wept. That's when I knew she's still in love with you. She went online to look for your other paintings at the exhibit. She saw *Farewell to Molly.* She was inconsolable."

"I'm sorry if I brought her pain. I must confess that I've painted two more paintings of her since then. One is titled *Reunion's First Glimpse,* and the other, *A Scene from Our Story.*"

"I'm aware of them. They've both been purchased."

I watched her face carefully. "As of an hour ago, they hadn't been sold. How could you know this? I didn't even know." I quickly retrieved my cell phone and saw there was an incoming message from Fiona. "My agent has called since I arrived here. Undoubtedly to tell me about the sale. How did you know they were sold?"

"An offshoot of our family foundation purchased them. We keep the foundation's multiple offshoots relatively silent for tax and profitability purposes."

"Your hidden philanthropic foundation purchased the paintings?"

"A family-funded entity."

I bristled. "What's your reason for purchasing them?"

"We treasure them because they are Molly. The soul of Molly. We're proud future generations will see her likeness. Jeff and I will ensure that they're placed only in leading museums. The foundation loans exhibits. My husband is a very gifted businessman. His appreciation of great art makes him a perfect benefactor. He believes your art is going to rapidly appreciate."

"Thank you for your patronage. But I don't consider myself a premier artist."

"You should. I talked with your agent when I called and left the message for you to call me. She told me she's been after you for years to move to New York so you might have more recognition, but you've refused. You were a relatively undiscovered artist. Until now."

"I wanted my work to speak for itself."

"Now it has and will, I promise. Jeff likes being in the forefront. He's selected a brilliant artist's work that also spotlights his beloved mother-in-law. It's a win-win situation."

I smiled. "You both seem to idolize Molly."

"Absolutely. Pamela died before I married Jeff. She had forbidden me to marry him. At that time, his family owned a nearly bankrupt aeronautic company. Her mantra was that one might select a rich man and be as happy as selecting a poor one. She didn't want me corrupted by poverty. I'm sure she was afraid her own wealth might be squandered on a needy husband. In her will, she instituted a clause that half her money was to go to Molly and the other to me, but not until I reached the age of thirty-five. By then, last year, I didn't need her money. The man I married has made me happy."

"What did Molly say about who you should marry?"

Samantha's expression brightened. "She stood by me. She warned me that I'd regret it for the rest of my life if I didn't marry the man I love. Just as she had regretted her choice."

"I can imagine that would anger Pamela."

"It did. We'd made engagement plans before she died. Although she passed away before the wedding, she knew I would marry Jeff. When his father died, the company was millions of dollars in debt. Unencumbered assets were nonexistent. Jeff was saddled with an out-of-control, spendthrift mother, a playboy brother who couldn't care less about the business, and an older sister who helped run the company into the ground."

"The company turned around?"

"Jeff was the youngest. Pamela thought he had no chance of keeping the business afloat. Together, Jeff and I decided to try to make it work. We restructured the company. Put my mother-in-law on a restrictive, yet certainly adequate allowance. Jeff's sister became vice-president of public relations. Amazingly enough, she was not only happier, she was extremely good at her new job. At any rate, we all worked together to rebuild the company and made it stronger than ever."

"It's a shame Pamela didn't see your victory."

Samantha shook her head before taking a sip of wine. "Pamela would never have credited us with anything. She could never be wrong, but she was absolutely right about one thing. Molly never did love her as much as she has loved you all these years."

"I never wanted Molly to be unhappy. Even after she left, it was important to me to believe she would be happier than I could have made her. Maybe that's the reason I finally accepted her leaving. Her happiness."

"Pamela made her unhappy. She put us both through hell."

"Blaming parents only creates negativity in one's own life. I know from experience. If Pamela knew Molly was still in love with someone else, perhaps that exacerbated her drinking."

"Your parents. Molly told me they separated when you were a child and are now dead."

"I once resented them terribly. My mother had an alcohol and drug problem. My father was too young for the responsibility of being a parent. I went through years of blaming them for what they might not have been able to control. When I finally realized that, I felt better about it."

Samantha seemed to let my words sink in. "Thank you, Danielle, I appreciate your insight. That wasn't something I had considered."

"You're too nice a person to live with pain. Whatever made you the person you are today was good. You're a lovely, decent woman, Samantha. You've created a terrific family, and you have love in your heart. That can't be anything but good."

"I only wish you and Molly had raised me."

I gripped her hand and said, "I think we all would have loved that. I know Molly must be so proud of you. I would have been."

Samantha placed her other hand on top of mine. "Will you call my mom?"

I tried to pull out of her grasp, but she held my hand tightly. "I'm not as sure as you that she wants to hear from me."

"And I'm sure that she does. Please, Danielle?" She squeezed my hand.

"All right. I'll call her."

"Do you still have her phone number?"

Sheepishly, I confessed, "Yes, I do, and you have my word, I'll call her." Of course, I had entered the number into my cell phone… as well as engraved it in my heart and mind.

Chapter 20

After leaving the restaurant, I strolled the sidewalks and mulled over the simple facts. Molly hadn't returned to me because of her worry for Samantha's well-being. And Samantha, the most innocent of all, now wrestled with her past. A child shouldn't have worn some faux anvil of culpability around her neck for all these years. My heart broke for Samantha's youth.

Childhood memories of haphazard hugs from drunken parents bombarded me, and a sadness about my own lost youth settled on my shoulders. I blinked the tears away when I reached the gallery, not even aware of how long I had walked.

Fiona pounced on me when I entered. "Why didn't you tell me you're working on another painting?" she asked, slightly hostile.

"What?"

"Esther dropped by early this morning. I mentioned that since you have a romantic interest, you've lost your craving to paint. The urge and surge that produced such great recent work has vanished. Anyway, she jumped to your defense by telling me you're working on a painting of Bethany. I'm in the dark. I know nothing about the new painting."

"I didn't mention it because I don't know if it will be very good."

"Let me be the judge of that. What pisses me off is that you let me think you had shut down your blizzard of work." She paused before gathering more steam. "Esther probably thinks I'm a fucking nincompoop because I don't even bother to keep up with you."

Her anger got under my skin. I had a question of my own. "Why didn't you mention that Franklin-Lewis is a branch of the Wesley Foundation? The Wesley family has purchased the lion's share of my paintings over the week."

"Jeffery and Samantha bought them?"

"You didn't know?" I scrutinized her face for any sign of deception.

"Hell no, I didn't know. Don't be a fool. You know everything I know. The minute I know it. Hidden foundations are just that—hidden. At least the paintings are in great hands. Their foundations exhibit in the finest museums. You should be pleased."

"I don't understand why they're being purchased by separate branches of their foundation, or however they're doing it."

Fiona shrugged her shoulders. "I'm not certain. I think maybe between the two of them, they're brilliant enough to realize that a diversity of many buyers brings competition. A marketing strategy."

I thought about it, and it made sense. "Sounds reasonable. They weren't attempting to keep it from me. I met with Samantha today. She confessed when I said I'd painted a couple new paintings of Molly. She said they had sold. I then guessed that they'd been involved."

"Yes. But that isn't all," Fiona said. "You've sold another four in the past day. I know the people who have purchased them. Some of your early work. A couple more that are in the New York Gallery are being held until paperwork is pushed through. Whatever the plan was by Jeffery and Samantha, it's creating a hot market for your artwork. A stampede. Danielle, I'm sorry I jumped you about your new painting. I'm damned pleased your compulsion to work hasn't turned off."

"On the contrary, I can't wait to get back to my suite and paint. But I'm not sure it'll be any good." Giving her a quick hug, I added, "I'll tell you the minute I'm pleased with it, Fiona."

"At least with Bethany's portrait you seem to be benefiting by some added bonus action," she said with a wicked grin. "The question is, does it increase your painting ability?"

"What do you think?" I waggled my eyebrows.

"Fluttering genitalia can't hurt creativity. Speaking of women, what did Samantha say about Molly?"

"I'm going to call Molly. Samantha's idea, not Molly's. I don't know what to think about it all, but I promised I'd phone."

If Fiona was going on a fishing expedition to find out information about Molly, I was not her catch of the day.

With precious timing, Max Parker and Spencer Murphy approached. Max blustered with his usual vibrato, and Spencer patiently heeled. Max grabbed me with a bear hug.

"Memorable, I tell you. I'm so pleased you'll be able to stay on another week. I predict an even better week next week than the blockbuster we have going now. Did I just overhear that there's a new painting to be previewed?"

"I'll let you all know when it's finished."

"Just call," Max said. "We'll send Spence up to get it. Is it another large format?"

"It's 44 by 56."

"Too big for you to be lugging around. Spence will pick it up the minute you're finished. Leave the varnishing for us. We have a fan system to dry it fast and get it framed and on the wall."

"Thanks, Max." I turned to Spencer. "And Spence. Thank you all, and please tell your associates thanks for me also."

We said our goodbyes. A sharp breeze slapped my face as I stepped outside.

As I walked, I thought about Molly. I dreamed we'd fall into each other's arms. Our embrace would be for all the years we'd missed. We had a chance to rekindle the love that had always been there because, according to Samantha, Molly hadn't stopped loving me.

My thoughts suddenly shifted. Bethany was also in the emotional mix. Implausible as it might be, I felt in some ways that I knew Bethany better than I knew the Molly of today. I set the thought aside by convincing myself that Molly probably hadn't changed.

Reflecting on the years Molly and I spent together, I thought of her when she was the keeper of my heart. Her little idiosyncrasies like waking with her holding me, laughing at our own simple jokes, the snap of her head when she was irritated. I recalled her constant kindnesses and considerations to everyone near her.

All of life was subject to its own metamorphosing. Souls had been modified. Perhaps time's shifting had become too great for us to resume a love affair. Or maybe no matter how enormously experiences had recast our separate lives, by episodes and by occurrences, perhaps love endured.

If I were to believe love wasn't capable of persisting for itself alone, I would be saddened beyond belief. For in the final analysis, what else was there?

Chapter 21

Bethany called to tell me she had a late meeting and wasn't sure when she might be able to drop by later. I suggested we order from room service when she arrived. That left a chunk of the afternoon to work on the portrait and to place the promised call to Molly.

I lifted the telephone tentatively and began dialing.

"Danielle?" she answered with such amazement I was certain Samantha hadn't told her I might call. "Samantha gave you my number?"

"I hope you don't mind. Molly, I would like to see you. Talk with you."

There was a long pause. "Do you really think that's a good idea? We were so long ago."

"It's a good idea for me. If it isn't for you, then I won't bother you again. After all, we shared a large portion of our early adulthood together. And I still have a lot of good memories. At least we can have a civil meeting and remember the past. The good times we shared. Catch up." I waited out another moment of silence.

"Danielle, I'm all caught up. You seem to know about my achievements and failures. There really isn't much else to say." Her voice softened. "I'm happy you've achieved success in your art."

"You've also succeeded as an educator and as a mother. I'd like to know more. How about we meet for lunch tomorrow? Just an hour or two of your time. It would mean the world to me."

"All right. I'd forgotten how persuasive you could be. Lunch would be fine."

"You tell me the place. I'm okay with anywhere."

"How about Fav's, a small neighborhood restaurant I love. It has a variety of choices on the menu. European fare." She gave me the address.

"I'll be there. Thank you for agreeing to see me. You've never left my thoughts over the years. I still recall our walks in the park, all the silliness, and certainly the love we shared."

"It was a long time ago." Her voice sounded tired and almost curt. "Everything has changed."

I let that go. We decided on noon. When I hung up, I experienced a dichotomy of emotions. Ecstatic that I would be seeing her again, I couldn't help but feel discouraged. She hadn't said she was glad to hear from me. I admonished myself not to expect any type of a romantic reunion. Perhaps it might not even be an amicable meeting.

There was a knock at my door. "Danielle, are you there?" Esther called.

I let her in.

"I have a little time before I meet with Carrie. How did your talk with Samantha go?"

I relayed the conversation and ignored her scowl when I told her about Samantha's request for me to call Molly.

"Did you call her yet?"

"Yes. She was distant. Didn't really want to meet me but agreed after I badgered her."

"Why is she being such a bitch? *She's* the one who derailed your happy home thirty years ago. That you're willing to talk to her at all is a miracle."

"I don't know. Samantha believes she feels guilty about dumping me. She also feels Molly is still in love with me and always has been."

Esther moved her chair closer to the one I had eased my dejected body into. "If that were the case, why wouldn't she be overjoyed to see you again?"

"I have no earthly idea. Samantha divulged some information concerning her home life." I told Esther about Pamela's alcoholism and the reason Molly stayed. "It's obvious that Samantha idolizes Molly. It's also apparent that her love for Pamela is minimal."

Esther pondered my words. "This makes more sense. Molly might have wanted to return to you early in her relationship with Pamela and couldn't because of Samantha. After all, Molly had started out as an elementary school teacher. Always loved kids. She mentioned often that she wanted a family."

"Funny thing is, I always felt she thought of my grandparents as her family. Her family had disowned her when they found out she was lesbian. But having a child for us was impossible."

"That could've been the attraction to Pamela then. Molly might have wanted a child," Esther said. "Got her graduate degree and an instant family."

"Then she worked her way up to professorship. Along with that, she became an alcoholic's nursemaid and a child's nanny-slash-protective parent. When we were together, Molly was strong, assertive, and certainly no one's doormat."

"What did Samantha have to say about that?"

"I didn't ask that question specifically. Only why she'd stayed. Samantha said her biological mother had been a beauty and brilliant. When Molly realized Pamela was a lush, she already felt like she was a mother to Samantha. And there was the threat of losing Samantha which would have endangered the child."

"And now," Esther said, "she's undoubtedly feeling some remorse and probably plenty of guilt. Life's storms. You're getting into choppy water with this one. You do have expectations. I can tell. It might well be a lost cause."

"Maybe. But here we are thirty years later."

"Bethany dropping by tonight?" she asked as she stood up.

"She's got a late meeting, so we planned on a room service dinner here."

"Are you going to tell her about tomorrow's lunch with Molly?"

"Of course I'll tell her. There isn't any reason she should know, though. I'm not promised to either of them."

"But you're already in love with at least one of them." Esther sighed dramatically as she reached for the door. "And I could say maybe both of them. Or is that an option you haven't entertained?"

"You don't hold out much chance for me with Molly, do you?"

She gave another huge sigh. "No. Molly's right in saying it was too long ago. Not that age totally remodels us, but time certainly rearranges us."

I tried to lighten the mood. "How are things going in interplanetary space? Found any space folk in the past twenty-four hours?"

"There's a Martian meteorite that shows microscopic formations. It suggests life might have created those configurations." She pursed her mouth as she turned back toward the door. "Earth is just one big womb for creation. Mars could also have experienced multiple pregnancies in the past."

I heard the swoosh of the door as it shut. Earth, stars, planets… Esther was right in so much of the histories about them. So why wouldn't she be able to sort out my dilemma? Why wasn't I able to sort it out for myself? For me, making decisions often resembled a personal hell.

As the country song went, it may not be hell, but you can see hell from here.

Chapter 22

Bethany was as charming and fun-loving as ever. After our shared dinner from room service, she patiently modeled while I pressed paint against the canvas, working to exact a duplication of her skin tone. Her eyes sparkled in a particular way that I could easily capture.

"Getting tired?" I asked her.

"Some. Today was grueling."

"Okay, I've got what I need. The rest I can finish up tomorrow morning. Relax."

She moved slightly. Then our eyes met. I went to her and eased my arms around her. The embrace was gentle, yet solid.

"You're the most tolerant model I've ever had the honor to paint." I rubbed the back of her neck. "Sorry it was a difficult day."

"Days seem to be getting longer and longer. If you reproduce anything but a tired old woman right now, I'd be amazed. After a day at work, I feel spent as to beauty." A laugh escaped. She had a charming, charismatic laugh, and it always amused me.

Together we studied the painting. The canvas was full, and her smile was certainly the focal point. The smile registered not only on her lips but within her eyes.

"I love it," she said softly.

I cocked my head as I studied it more thoroughly. "Although it's realistic, it has a touch of capriccio in it."

"Capriccio?"

"In art it mixes elements of fantasy with actuality."

"It's also a short piece in music. I'm not certain what kind. Just short."

"I wasn't aware of that. Did you study music?"

"No." Her smile slowly faded. "We lend one another knowledge when there is love. Just like with us, we're teaching one another all kinds of things. At least you're teaching me something about art. You paint with such ease."

"I confess the first five hundred or so of my portraits weren't as easy. But, yes. It gets easier with each swipe of the brush. Maybe I just build on recognizing mistakes. Success is knowing what not to do."

"That's perfect. If it doesn't work, don't do it again." She glanced back at me. "With the exception of love. Love always works. Not always the way we want it."

I nodded in agreement. I then swallowed several words before I said, "Bethany, I'm meeting Molly for lunch tomorrow. At her daughter's request, I called her. And for what it's worth, I talked her into seeing me. I'm not sure why. It's hopeless. But I wanted you to know in case you want to leave."

"Luv, at this precious moment, we are together and I'm here. If I wanted to be elsewhere, I would leave." She reached for my waist and tickled me, causing me to giggle. "Please don't look so serious. So lumbered."

I hugged her. "Thanks for understanding."

"You don't owe me an explanation or an excuse," she said as she withdrew from our embrace. "I reject constraints within my life, and I'm not likely to place constraints on anyone else's life. I'm rather a fatalist. I believe love is finite when it isn't meant to be. And infinite when it is."

"I agree."

"Too many lovers wish to become puppeteers. That has never worked for me. Maybe that's why I understand you." She glanced away. "And in truth, life has taught me that sharing time with someone you love is enough. If there isn't more, I accept that. Or if it's gone from me, I also accept it. Yet still love." She reached out her hand and wiped my face. "How did you get blue paint on your chin?"

"Blueberries for dessert?" I said in jest.

"Good. I was hoping you hadn't broken into the Smurfs' Village again."

Chapter 23

The following noon I sat across the table from Molly as we sipped our wine, awaiting our lunches that we'd ordered. Her smile was courteous, not the smile of someone wanting to be with me. She seemed still and uneasy. We'd hugged each another so briefly that I felt the spring-like motion as she moved away from me. She obviously was reticent to share even a brief graze of our cheeks.

Fav's was an upscale neighborhood brasserie with a cozy terrace and river view. We elected to sit on the terrace, although the sky was cloudy and there was a chill in the air. The décor was vermilion, navy, and white, colored with a wide array of floral art. Brass-hued tables and chairs were circular in design and ultra modern. Autumn foliage and flowers cascaded down from hanging planters. They lined the short brick wall that surrounded the outside dining area. It was charming and yet a bit cold.

After we ordered, I'd hoped that Molly would become less apprehensive. Perhaps that was what kept my own nerves in check. Conversation remained chatty, yet strained.

"Your friends back in Colorado, are they well?" she asked.

"Our friends are fine. As I mentioned, Esther is here in England but lives in Denver. Still single." I paused. "And they truly were *our* friends. Not just mine."

"*Our* friends all sided with you. They never stayed in contact with me after our breakup." Her golden brown eyes clouded over.

"Molly, I never bad-mouthed you. Maybe we all felt abandoned."

"It wasn't my intention to make you or them feel abandoned. I fell in love with someone else, and I moved away."

The words seemed like chunks of great rocks falling in on me. "I realize that. All I ever wanted was your happiness."

"Happiness," she repeated. "Kant states that happiness is not an ideal of reason but of imagination."

"Still quoting Kant?"

"Yes, although so little philosophy seems relevant as I age. I often hope that my life hasn't been a dismal failure as I searched for empty truth and useless wisdom."

"You were an educator. As you aspired to be. You have your lovely family. Samantha is a treasure. That's a great deal to show for your life. There's nothing better. And you've made your family happy."

"We're back to the subject of happiness." She swallowed the next sentence as if it were an egregious enemy. "I find it astonishing that there is any happiness at all in the world. Things are always so complex."

"I don't know if you recall my grandfather's philosophy of happiness. He used to say happiness is a good sense of humor and a bad memory."

Smiling, she said, "He was a wonderful man. I think of your family often."

"I think of you often, Molly."

"It's too bad you don't have a faulty memory. You might be happier now."

"Please don't say that." I felt wounded.

She brushed hair away from her face that the breeze had caught. She wore her hair back in a stylish roll. Her eyes were slightly puffed, and she looked tired. She waited before she responded. "Danielle, when I was thirty it was suddenly as if everything was passing me by. I wanted to do something with my life. That was why I applied to every university I could in order to get into a master's program. I selected the most prestigious university that offered me the best grant. It happened to separate us. If I had believed it might have changed our lives, I would've opted to go to Colorado University and stay near you. I didn't go searching for an affair. It just happened."

Her head lowered. She fiddled with her multicolored blouse's collar. The dark jacket and slack set was chic. Matching shoes and handbag were also elegant. My own beige jacket didn't match with my darker slacks. And the blouse I had selected was several shades of browns and tans.

I looked away. "I understand. I wasn't much of a catch."

"This is exactly what I had hoped not to get into. You were perfect, and I loved you. It's difficult to explain what I did thirty years ago. End of story." Her jawline was set, and her eyes quickly flickered. "Forgive me. I'm so sorry."

"Molly, I've always forgiven you." I tried to keep my tone friendly, fearing my words might sound abrasive. I changed the subject so we were both more comfortable. "I love London."

The tension fell from her face. "It is lovely this time of year."

Finally, after discussing weather, London, and the British, I said, "Thank you for agreeing to see me. You've always remained in my mind and my heart."

"I've thought about you as well, but it hurt to think of you."

"I've never forgotten our life together, regardless of how much it hurt. You've always been with me." The silence became uncomfortable. "I'm being honest. I've never stopped loving you."

"And I'm also being honest. Unfortunately for both of us, there isn't a love do-over. There were so many times in my life when I wished there might be another chance. There wasn't."

"My body is greatly depreciated," I joked. "But it hasn't yet collapsed to obsolescence, so there's always a chance."

She laughed, and it was lovely. "You've always known how to make me happy. And you're still an idealistic optimist."

"I hang out with optimists," I told her. Thoughts of Bethany filled my mind.

"There were times you played the part of a moody artist," she said with a note of challenge.

"Maybe I wanted to appeal to you however I could."

Torment flickered across her face. "You always appealed to me."

"I never felt it was always."

She stiffened. "Maybe you didn't try to feel always."

I attempted to mitigate the alienation I felt. "Molly, let's begin as if we just met. Put the bad parts of thirty years ago behind us. I apologize for anything I've done wrong."

"You've got to know how terrible I feel about leaving you. I let you down. I don't question for a moment that you'd never have let me down."

"Samantha believes you were seduced away by Pamela. I can understand that."

"It was much more complicated. Danielle, I found someone else, and I've regretted it for the past thirty years. Pamela was the wrong choice. But there were layers and layers of unresolved problems we never faced."

"Are you saying we had problems that couldn't be fixed?" I asked incredulously.

"You know we did."

"No, I didn't know. If there were difficulties, why wasn't I aware of them?" I took a gulp of wine, a little too much as it burned my throat.

"I thought you knew. There was a list of shortcomings on both sides. I was a teacher. Although you didn't have a radical gay agenda, you lived your own life honestly. Back then, and in Denver, Colorado, it was difficult for me."

"I was never obvious, but I never denied who I am."

"That was part of you. Being honest with who you are makes you a gifted artist because you're also honest with your art. I could never compete with your art. Be honest about that. No one can. That's also what makes you a great artist."

"I'm not a great artist. At best, I'm borderline."

"You are far better than borderline," she said with a knowing nod. "And you're coming into your own as a very important American artist." She played with her napkin. "Danielle, I apologize for being contentious."

"A little late for both your commentary on our relationship and for my becoming a world-famous artist."

"No, it isn't. Not at all. I'm so proud of you. I Googled you and looked at every single work you've done. Those paintings are brilliant. I'm sublimely pleased you've painted me. Perhaps I'm the only person who can see through the jubilation to the torment. I understand your anger because I left. But in your work, I see that you're never going to get over it. Perhaps never really forgive me."

"Molly, I've already forgiven you. I've never stopped loving you."

"You have never stopped loving what we had, Danielle. I strongly suspect you stopped loving me years ago. If you'll be honest right now, you'll admit that I've caused you years of pain. And you can't be expected to forget that."

"Molly…"

"Admit that you don't feel a deep rage when you allow memories of our breakup to resurface."

As my sealed secrets, even well-kept from myself, began unveiling, I felt my heart clench. My eyes pinched shut to bat away tears that were beginning. When I saw her face, tears were also forming in the corners of her eyes, and I knew she was right.

"But I love you in spite of the past," I told her.

"Loving in spite of is almost worse than not loving at all."

As the waiter placed our orders in front of us, I knew I had to pretend to enjoy the lunch. But I had to force myself to eat.

"Everything looks delicious," I said without great enthusiasm. We had both ordered the Fav's special of tournedos with mushrooms and Parmesan cheese on wild rice, accompanied by an endive salad. I took a bite. "Mushrooms and Parmesan are perfectly blended."

"I come here often when I'm in London. I usually order the sour cream pound cake with a strawberry topping and it's delicious. I restrict myself to half, so perhaps we can share an order for dessert."

"That would be wonderful."

"I see neither of us has changed when it comes to weight. I'm still monitoring and restricting. And you aren't a bit worried about it, are you?"

"Sorry. Must be my nervous energy. I exercise when I'm home. Walking, biking, and hiking."

"If I remember correctly, you used to jog in the mornings," Molly said.

"It's a walk now."

"Samantha and I played tennis until about a year ago."

"Why did you quit?"

She looked away. "Time marches away with us. My grandsons' schedules are filled. Keeping up with them is like a three-ring circus."

"Samantha showed me their photos. They're adorable."

"They are, aren't they? They're my life. Samantha and Jeff are also my joy. They've allowed me to be such a large part of the boys' lives. From helping to name them, to being there with them since their birth, I've cherished my grandsons. I'm fortunate to have them all." She hesitated. "Are your brother and his family well?"

"All wonderful. I'm blessed." Small talk was dragging us away from what I wanted to tell her. I blurted out, "I'm also blessed you were in my life."

"I also feel that way. For what it's worth, I've never loved anyone as I loved you."

"Your love may be past tense. Mine remains present."

"Please don't say that. It breaks my heart to hear you tell me that. There's no longer anything between us. Can't you see?" Her eyes were imploring me.

"You truly want my love for you to end?"

"It has to end. For both of us."

"It ended for you thirty years ago."

"That's not true." She wiped the side of her mouth with her napkin and tossed it on the table. "See, this is why it wasn't a good idea to meet."

The waiter placed the sour cream pound cake down with an extra plate. Molly divided the cake, handing me the larger share.

Trying to diffuse the sadness of the conversation, I thanked her. "I see you're trying to fatten me up."

"I'm trying to maintain my weight, actually. But a few pounds couldn't hurt you."

"Well, I might forever love you, but don't think I haven't tried to forget you." I waved my fork at the cake. "And to gain weight."

Her full laugh was as I remembered it. "I always lectured my students to be unremitting in their pursuits."

"But your students weren't as impossible as I am."

When we finished eating, we hugged with the same brevity as when we began the luncheon. Although the ebb and flow of life was compelling, it produced mixed results. We were to say goodbye yet again. This encounter hadn't set me free. My soul was more claustrophobic, yet searching, than ever. My love was more permanent.

The one request she asked of me I was unable to give her. I wasn't able to forget her. We stared at each other as we parted. She was aware of my inability. Like some ancestral ceremony revisited, for me to stop loving Molly was preposterous.

Chapter 24

Once safely back at the hotel, I barricaded myself in my room. I left a message at the desk that I was not to be disturbed. I had closed the blinds, and when I finally decided to paint, I opened them again. Light bathed Bethany's face in the portrait. It was a welcoming force. For the moment, I felt safe.

Exploring the expression on Bethany's face, I realized I couldn't allow myself to have feelings for her. I couldn't relinquish my emotions. Look what happened with Molly. My pain had only increased by seeing her. Molly delivered the message I should have understood decades ago.

Those friends surrounding me must have thought my thirty-year absorption with love devoid of reciprocal emotion to be ludicrous. Had that made me a long-term, faraway stalker of another's soul?

In Molly's estimation, we were never right for one another. Years ago, I had tallied my shortcomings. An unknown artist had no prospects. It became clear she wanted more when she upped her ante by going back for her master's degree. I hadn't bettered myself or elevated my status. I hadn't even expressed the desire to become wealthy or renowned.

And Molly's other accusations were just as accurate. Admittedly, I was selfish about my time when it came to creating. Looking back, I could now see where I had ignored her when I was working, but at the time, I didn't realize it.

She said she couldn't compete with my art. My mind continued to rerun her statement. Now, in the solitude of my boxed-in loneliness, for the first time, I admitted I could never give up my art for anyone. I had always had a hunger, a compulsion, that made me strive to create art.

Back then, my plans were simply flimsy dreams. Part-time jobs paid my share of the expenses and provided enough money to buy canvases and paint. That couldn't have been good enough as we entered middle age.

I uncapped a tube of paint and watched an intense cadmium red ooze onto the palette. I opened one tube after another until the palette's surface was speckled with colors. As I lifted a small fan brush, a sharp aching gripped my arm. My fingers clutched so tightly that the brush broke. I held my face in my hands. I wept for at least half an hour, but it seemed like it had been the entire night.

A hard pounding at the door jolted me from my cavern of pain.

"Danielle, open the damned door," Esther yelled.

I slowly walked to the door and reached for the knob. "All right," I yelled back at her.

She blew into the room. "For god sakes, I've been trying to rouse you. You haven't answered my phone calls. Are you okay?"

"Just a minor crying jag."

"Nothing minor about it. I heard you from the hallway. Sit." She pointed at the chair on her way to the liquor cabinet. She poured us each a shot of whiskey and handed me a tumbler. "Drink."

I lifted it to my lips. "I never drink straight liquor."

"Just drink it, Danielle. You look like crap. Bethany is supposed to be coming later, and Carrie wants to go out. My best plan is that I call them both and cancel. Then we can talk."

"I'll be fine." I took another gulp and grimaced. "This stuff tastes ugly straight."

"Just finish it. I'll call our dates and reschedule for tomorrow."

"No. I'm better now," I said sharply.

"Better than what? Look at you!"

"It'll be okay, Esther." And I had thought that my childhood made me resilient to anything. I was woefully wrong.

"Bad time with Molly, huh? Come on, we can talk about it." She sat down in the other chair across from me.

"Not much to talk about. It's all over."

"For shit sakes. It was all over thirty years ago," Esther shouted as she enunciated each word. "As Carries says, it's all bloody done."

"All bloody done," I repeated. "Well, the truth is I'm still trying to stop the pain."

"Get over the pain. Even if you loved her then, she's not the same person. People change in thirty minutes. In thirty years, the person not only changes but damned well converts to another human being. She's no longer the Molly you loved, and you aren't the Danielle she loved."

"That's exactly what she said. Nearly verbatim." I stood and went to the bar. From another small bottle, I poured Esther half and the rest in my glass. I then took two big gulps. "You're both right. So let's party. When Carrie calls, ask her if she'd like to double. I'm sure Bethany would be fine with going out for dinner and dancing."

Esther lifted her glass. "Ladybugs Rock!"

"Ladybugs Rock!" I lifted my glass and drained it. "Maybe I can make one woman in this flipping world happy. If only for a few nights."

"Some people don't even do that. Living metes out precious little complete love. Connection is rare. Seclusion is not rare. And art truly isolates you."

"Although I live in this sanctuary of seclusion with my art, I've never sought to be cloistered. I've wanted to belong, Esther."

"I can't even belong to the damned immensity of outer space, and you're concerned about a tiny planet."

I felt a little lightheaded and was amused at her words. "I knew we'd get back to interplanetary allegory."

"I'm always amazed intelligent life seems confounded by the heavens. Understanding human relations has always seemed far more perplexing. Give me starbursts and good old cosmogony anytime." She became wistful. "I find more is sacred when I look up than when I look around. Space is less encumbering."

I ran a hand over my forehead. "I've always wanted to believe in all the structures of love here on earth. I paint the faces and forms of human beings. It's my own diary of being here. I desperately want to belong and to have another human soul be a part of belonging to me. I still want Molly."

"I doubt if you could have helped yourself," Esther said. "I don't think I'd ever seen anyone more in love than you and Molly. It might even have influenced my own life. If the two of you seemed that in love, and your relationship dissolved, what chance did the rest of us have?" Her eyes were so mournful, I had to turn away.

"I always believed she'd return. It was my dream."

"Dreams don't end how we want them to end. It doesn't mean things won't end happily. Scratch the decades-old dream from your scorecard. I've been telling you to do that for a million years. Now that you've heard it from the horse's mouth, get on with it."

"Horse's mouth?"

"Okay. I'll rephrase it. Now that you've got the scoop from Molly, get on with your life."

Suddenly overcome with sadness, I felt a tear winding its way down my cheek. I swallowed hard before speaking. "I can't get over this feeling of desolation."

"You're not desolate as long as you've got your friends. Bethany is there for you, and she's there as a lover or a friend."

"Esther, I don't want to hurt her, or get hurt by her."

"We are earth's bio-props. Even though we might try to be one another's prop, it's transitory at best."

"Where are the most brilliant stars going to be seen in tonight's sky?" I asked.

"No damned scientific measurements of the brightness of celestial bodies for me tonight. No." She breathed deeply a moment. "Albedo is the amount of light reflected off a celestial object."

"And what object will be sparkling the brightest albedo tonight?"

Esther didn't answer. Maybe she knew the secret. Most of the night stars probably wouldn't be coming out. Maybe my tears kept them at bay.

Chapter 25

Esther and I met Bethany and Carrie at a small Irish restaurant.

There was Limerick ham with baked parsnips, steak and Guinness pie, Irish roast pork, and steamed cod boxty. Breads included buttermilk scones, soda bread, and oatcakes. Clouds of steamy spices bloomed. We traded samples across the table, and each seemed more superb than the last.

They teased me about my Irish roots and Irish dialects, until I diverted the conversation to space aliens. Did extraterrestrial beings have different dialectal communications? We zeroed in on Esther. Naturally, she jumped right in.

"It isn't a silly joke," she said with a serious expression. "Proof is coming. There are small traces on Jupiter's moon, Europa, which might very well be waste products of underground bacterial colonies."

"What?" Carrie exclaimed.

"It's true. It might be a sign of alien life."

"Esther," I said, "I might not be a scholar, but have you got your facts right on this one?"

"Of course I'm right."

"I'm not so sure," I told her.

"You know I'll go to my computer tonight and pull it up for you. Sometimes, Danielle, I think you're one brain cell short of a chunk of granite."

Carrie jumped in. "Come on, Esther. Bacteria crap on Jupiter's moon? Now that's bizarre. I never heard it on the news. Bog-trotting bacteria."

As we chuckled, Bethany tried to help Esther. "It's possible. She sounds very convincing."

Carrie elbowed Esther. "I think she's just fresh out of nonsense and made it up."

"Made it up?" I asked. "Wait a minute, she couldn't have. She's a scientist. There's not an ounce of make-believe in her. Maybe she's exaggerating."

"Danielle's right," Esther said. "I don't have one iota of imagination. One bit of truth, though, is I'm ready to hightail it out of here and party."

We agreed and grabbed a cab to a small club that Carrie had selected. One not at all fancy but cozily trendy.

It felt good to be on a dance floor holding Bethany... and being held by her.

"Loved the touch of Ireland tonight," I whispered in her ear. "But I think I had a drink too many. Now the truth comes out. I am indeed a barstool Mick."

"Canadians love the Irish."

"I'm glad." And I meant it.

During the trip back to the hotel, my thoughts of the evening tumbled over in my mind. I'd attempted to stay high-spirited, but I hadn't fooled Bethany. Esther might have briefed her. She was kind, considerate, and supportive.

I felt Bethany's warm arm around my shoulder as we walked through the lobby. When we arrived in the suite, she immediately went to the painting.

"You make me look terrific."

"You provided me with the image. Sorry I wasn't as chipper as I might have been tonight."

"Danielle, you have every right to be emotional. I take it this noon's gathering didn't go well?"

"Molly said what I should have already known. It's over." I hesitated and added, "Thank you for being so understanding."

"I've been through a breakup or two. Loss is excruciating. All loss."

"And how did you make your way out of the darkness?"

We sat next to each other on the sofa. She reached out and took my hand inside hers.

"I spent a week or two in fully anguished diva mode. Then I told myself that I needed to get over it." Pain filled her eyes. She had obviously experienced an overwhelming breakup. "Getting well is the primary option."

"Bethany, you're very special. I wish we had met thirty years ago."

"But we've met now."

"And *now* I'm a golden girl."

"You're one of the most extraordinary women I've ever met. The past is over. I can't change it, nor would I want to change it. It's part of you."

"Persisting memories aren't always easy."

"Danielle, you've come to mean a great deal to me. Often love travels in separate coordinates. Maybe our timing isn't spot on. But maybe the goddesses have recruited me to be your special envoy."

I caressed her cheek. "You do make me happy."

"And you make me feel as though I've been made whole. I'm free to love again. Perhaps my daydream is even more impossible than yours. I wish I could return to your lovely Colorado with you and be part of your life."

I sat back, a little stunned. "There are a million reasons why it wouldn't work."

"As long as there's one reason why it might." She lifted my chin and leaned into a gentle kiss.

A warm glow filled my heart. "I want to begin another portrait of you. And I want your face, your smile, to take up the entire canvas. I'll title it *Bethany's Smile*."

She pointed to her portrait I had just finished. "What are you naming this one?"

I thought about it a moment. "Maybe *Arrival of Hope*."

"I might have a shot at making you happy for the rest of our lives, Danielle. If you'd let me."

"I don't know. Considering how my day went, I'm much more interested in bringing the happiness than receiving it."

In her high-tone Brit accent, Bethany said, "I'll settle for a bit of both. Indeed. A little bit of both."

Chapter 26

The night was calming and tender as Bethany soothed me with her soft touches. In the morning, she gently kissed my temple before she left. I had wanted to get up and have an early breakfast with her. She wanted me to sleep in. She won the debate easily.

After she left for work, I finally crawled out of bed, consumed with thoughts about my latest portrait. *Arrival of Hope* was dry enough to take to the gallery, but I didn't intend on putting it in the show. When Fiona phoned, I merely told her it wasn't ready. In truth, I wasn't ready to relinquish it.

I would paint my next work, *Bethany's Smile*, on a large canvas. Glancing over at the 24x36 canvas, I decided it would become a self-portrait with Bethany. She had jokingly asked me if I was going to give her a photo or a painted portrait of myself when I left her behind. I asked which she preferred. She replied she would enjoy the one I painted, which would be the true me. I asked if I might include her at my side in the portrait, and she agreed.

A knock at the door interrupted my thoughts. As I opened the door, I said, "Esther, I…"

Fiona stepped in. "Wrong wing-chick. Sorry to invade your temple, but I was curious to see your latest work." She whisked past me and toward the painting. "The canvas is blank." As she turned, she saw *Arrival*. It was leaning against the wall. "You're done. It's magnificent."

"Not done, really," I said. "Just wanted to give it a rest."

"See my hand?" She shoved her palm in front of my face. "I can count on these few digits how many times you've left a painting and started another." She peered at the bottom of the painting. "And you've signed it. You never sign a painting until it's complete. Going to give me a clue as to why you didn't tell me it was done?"

"It's my prerogative to finish when and if I decide."

"And it's my responsibility to monitor each of my clients. I'd be remiss if I didn't know what my clients are painting or, for that matter, thinking."

"I'm thinking that whether I sell it is going to be my decision this time."

Fiona rolled her eyes. "I also came up here because you weren't answering your messages."

"I've been occupied."

"Danielle, I tried to contact you to see if you think you can replenish your work in a few months for another show. A major show in Boston in May. But with the way you're acting, I'm not sure I'll be handling you as a client in a few months. So, I damned well may *not* need to know."

I quickly tried to diffuse her anger. "Fiona, please don't think of dropping me. Forgive me. Of course I want you to be my agent. You've been the only one in the world who has always believed in me." I gave her a hug. "I'll be ready for a new show in a few months. I'm bursting with ideas about subjects and themes."

"Well, keep me informed. I have to say it was easier keeping track of you before you became a playgirl."

"Yes, but I make a very productive playgirl," I joked back. I would try to remember to tell Esther about Fiona's 'playgirl' comment. She'd enjoy it far more than I had.

"Danielle, are you listening?" Fiona broke into my thoughts. "We're talking a dynamic catalogue. I've booked a printing company." She walked to the painting. "Got a new muse?"

"I may have. I want my next portrait to be Bethany's entire face. I want to capture the sparkle in her eyes and her smile."

"Hope you've got plenty planned. The exhibition requires the creation of an entirely new show. Four or five dozen minimum. Can you paint that many?"

"Yes. I have about a couple dozen in my studio that are ready or nearly ready. If we get in a bind, I can always remove a few from my walls."

"I'm damn glad you've become so prolific." She hesitated. "At least you're prolific when a muse is near. Like Molly. I always felt she was your impetus."

"Esther chatted with you about my lunch with Molly yesterday?"

"She did. And that was the first thing I thought about. Who was going to take over muse duty?"

"I paint because of my need to paint."

"Still, you churned them out when Molly reentered your life a week ago. Now you're painting Bethany at a fever pitch. I assume that will dwindle once you return to the crotch of America."

I laughed. "Agreed, Denver is not as cultured a megalopolis as your own New York City. But we are somewhat gentrified."

"Like California, Colorado gives a poor imitation of New York culture."

"Fiona, as far as you're concerned, outside of Europe and the East Coast, there is nothing."

"Absolutely nothing."

"Hey, I love my space of the world."

"You'd do much better surrounded by a little civilization."

"You are so egalitarian," I said, my voice dripping with sarcasm.

"Go paint, bumpkin hick."

"City slicker," I shot back.

Fiona believed I had replaced or exchanged muses. And within days, the emptiness of Colorado would replace my newest muse. Knowing I was leaving behind the two women of my London odyssey, I thought perhaps Fiona had good reason to be concerned.

Chapter 27

Within the hour, Esther's phone call interrupted my morning. I was certain Fiona and Esther were conspiring against me.

"According to Fiona, without Molly or Bethany, you'll be muse-less." Esther must have been shouting into her phone. "Carrie said you need to buck up your ideas or you'll lose Bethany."

"So now Carrie is in the mix."

"Damned right. She's been Bethany's friend for years. And she thinks the world of her and doesn't want Bethany hurt."

"My ears are wearing out from your beleaguering the subject, Esther. Why don't you come to my suite? I'll order something for us to gulp down. Might improve your mood."

"Because I'm about to hop in the shower."

"How about this. I'll order some room service delivered to your room. By the time it arrives, you'll be out of the shower. We can chow down. And talk."

"Then bring your checklist because I want to go over it with you."

"Is that a yes? We'll have breakfast together?"

"Why are you doing a late breakfast? You usually eat earlier."

"I'm off schedule. I'm painting."

"Don't be late coming down. Twenty minutes tops."

"You'll only have half my arse to kick into submission. Fiona just left after having kicked her share, as I'm sure you know. You two are in cahoots."

"You got that right. Fiona knows what I know."

"I'll be there in twenty minutes. And, Esther, thanks for being a great friend."

I tucked my phone into my breast pocket and ordered room service. I picked up a soft graphite sketching pencil and stood in front of the white canvas for several moments. I sketched the contours of Bethany's head. After proportioning her face, I stopped.

Glancing at my wristwatch, I noticed it was nearly time for me to take the elevator down to Esther's.

Room service was being delivered as I arrived. Esther waved her hand for me to sit down. That was a warning sign she was about to go on the offensive.

I sat, placed my napkin on my lap, and lifted the stainless-steel cover. "Yummy."

She poured coffee and stirred it vigorously. "Are you planning to phone Molly again?"

"I'm not sure. She made it quite clear that she'd rather I not contact her."

"Not sure? I know that you're over the initial shock and now you'll call her. Innocently, you'll ask if she's okay, or some other lame question."

"Probably not. My best guess is that Molly is no longer in the equation."

"Danielle, I've talked with Carrie about how Bethany is feeling about you."

"How are you feeling about Carrie?" I asked, to deflect Esther's attack.

"A little early in the conversation to rotate our talk, but nice try. Carrie and I are going to be friends for years. She plans to visit Denver on her next vacation. Neither of us has any illusions about a future together."

"Carrie's a nice person."

"You and Bethany could have a future." Esther was relentless.

"You don't know that. Bethany is an independent woman. I'm not likely to break her heart. Carrie doesn't need to worry. Bethany knows I'll be returning to my home."

"What makes you think she wants to be left behind?" When I didn't answer, Esther posed another question. "Do you think you'll e-mail a few months and then it'll become some makeshift, platonic relationship?"

"Probably. Possibly."

"You both want more."

"Esther, I'm really on edge right now. You want to know what Molly's indictment was? The part I didn't tell you? She told me Pamela wasn't the only reason she left me. She left *me*. That's the deal. I'm no longer certain I'm relationship material."

"I don't follow you. I've told you before—you and Molly were the most solid couple I'd ever seen."

"She tells me now that she was sensitive to my being out. Not hiding my lesbianism. At least not denying it."

"That's a crock. You were never obvious. Never a dyke. That butch crap is a bogus charge. It shouldn't matter anyway, as far as that goes. We're all women."

"I never hid it the way she did. I've only been ever so slightly androgynous. I like comfortable clothing, and I'm not fussy about being all girly. But I was careful around her educator pals. That pretend junk made yesterday's self-intolerance even uglier than street or church bigotry."

"If it bothered her, why did she stay eight years?"

"I'd be guessing if I answered that."

"Why else did she say she left?"

"Because she was always in competition with my art. Competing for my time. Maybe she had a valid point. I did spend huge chunks of time on my art. Maybe she questioned if the sacrifice was ever going to be worth it. Perhaps she felt I hadn't realized my potential and wouldn't. Maybe she thought I loved art more than I loved her."

Esther took a drink of coffee. "Did you?"

My hesitation was longer than I would have liked. "Maybe I do love art more than anyone. I love art more than I love myself. Perhaps my art is me, and I love that part of me more than any other parts."

"I'd like you to tell me why you believe you couldn't have a life with Bethany."

"First, Molly's complaint. I love my art too completely. Bethany deserves more."

"You can't believe a woman could understand about your art. That's part of the human condition to want to be the most important part of a lover's life. But some women can admire and respect talent. Okay. What's the other reason?"

"Second, I'll always love Molly. Although I've resigned myself to our love being impossible, I can't ever stop loving her. How is any woman going to accept that, along with being ignored by me and my art?"

Esther slammed her coffee cup against the saucer. "Bethany isn't just any woman. She's a woman who has already fallen in love with an artist—an opera singer. And they struggled together for her lover's dream. For the nearly twenty years they spent together, they shared that hope. They achieved that dream together. Then six years ago, Bethany's lover was killed in a car crash. That leads me to your second qualm. If you think you can accept the fact Bethany will always love her dead partner, she can certainly accept that your love for Molly can't end."

I sat back in my chair. "I didn't know…"

"I believe you and Bethany just might have a wonderful foundation for love," Esther said. "You both come with a boatload of baggage."

I couldn't remember much else about our conversation. A solemn shadow accompanied me back to my suite. Painting the duration of the day was not only my passion but also my therapy. By late afternoon, I was exhausted.

The telephone rang. I was expecting a change of plans about this evening with Bethany or maybe Fiona reporting gallery business. I hoped that it might be Bethany, and I would suggest a quiet evening of dinner in and conversation.

It was Molly.

"I must talk with you again. If we can arrange lunch for tomorrow, I'd appreciate it. I was unfair and would like to explain."

"Of course." My hand gripped the telephone as if it were a lifeline.

We hung up after making arrangements. I sat for a long time staring across the room at Bethany's portrait.

I didn't want to navigate my way through a lunch where strained conversation was on the menu. But I also didn't want to miss an opportunity to rekindle the flavor of life I once knew. I surrendered to the fantasy that I'd once again feel enriched by Molly's love.

Chapter 28

Having sent a text message to Bethany earlier mentioning Molly's surprising phone call, I half expected her to break our date that evening. But I needn't have been concerned. She arrived on time.

"No worries." Bethany's arms surrounded me as she entered the hotel suite. "Danielle, there have never been any expectations on either of our parts. You've certainly made that clear. I've accepted the fact that you have feelings for Molly. And if there might be a chance of reconciliation, I know you would be there in a shot."

"We aren't talking about reconciliation. She said she wants to meet for lunch tomorrow. Maybe she wants to leave it on a less final note. A friendship. Or maybe Samantha talked her into it."

"I find that rather dubious." Bethany took off her light raincoat and tossed it on the back of the sofa. "It isn't a problem between us. I'm resigned to the fact you'll always love her. If it is love to begin with, it remains."

"Are you talking about Molly or from experience with your lover?"

She looked surprised. "I thought Carrie might tell Esther about Tricia."

"Why didn't you tell me? I'm feeling as though I'm constantly the one in the dark."

"I didn't mention it because it always hurts. I've chosen not to hurt by not going through it all again. Tricia had been my life for twenty years. It's taken six years to get to where I am now. And where I am now—well, I'll always love her. Knowing what a splendid human being she was, I'm aware she would want my happiness."

"Would it be too painful to tell me about her?"

"No. You've divulged your relationship with Molly. I feel I owe it to you to tell you about my life with Tricia."

The dinner that I'd ordered arrived. Fortunately, Bethany began as if taking the bookmark out and reading her life aloud.

"Tricia and I met twenty-six years ago. We fell in love, lived together. We made every effort to see that she attained her goal of achieving stardom as an opera singer. Great reviews, notices, a couple of terrific CDs. And she had leads in several important operas.

"I'm a people person, and if I say so myself, excellent at what I do, but I have no aptitude for the fine arts. I have enormous admiration for those who possess creative talent."

"I would imagine Tricia also had enormous appreciation for your support."

"She was a great deal like you are, Danielle. Compulsively drawn to find her very best. I have a great respect for those willing to give their lives over to their arts. You give a gift to audiences, to spectators, to celebrators, or to lost souls. To all of humanity."

"It isn't so much that I've been willing to give my life to art. I've needed to do so. Tricia probably couldn't have helped being a singer. She was fortunate in having you at her side."

"Tricia was so full of life. I was blessed to share her exuberance. Although there were times when I felt left behind, I wouldn't trade a single day."

"She sounds like a wonderful person, Bethany. To be with you, she must have been wonderful."

"I remember the last morning I spent with her. I insisted she take our auto, telling her I would take a cab to the airport. She wanted to do some shopping for my birthday gift. We kissed goodbye, and I told her to be careful. A car filled with teenagers sped through a Yield sign. Our auto was broadsided. Tricia was killed upon impact."

I reached across the table to hold her hand. "Losing Tricia must have been the worst time of your life."

She swiped her wet cheeks. "Thankfully, I had Carrie's support and the support of other friends. For the last six years, it seems as if I've been waiting for Tricia to come back. So I know how you feel about Molly. At least Molly's return is a possibility. Tricia isn't coming back. But it was so hard. For the first couple of years, I'd see something relating to music in a store and I'd want to buy it for her. Then it would strike me. She's gone."

"I'm glad you had people around you who cared for you."

"Friends and family. Carrie was especially wonderful. Like a younger sister to me."

"She and Esther have an excellent relationship. I think they'll visit one another."

"Travel is nearly all paid by both my profession and Carrie's travel agency. So I'm sure she'll be traveling to Denver."

"And you'll visit me?"

Bethany smiled. "I'd like that very much. Danielle, we're all frightened of giving our love. I have been. Until now there hasn't been anyone I truly wanted to love."

We were quiet for many minutes. I tightly held her hand in mine. I then stood in front of her and leaned down. She wrapped her arms around my shoulders. We embraced as if we might lose one another if we let go. I was acutely aware of how complete she made me feel.

Chapter 29

It was noon. Same place—Fav's. Same woman—Molly.

I looked across the table and into her somber brown eyes. We'd greeted each other cordially.

She'd dressed casually, yet with elegance. I'd also dressed casually but didn't pull off the same sharp fashion look.

Our server brought our lunches of pheasant salad with cranberry vinaigrette

She tasted hers. "Yes. It's as delicious as I remembered. Since I recommended it, I hope you like it. This is my favorite restaurant in London, as well as my favorite lunch."

I trickled a dollop of dressing over the variety of herbs and greens and placed the slices of pheasant breasts onto the salad. I took a bite and my taste buds ignited. "This is absolutely the best salad I've ever had. Great choice."

"I'm pleased you like it."

"We've always liked similar things."

There was a moment's pause, before she finally spoke. "After meeting with you last time, I realized I might have heaped some cruel accusations on you. I wouldn't want to do anything to hurt you. I tried to explain my feelings to you. Certainly not to bring you pain."

I decided to be honest. "Naturally, I'm wounded. I honestly had no idea there were problems in our relationship."

"I didn't realize you had no idea about what I was experiencing. Even if you had recognized the difficulty, there wouldn't have been anything you could have done." She hesitated. "When I got home after our meeting, I spoke with Samantha."

"Samantha is a lovely young woman. She looks like her mother."

"How do you know?"

"I saw Pamela's photographs on the jackets of her books. Their resemblance is close. But when we met, I wasn't thinking in terms of a book's dust jacket photo I'd seen thirty years ago."

"You were right that raising her is the best contribution I've made in life. At any rate, she took your side. She thought I'd been heartless in how I treated you. She's very fond of you."

"You pointed out my shortcomings. They're accurate."

"I knew how much you loved me, Danielle. My intention in seeing you was to give you closure."

"*Love* you. Molly, I still love you. I might've been young and arrogant about the breakup and wrongly placed blame with you. It doesn't matter who was at fault. It was my responsibility to pick up the pieces and go on with my life. I wasn't successful at continuing on. You aren't responsible for closure. Your truth is your reality, and you owe me nothing."

"I should have known how *my* truth would impact you. When I left, I believed I was leaving to make it best for both of us. Maybe so we wouldn't need to begin battling to save our relationship. There's agony in that."

"My parents gave up on their love and their marriage," I said. "If you'll recall, I told you I'd never give up. No matter what happened, I would never have left you."

She suddenly became angry. "Ah yes. I recall how you forever sanctified fidelity and hated betrayal. Do you think your life would have been better if your parents had remained in a loveless marriage? That Samantha turned out as wonderfully as she did was a miracle. I was in a loveless relationship. Believe me, it's toxic."

"I suppose it was best that I wasn't raised by my parents. For many reasons. But I didn't consider our relationship loveless, Molly. Everyone we knew believed our relationship was good."

"It might have been good. But it wasn't great. I opted for great. After I left, I discovered great doesn't exist. Maybe I shouldn't have left you. For my own reasons, I did. I regret having left you. Well, I regret everything with the exception of Samantha."

"I believed you loved me. After you left, I found that reclaiming the innocence of trust was difficult if not impossible. I've still never loved anyone as I love you."

"Nor I you. I did find that perfection is unattainable." She took a bite of salad but probably wasn't enjoying the meal anymore than I was.

"I'll always believe there was only one completely true reason for your leaving," I said. "You found someone better."

"Pamela was certainly not better. I found someone who needed me. Emotionally, she was an invalid. You never needed me. You had your art."

I scrunched my napkin and dropped it on the table. "If I had been needy, would you have considered staying with me? If I had been an alcoholic? Maybe I could have thrown in drugs along with an alcohol problem so that we might have remained together. That would have made me even more pathetic. As well as more like my mother."

She dabbed at the tears in her eyes. "I'm sorry you went through so much pain."

"I'm pathetic enough and empty enough to still be experiencing that pain. Did you ever experience hurt?"

"You were the only woman who was ever in love with me and that I was in love with. Have you ever considered the consequence my leaving had on me? But I needed to leave." She held her left arm out. "The itch is here." Then she held up her right arm and said, "You only scratched here. You were always a mile from where I needed reassurance. Sadly, you didn't even realize I had unfulfilled needs. But if you had concerned yourself with my emotional deficits, maybe you wouldn't have found the depth of your soul that you paint with such eloquence now."

I picked up my napkin and smoothed it into its original shape. Would that this situation could be smoothed as easily. "Have you ever considered I might have reached success faster with you at my side? I wanted my success for you as well as for me. Instead, my struggle has been a lifetime's suffering. There were times when I didn't even want to live. So please don't insist on playing some guiltless what-if game. I confess I was too preoccupied with my art. I concede I wasn't delicate enough about my sexuality. I have the feeling that no matter what I changed, it wouldn't be enough. I begged you not to leave me. And I would have done anything for you. I would have tried to help you with your emotional deficits if I had known they were there."

Molly poked at her salad. "That was the problem. You couldn't have helped me. We weren't on the same path. We lost our way. I didn't understand your commitment to art. And you didn't have a clue about my passion for philosophy." She stabbed a chunk of pheasant with her fork. "We were going in separate directions. Growing apart."

"Molly, I agree I didn't get philosophy. I always figured we're all philosophers. Each individual. One's own belief system. Not the universal kind that elevates those who espouse other people's philosophy. But we accepted one another's chosen fields."

"Did it ever occur to you that I revered philosophy as much as you did art? Philosophy has saved me. It gave me a way to interpret life. Philosophy is my way of viewing life. When you marginalized philosophy, you marginalized me as well."

"I recall a time I attacked philosophy because you mentioned how a photograph could capture people's spirits as well as an artist. I spoke out of frustration and anger. I apologized."

"And I told you back then I was sorry for what I'd said, Danielle. I didn't mean your art in particular. Don't you see, even now we're arguing over past hurts. The truth is, I felt at home in my field. Pamela was a renowned writer and professor in my field. She was there, and I sadly believed you weren't. But none of that matters now. I can't undo it. It's all too late."

"Why is it too late? A chance meeting here in London. Maybe it's meant to be. We could be kinder to one another. More understanding. We could make it all better. Age teaches how to be mellow. So why not another chance?"

"Listen to yourself. We're sixty years old. Each year we circle the track, and each year we hope for another. We'll never again be thirty." Her eyes held an enormous pain.

"We could try to be sixty together. Is it too much of a stretch to believe love doesn't just vanish? I want to believe love remains."

"It may very well remain, but it doesn't always stay the same. It changes."

"Molly, we've changed, yes. But love is still there."

"This is why I didn't want to meet with you again. You seem convinced that we can have this reconnect. That's impossible. We have different lives to live. They've been different for thirty years. It can't happen."

"Can't happen and won't happen seem to be your mantra. But it could happen. And as far as I'm concerned it could." I waited for her to meet my eyes. As if in another world, she blinked rapidly and then faced me again.

"Molly," I said, "don't you see, we could work it out. Maybe we could live in California half the year and Colorado the other half. Why not take a chance?"

"There are complications. It didn't work thirty years ago. It certainly wouldn't work now. Why can't you see that?" Attempting to convince me seemed to have depleted her. "Please."

"I can't."

"You won't. But you must. What can I say to dissuade you from believing this absurd idea of us together?"

"Maybe I can't ever be discouraged for the one simple reason that I have no control over. I'm still in love with you."

She stood. Tears filled her eyes. "And I'm still in love with you. But it's too late." She sobbed as she rushed from the restaurant.

Stunned and with blurred vision, I quickly asked the waiter for the bill as I made my way to the exit. He waved me on, reporting that my friend had taken care of it before we dined.

I hastened to the street. Molly looked back at me as she was entering a limousine. There was great pain in her eyes. I saw her outline in the darkened window as the large, pearly white vehicle pulled away from the curb.

I felt as if my existence was also pulling away. "Molly," I said with such deliberation that it frightened me. How could I live if it was too late for love?

Chapter 30

Fiona furrowed her brow. "Danielle, are you okay?" she asked as I entered the gallery.

The glare from the gallery's fluorescent lights made me squint in an effort to dim their brightness. "I was passing by and thought I'd drop in to see how the show is going."

"It's going splendidly. But you seem upset. Can you tell me about it?"

"The second lunch with Molly didn't go any better than the first."

"There's absolutely no benefit for you feeling as you do. You're getting nothing out of it. Unless you're clutching worn-out old memories to ease your fear of aging. How many times, and in how many ways, is she going to have to tell you she doesn't love you?"

"She just now told me that she's still in love with me."

Fiona let loose with an enormous gush of expletives. "That fucks my theory all to hell!" She put her arm around my shoulder. "So are you going to see her again?"

"She ran out of the restaurant after she delivered her line of devoted love." I heard someone enter the gallery.

"Do you even want to see her again?"

"If I were prudent, I wouldn't want to be within a gazillion miles of her."

"Don't use prudence as being anywhere near your personal attributes. You aren't at all fitted with a single bit of prudence. Let me repeat. Are you going to see her again?"

Before I could answer, Esther greeted me. "I couldn't help overhearing. Well, are you going to see her again? I presume we're talking about Molly."

Fiona answered before I had a chance to. "Molly told her she still loves her and then made a beeline for the nearest exit. The fool."

Without her usual restraint when it came to issues concerning Molly, Esther whirled toward me. "She a shrew. That's it. She keeps you emotionally bouncing from hope to despair. She is an absolute sadist."

"Don't get ratty," I said. "It's so complicated. I honestly think she's as confused as I am. Her daughter insisted that she contact me to apologize for what she said before. And yes, she said she also loves me but that it's too late."

"So now she's got multiple personality disorder," Esther said. "Playing the roles of protagonist and antagonist. Smacks you down, picks you up. Blames the breakup on your bogus defects, sees you next time and is sorry for screwing with your head. How much more are you going to take?"

Fiona piped in, saying, "In love, out of love, in love."

I was outnumbered, so I opted for a change of topic. "Fiona, have you tallied the sales for the exhibit recently?"

"Yes, and you need to be awarded a trophy. You're getting a bundle of money richer, even as we speak."

"Why did I have to come to Europe to be discovered?" I hoped they didn't notice I'd steered away from all talk of Molly. "I'm making more on this exhibit than I made in the past decade. Or ever made."

"Good press, good initial sales, and great paintings," Fiona said. "You're finally being recognized. As far as why we're triumphing in Europe—location, location, location. You see, Europe is slightly more cultured than New York." She measured a quarter inch between her thumb and forefinger.

"I guess I don't get it," I told her. "The United States has always considered me a very minor artist. Very minor price tag as well."

"After our Boston exhibit, all that will be put right. I'm thirsting for a cappuccino. How about I take you two crazy Saphs to Crumpets and Brew for a double cappuccino. And we can sneak a trip under the glass of their extraordinary pastry cart."

As we left the gallery and neared the coffee shop, I asked, "Are we going to be able to change topics and find out about you two? I want to know the latest cradle-robbing stories. Are the cougars ready to divulge some splendid stories?"

"I'm overjoyed," Fiona said. "What stamina. I may take my toy boy with me on the next exhibits. France and Germany. Germany, I'll need my stress relieved. The artist there is a major pain."

"Yes, I believe you'll need your lad if what you say about your German artist is true."

"It's all true. The artist's work sells. I have a long-standing arrangement with him, or I'd dump him like a rodent."

Esther and I howled as she described her bedroom scenarios. We selected yummy lemon croissants from the tray and began to munch.

"Now let's discuss Carrie, Esther," I said.

"Fun at forty." Esther took a huge bite of her pastry and a swig of cappuccino. She did divulge that Carrie liked to cuddle.

We bantered back and forth until we'd finished our snacks and coffees. I laughed at Fiona's and Esther's escapades. It was clear Esther's feelings for Carrie were precious and just as clear that Fiona's emotional ties with her toy boy were on the other end of the spectrum.

Chapter 31

Leaning the phone to my ear, I listened to Esther's diatribe on most of the day's news. She was waiting for Carrie to finish with her shower, while I was waiting for Bethany to arrive at the suite.

"Bethany hasn't called," I said.

"So she's late. She'll call." Esther continued with her rant as if I hadn't interrupted. "I'm an analogy kinda gal. There's this breakthrough. An X-ray ghost seen after the demise of radio-bright jets. Astronomers actually caught it. Ghosts remained after a black hole's eruption. Now here's why I mention it. Love is analogous to black holes."

"What in the heck are you talking about?"

She interpreted. "Affairs leave ghosts, too. Memories are jam-packed with them. The yesteryear Molly ghost leans heavily on your mental retention. Ghosts become like little brain souvenirs—keepsakes. You've got them going on. You need to shut them down. Take all those memories of Molly and let amnesia have its way with them. Don't be sad. Bethany will call."

I checked the clock. "I need to immerse myself in the painting. Hear the whoosh of my brush against canvas. Listen to the scraping sound of my pallet knife as it applies paint. Paint spreading like wings across the white."

"Fine, but remember the damned ghosts."

After hanging up, I returned to my easel. I had spent half an hour with brush in hand when Bethany finally called. A major disturbance had occurred at Heathrow. Security hierarchy, which I suddenly realized she was part of, had all been called in or were on standby. She would have called earlier, but she explained that when she was on alert, there just wasn't time. The moment the emergency was over, she had phoned me. She asked if I might forgive her. I did, and we disconnected. I ordered a sumptuous dinner for us.

She arrived before the dinner delivery. After pouring her a drink, I showed her the latest work on her portrait.

We sat down, and I said, "I didn't know you were in security."

She gave me a secretive smile. "It isn't what I talk about."

"Not even to a lover?"

"No one. I'm a part of the security team. In fact, I head a section. I haven't even gotten into specifics with my family. Of course, Carrie is aware of the basics, and I've now told you the basics. Haven't you ever wondered why I carry two mobile phones? When I ring someone, it's always with the more colorful one. The other is always open unless it's an emergency. I place them both on the bed stand every time we go to bed. If a call had come in on my company-issued mobile, you would have seen me rush."

"I promise your secret is safe with me." I crossed my heart.

"I know that. We're required to pull background checks on people we're intimate with. Security precaution. You've been vetted. Danielle Eve O'Hara. Born in Topeka, Kansas to Eve Marie and Norman O'Hara. One brother, Dylan Patrick. No criminal record. No civil lawsuits. Lived in your current house nearly thirty years. No foreign ties. Travel has been minimal. Never been to a country on a restricted list. Never affiliated with a militant or subversive group."

"You mean to tell me that my women's rights, civil rights marches, and anti-war efforts went unnoticed? My 1960s were a lost cause?"

"Apparently so. You must not have been arrested. No record. Nothing. You're a perfect citizen of your country. You're obviously, other than your marching in a parade or two, or burning your bra, rather dull. At least your actions haven't been nefarious enough to attract attention."

"Busted." I chuckled. "I'm dull."

"Clover is even dull," she said with amusement. "She has never run away, nor has she been reported for any canine transgressions."

"You didn't really check her out, did you?"

"Not at all. I could tell from her photo she hasn't a covert move in her playbook. Completely trustworthy is little Clover."

"I'm glad I cleared. And I promise I'll refrain from delving into your work. Besides, I wouldn't have any idea what secrets I'd be looking to find."

"The obvious might be that I've been briefed on the arrivals and departures of high-profile travelers. Or possibly information about any deficiencies in our systems or policies concerning possible breaches of security. Not that we have any. When they transferred me to security, I even signed a pledge, along with a full disclosure of my sexuality. So there's nothing I can possibly be blackmailed about."

"Don't worry, I won't ask any questions about how your day went. Actually, I stopped asking about your profession when your details were so brief they were almost curt. I guessed that some people like leaving business at the office. Then I thought you might consider your job boring."

"Boring? I think not. My life revolves around emergencies. Like crisis traffic lights—red, amber, and green critical stages. That's a summation of my job. When my larger cell phone rings, my heart races. Followed by my body. I can still do a fairly adequate sprint."

"I suspected you used two phones for different women." I actually had noticed the two phones but thought it was common for airline workers.

"There are no other women in my life, Danielle," she said softly.

"I do have one question."

"I had a sneaking suspicion you might be an undercover bad sort."

"When you hear the question, you might well have me in cuffs."

"I'm really not into that, luv."

We chuckled a moment, before I asked, "Will you accompany me to dinner tomorrow night? As Fiona's guest?"

"Certainly. I know it isn't your birthday, so why is Fiona splashing out?"

"She promised me and my date an evening at an elegant restaurant of my choice. She also invited Esther and Carrie. Reward for the success of the exhibit. Any excuse for a celebration is fine by me."

"Where are we going?" Bethany asked.

"Where would you suggest?"

"There's a place called The Scripted Banquet. Very elite. It does rather separate you from your money. They're so exclusive that Carrie doesn't even receive comps."

"That shouldn't be a problem since Fiona has plenty of money. She's not squeamish about opening her vault, either."

"A great many gay and lesbians frequent The Scripted Banquet. Will Fiona be all right with that?"

"Not that she swings both ways, but she has explored both worlds. I'm only interested in women."

"I'm only interested in one woman."

Our eyes met until I looked away. "I hope that's me. I hope tomorrow night at The Scripted Banquet is to your satisfaction."

"If you're there, Danielle, I shall be more than satisfied. I'm certain the nosh will be absolutely superb."

Chapter 32

Bethany left my hotel suite early in the morning. Although she tried not to wake me, I rolled over into her goodbye kiss. After she departed, I touched the warmth of the spot where she had slept, feeling the indentation in her pillow. I dropped off in a pleasant, drifting sleep.

By midmorning, I awakened and reached to check my alarm clock. I wished Bethany hadn't left. Happily, the next best thing was elevenses with Esther. I heard her rhythmic knock and opened the door. She stood with sack in hand and two paper cups of cappuccino.

"Elevenses," she chimed as she placed them on the table. Looking back at me in my sky-blue terrycloth night garb designed somewhat like a toga, she grimaced. "Elevenses are stretching it some for you. In your case, it looks like you're ready for brekky. Or not. Do you have one single negligee in your entire wardrobe?"

"Nope." I was not willing to discuss my state of fashion in a barefooted moment.

"A very grotesque nightie. Just rolled out of bed, did you?"

"I did. Late night. The planets were aligned for a late, late night."

"They say there might be another planet beyond the orbit of Pluto. Lurking out there. Planet X. Bigger than Pluto. It could explain some of the goings on with the Kuiper Belt. Bet if it does exist, it is one cold, flipping planet."

"And?" I tried to sort out how this Planet X might be relevant to our conversation.

"If it exists, you had one chilly, frosty planet aligned with your sweet affair last night. I doubt the temperature of your bed got much above boiling."

I flipped the top from the steaming cappuccino and took a quick taste. "Hot. I can warm my frost-bitten lips, still frigid from Planet X's influence."

"Must have been some scalding sex last night." Esther spread napkins and dumped her favorite overly gooey pastry on them. "Was the night long, sweaty, *and* hot?"

"Yes, I had to sleep in. Have you noticed our decomposing bodies don't regenerate as quickly as they used to?" I bit into the crispy turnover. Hidden within were tart cherries, the kind with a delicious bite. "I need to conserve energy."

"I don't consider it conserving when sometimes there's nothing left to conserve." Esther lifted her coffee into the air and said, "To us and our energy."

"Or lack of it." I had a foamy sip of the cappuccino's topping. It had been wonderfully blended. "However, I'm happy for the good health I've been blessed with. When we get to be this age, it gets dicey health-wise. So I've got to say, we're holding up pretty well."

"It's a puzzle how you've gotten this far. Usually heartbreak is a killer. And you've been heartbroken nearly all of your life. Unhappiness can knock off a few years. Stress, too, as far as that goes."

"I've had my art. That's kept me going. They say pets keep people healthier."

"Sadie and Aggie want to keep me healthy enough to be their servant."

"Speaking of bosses, have you talked with Fiona?" I asked.

"Just left the gallery. I stopped by on the way to pick up the goodies. She confirmed dinner tonight. Where have you selected to celebrate?"

"It was Bethany's choice, actually. A truly great place. The Scripted Banquet."

"Sounds fine. I like Fiona. I remember when you first met her. She'd seen your work at an art fair in Santa Fe."

"Yes. Best break I ever had. Told me she would like to represent me. When she gave me her card, I did a double take. I'd heard the name, of course. Although she wasn't as prominent as she is now, she was certainly a force with which to be reckoned."

"A force and a dynamo," Esther said.

"Over the years, I've gotten to trust her. I liked her from the first. Sometimes I can tell about people by studying them as if I were going to paint them."

"You must have had that kind of feeling with Bethany."

"Pretty much. I was mostly concentrating on Molly when I met Bethany."

"We all know that. So is Molly still weighing heavily on your mind?"

"Yesterday, Molly was so insistent that I forget her. So final. I even offered to live part time in California."

"You what?" Esther almost jumped out of her chair.

"I suggested we live six months in each locale."

"I can't believe you'd agree to that."

"It didn't do me any good. She just isn't interested."

"Danielle, love isn't always a forever deal."

"I do care about Bethany."

"Now back to the activity report on last night. Lovemaking for hours, were we?" She sniggered so loudly she snorted. "Don't hold back the good parts."

"We talked most of the night. I told her about Molly's declaration of love."

"What did she say?"

"Again, we don't own one another."

"Bethany's a sensible woman."

"I appreciate that about her. She said she's glad I'm honest with her. She's aware that Molly has dumped me for good and that I'm still in love with her."

"What I admire about the death of stars is their clean breakup. They explode and then just blink out of the sky. Boom, goodbye. Relationships should be so blessed."

"What does Carrie have to say when you explain crap like the death of stars?"

"She says, and I quote, 'It's all going on up there, isn't it, luv?'"

"Your reply?"

Esther giggled. "I tell her, not all. A lot is going on down here in London, as well. I told her I could open doors for her she never knew existed."

"She didn't buy that tired old line, did she?"

"She called me a saucy muffin, so I do believe she caught the gist of my statement."

Chapter 33

I spent the day's remaining hours painting. As I painted, Molly and Bethany consumed my thoughts.

Although I wasn't quite finished with *Bethany's Smile*, I had made enough progress to feel it was nearing completion. When I finally placed my brush down, it was time to clean up my work space and myself. I showered, applied a slight amount of makeup, arranged my curls, and dressed in a new pantsuit.

I appeared at the gallery where Fiona was waiting. Esther had spent the afternoon at Carrie and Bethany's apartment. Fiona had suggested that I stop by the gallery and we would drive together to pick up the other three women. It was, she diagrammed in the air, on the way to The Scripted Banquet. She explained that she loved driving her rented Bentley. All the younger men, she claimed, were wild about flashy cars.

She had staged a little get-together at the gallery with wine, cheese, and all the promotional adornments served throughout the afternoon. She had more than adequately sampled the wine. Perhaps she had, I thought as I sniffed her, bathed in it. Clearly, if it were not the fault of osmosis, she had imbibed. Normally, I balked at being driven when a driver shows signs of booze. But on a few occasions, I'd seen Fiona drink the bar empty and still be functional. Thus, I relented.

The dark tan Bentley was impressive. We were dressed to the nines, and so all was festive. Fiona was in a particularly elated mood.

Sales had been brisk. Each time the stock appeared meager, Fiona called Roxie. Roxie took photos of some of my remaining works that were scattered in my studio, garage, and assorted closets and sent them to Fiona via email. Then Fiona would direct her to pull and ship the ones she wanted.

After we arrived at Carrie and Bethany's apartment, Bethany gave me a guided tour. The place was stylish and chic; she'd decorated it in extraordinarily good taste. I found the art on the walls to be excellent.

Once in Bethany's bedroom, my glance moved toward the antique desk to a photograph of Bethany and the woman I presumed to be Tricia.

I picked up the photo. "Is this Tricia? She's quite lovely." Bethany didn't answer immediately. I turned and saw her wiping her eyes.

"Yes," she said softly.

I put the frame down and took her into my arms. I understood her better, now, I thought.

Before we were ushered into the Bentley, Fiona offered up the keys. Because she had imbibed, and it was truly beginning to kick in, Carrie drove. Carrie bemoaned the fact that she had never driven such a lovely motor as a Bentley. We screeched away. Within two blocks, I wasn't so sure that it'd been a good tradeoff. But we arrived unscathed fifteen minutes later. And we were on time.

The Scripted Banquet was indeed ritzy. Textured walls were plum-colored fabric with plush designs. Enormous crystal chandeliers hung from vaulted ceilings. A brick wall with arches housed what looked to be enough bottles of wine to produce several drunken countries. Each of the small dining room areas was separate and private. Each had an antique fireplace with gilded gold trimmings. Alabaster-colored tablecloths and napkins polished off the posh décor.

The hostess seated us at an enormous round table. When our wine steward appeared, Fiona took the lead in ordering a staggeringly expensive array of dinner wines. Then she began selecting after-dinner liqueurs that would pair perfectly with various desserts.

Carrie threw her arms out wide and squealed, "Cheers, a keg party."

"You Saphs have fun," Fiona said. "I'm going to. But then I always do. It might be a new emotion for Danielle."

I gave her a mock scowl.

"Anyway, the rest of us are celebrating the success of her show," she continued. "Enjoy a culinary delight."

We clapped. I thought I'd better not drink too much, for I might have to guide my fellow Saphs home. After the toast, I began sipping water and taking only a taste of the wine. It was to be a jubilant evening. With or without wine, I planned to be high-spirited. Or at least give the impression of elation.

Bethany took my hand. "I hope you'll all enjoy the feast. I feel responsible for having selected the restaurant."

"I've been here before," Fiona said. "I've been everywhere that is anywhere. And it has an excellent menu selection. The fare couldn't be more sumptuous."

We ordered dinner after a discussion about what sounded good. Every meal served at the tables surrounding us looked delicious, and the fragrances were divine. Although torn between beef bourguignon with whipped potatoes, and broiled lobster, I decided on the beef bourguignon. Esther and Fiona opted for the broiled lobster. Carrie ordered the grilled quail, and Bethany decided on chicken rouennaise.

After the server took our orders, Esther lifted her wineglass. "I'd like to toast to this evening of fun and friends. Ladybugs Rock!"

Simultaneously, Esther and I tapped our glasses and in unison said, "Ladybugs Rock!"

"What's that mean?" Fiona asked.

"Ladybugs Rock is our little coterie of friends," Esther told her. "A closed membership organization. Very exclusive. It's a circle of the best women in the world, if we do say so ourselves. Twenty years ago, we congregated and decided to call ourselves Ladybugs. Then we added Rock. Ladybugs Rock became our battle cry."

Fiona took a large gulp of wine. "Can we join?"

With a quick, frisky wink in my direction, Esther said, "Bethany and Carrie already had their initiation into the club. With you, it would be more difficult. You need to be a devoted fan of Colorado. That's part of the initiation rites. In fact, you would need to express allegiance in a pledge. New York would no longer be number one in your heart. You would belong in spirit to Colorado."

Fiona slammed her wineglass onto the table with a little too much force, causing some of it to spill over. "How could I do that? My allegiance is to New York. Always has been and always will be."

"Then you can't be a valid, authentic member of our organization. Bylaws of our organization are very strict regarding one's affiliation with Colorado. Sorry." Esther's expression was grim.

"Not to worry, Fiona," I said. "You probably wouldn't be able to make it through the criteria listed to become a member. Even if you were to become besotted by Colorado."

Esther stood with drink elevated and said again, "Ladybugs Rock!"

Fiona was bewildered. She waved the waiter over. "Bring another bottle of this flipping wine. I see I'm going to need it."

"What's wrong?" Bethany asked.

"I'm all alone with a batch of crazy Saphs. I'm only a small portion Saph myself. A sampler Saph. I'm completely outnumbered by all you Ladybugs Rock people." Frowning, she asked, "And how did you two become members?"

"We absolutely love Colorado," Carrie said as she joined the hoax.

We all awaited Fiona's outburst. I'd seen her smashed before, and she could become hilarious.

But this had been overwhelming for her. Suddenly, tears formed in her eyes. "But I thought you were my friends. Just because I'm from New York and not a true Saph, you're blackballing me. It isn't fair. Not one bit fair."

I quickly interceded. "It's okay, Fiona," I said as I patted her arm. "You're our friend. How about if we say because you like Colorado and have at least sampled, you're allowed to become our international club mascot. Lots of members, only one mascot. You."

We all stood, raised our glasses, and toasted, "To our new mascot, Fiona!"

That seemed to lift Fiona's spirits for the evening.

There was indecision on dessert. I selected hazelnut parfait with candied violets. When the waiter placed it before me, I felt a tinge of homesickness. I had herbs and tiny violets in pots surrounding my deck. Looking into the small faces of the violets, I swallowed hard. I missed my home and, most of all, Clover. By now, she probably wondered if I'd fallen off the face of earth.

I tried to pick up my mood by teasing Fiona. "Fiona, you're getting a little flirty with the waiter."

"I hope he heard me when I said I could blow the ears off a donkey. Then added, or a waiter."

"And can you?" Esther asked with total decorum.

"Does an alligator pee in the swamp?" Fiona retorted.

Chuckling, Bethany said, "We don't have many alligators in Canada."

"Or England," Carrie chimed in. "Not that I'd be looking for one. But we do have lots of randy art agents visiting England."

"And this randy art agent is also *the* official Ladybugs Rock mascot. A mascot without a man!"

"That being the case," Carrie said, "let's get your waiter back. Have him take our photo. Danielle, you have your phone handy. Under the pretext of having him snap a shot of all the Ladybugs Rock members, we'll ask him to do the honors."

The waiter was willing to take our group photograph, however unwilling to do additional honors for Fiona.

We again cheered and toasted Fiona. Tapping my wristwatch, I suggested we close down the wonderful party. We all thanked Fiona as she got the staggering bill.

Carrie's eyebrows shot upward. "You're going to need some dosh for this evening. No comps here."

"Not to worry," Fiona said.

Esther again reminded us that we'd better head back. Because of the late hour, and needing to work in the morning, Bethany had decided to stay at her apartment, along with Carrie and Esther.

Delivered safely, they piled out of the Bentley, and Fiona collapsed in the backseat. "Here you go." Carrie handed me the keys. "You and Fiona are the last broads standing." She motioned toward Fiona. "And she's barely standing."

"I've never driven a car like this."

"Come on, Danielle, it's a straight shot back. Fiona's hotel is only a couple blocks from ours. Park the car in her hotel garage, haul her in, and then either walk, call a cab, or stay over with her."

Bethany said, "Stay with her. I'm sure her penthouse is big enough for a guest."

I pouted slightly. "Probably large enough for a fleet of sailors. By the way, where are all the gigolos when we need them?"

I pulled away from the curb as I heard the chanting chorus behind me. "Danielle, don't forget to drive on the left-hand side. Ladybugs Rock!"

Driving the Bentley was an experience, and I took it very slowly. The trip allowed my humor to return. Once in Fiona's luxury suite, I got her safely slung across the king-sized bed.

"Thanks so much for the lovely evening." I tucked a bedspread over her.

"Danielle, I'm so proud of your painting." Her words slurred as she threw her arms around my neck. "I'm happy you'll be solvent and even rich soon. I saw how you've struggled."

"I haven't ever thought of myself struggling. Just sometimes doing without." I sat on the bed's edge.

"Now you won't have to do without much of anything."

"I feel fortunate. And I'm thankful you've been there for me. Promoted me all these years."

"I knew you had it. Even Spencer knew when he was a little boy."

I suddenly sat up straight. "You knew Spencer when he was a child?"

Fiona frowned as she reclined against the mountain of pillows. "Well, I can trust you." She took a deep breath and let it out. "Spencer is my son. I knew I wouldn't be able to take care of him back then, twenty-five years ago. His father desperately wanted him. He was an art dealer. I declined his proposal of marriage when I was pregnant. He married a woman who couldn't give birth, and I agreed they could raise Spencer. It was amicable. They adored him. He was always aware I was his biological mother. I saw him on vacations and whenever I was in the upstate New York area. He went to boarding school, university. Then I gave him a job."

"Spencer is your son." I was shocked. "But why didn't you tell anyone? I mean, Spencer's a wonderful guy."

"It isn't that I'm not proud of him. I'm prouder of him than anything else in my life. I wasn't cut out to be a hands-on mother. Not really. As he grew, well, honestly, I wanted to hold onto my youth. That's why I get a little work done." She patted the sides of her face. "Lifts. I want to chase younger men. I've never been through with party life. I'm not mom material." Her voice shook.

"Not everyone is," I said as I patted her leg. "But you are one hell of an agent."

"Yeah. I am. I hope you don't think badly of me because I'm not a proper, traditional mother."

I gave her a quick hug. "I think you're the best kind of proper, traditional mother. Proper mothers do what's best for their child. Spencer obviously admires and respects you."

She sank into the pillows as her eyelids fluttered shut. She mumbled, "You're my favorite artist ever. You crazy Saph."

"Thanks. And you're my favorite agent, and mascot." There was a slight smile on my lips as I turned down the light. Then the smile eased into a moment of pain.

It had all turned out, no matter what. For the best. And now I yearned to paint.

As I walked the streets to my hotel, I thought that I might spend some time beginning the self-portrait with Bethany that I'd promised I'd do for her. Planning it as I entered my hotel suite, I heard the telephone ring.

"O'Hara," I answered.

Bethany's sweet voice was on the other end of the line. "Any trouble getting back to the hotel?"

"Nope. Fiona was done partying, finally."

"The English say she was squiffy to begin with and she became sozzled by night's end. To us, it would be going from tipsy to drunk."

"I sometimes forget you're Canadian until you refer to the English."

"As I always say, Canadians are more like Americans than they are English. My own accents vary. I've become more English because when I was a flight attendant, it took up so much time being asked about where I was from. Anyway, tonight was special. Fiona's special, too."

"More special than I realized."

"Please thank her again for a lovely night."

"I did, and I shall again in the morning. She might not be aware of much tonight. She does enjoy life. Knows how to splurge, that's for sure."

"She must have spent an enormous amount."

"Fiona is generous. But more than that, she's always been there to encourage me. Over the years, our friendship has grown. Anyway, I think the world of her."

After a slight pause, Bethany said, "I miss you, Danielle. I should have returned to the hotel with you."

"I'll be busy painting the self-portrait with you included. I thought I could use the photo on my phone. The one Carrie snapped of us. I'd like it to be of the two of us. I thought I might paint the portraiture from that image."

"You truly are going to paint us together?" She sounded surprised but pleased.

"I thought it would be nice."

"It would be magnificent to be with you. In any context— painting, photo, or real life."

"I'll start on it immediately."

Before we hung up, I found it difficult not to tell her I loved her. Holiday romances tended to connote triviality, and my feelings for Bethany were anything but trivial. But the truth was we were an enormous pond apart. Half a globe apart, actually.

As I set up my paints, I tried to come to terms with the evening. I lifted my brush and daubed it into a small mound of paint. I'd selected a fresco liner brush. It would work for the delicate outline I wished to paint. I truly didn't want this painting to be an inert image.

Chapter 34

After sleeping for a couple of early morning hours, I was awakened by a troublesome and absurd dream about being colorblind. As I unwound my tired limbs, I gazed across the room to examine what I'd placed on the canvas throughout the night. Or more precisely, early morning. I had selected the remaining small canvas. Upon a 24x36 space, I'd dabbled paint in all the correct places, but it still needed a great deal of work.

As the morning progressed, I became more and more emotionally conflicted. I had waited thirty years to hear Molly say she still loved me. My deepest emotional response was to call her. I wanted to hear her voice. I wanted to hold her in my arms. I wanted to believe she still was in love with me. The euphoric moment seemed perilous. There were her words, and then there was her hasty retreat.

Knowing Molly as I had, I also saw a flicker of fear in her eyes. I speculated it might only be that she was uneasy seeing me. Anxiety was a form of fear. I wished I could've made her laugh, smile. I wished I could've interpreted her better during our luncheon.

Amazed, I contemplated how we misrepresented, mispronounced, and even failed to accurately visualize the past. We often enhanced memories and perhaps just as often corrupted them.

Youth, however, was bulletproof. We became youth with uncertainty, a bit of mirth, and whimsy. Perhaps there was nowhere else to hide. So we became indomitable youth. Striving for conviction, knowledge, and confidence, as we began to learn love. Love, the most elusive of enigmas, came at us like a rushing torrent.

Early adulthood was a reckoning time. We groveled for love. We strutted with the glory of love, and we staggered with its burden. When love appeared, we treated it with as much of ourselves as it seemed to require. We sometimes got it right. Often got it wrong. When it went out from under us, we peered into oracles of tomorrow.

I believed in my own prophesies of being able to one day resurrect lost love. Engendered memories chased me throughout the morning. One thing youth hadn't taught me was to inspect my own presumptions more carefully.

When the telephone rang, I was glad it was Fiona's raspy morning-after voice.

"And how is our semi-Saph, Colorado lovin', Ladybugs Rock mascot this morning?" I asked with a chipper voice.

She laughed her familiar aria. "Damn that was fun."

"Thanks again for the great time."

"They could have charged a hundred times what I paid for all those laughs."

"How's your head?"

"Sore. Carrie promised I'd have a wonky brain today. And I do. But my only regret is that I didn't find some young stud."

"As I was driving that magnificent car, I wished you'd found a guy to lay you, Fiona. I'd have had a chauffeur, and you'd have had an orgasm."

"Are we going to be a Saph bitch today?"

"I work on being a Ladybugs Rock, Saph bitch every day," I teased.

"Are you sure being a mascot is more special than being a member?" she asked with a note of skepticism.

"I am. We have at least a couple dozen members, and you're our only mascot."

"Okay, I like the thought. On to more important matters. When am I going to see all of your last paintings?"

"You can come by anytime to see them. I'm also working on one of Bethany and myself together. I just started it. But, I warn you. I've promised it to Bethany. Let's call it a modeling fee."

"Modeling fee, my ass. Or I guess hers." Fiona's hangover obviously hadn't dulled her sharp tongue.

"Be that as it may, she's been promised it. But you can take a gander at the others I've finished."

"I loved the good old days when you'd rush the canvases to me and beg me to sell them for you. Maybe you could snag that adorable Bethany and take her back to Colorado as a full-time model."

"We do live on different continents. I'm on her turf."

"That's it? That's all that's stopping you?" The seconds of silence must have made her realize she'd hit a nerve. "You're uncertain about Molly? Right?"

"I'm uncertain about what to order for breakfast."

"Leave it any longer and you'll need to order lunch. Let me give you a bit of advice. After all, my fifteen percent should include helping you hike up those bootstraps. Okay. First, order a deluxe, giant-sized breakfast. Second, call Molly and tell her if she's really in love with you, she'll come back to Denver with you. Third, beg Bethany to fly back to your home with you."

"Suppose they both agree?"

"You should be so lucky. Or as they say here, you should be such a jammy Saph."

"Fiona, are you planning on coming up to see the paintings any time soon?"

"If you call soon 'immediately,' then yes. I'll be there within the half hour. Order me toast, scrambled eggs, and tea. That ought to do it for hangover food. Tell them no greasy fry-up meal. These limeys can truly fuck up food." With a huge sigh, she added, "But the Americans can truly fuck up a rock fight."

"I think I'll just put in our order. I'm not giving any food reviews."

"See what I mean. You are a crazy Saph."

"You really should have found a good man last night."

"I would have settled for a bad one, young enough to be trained."

"What's the word I'm searching for?" I paused. "Oh yes, now I remember. Nymphomaniac."

She roared. "That's the word. I'm the cougar poster child."

"Well, you're a damned fine one."

"I'll be right up."

She hadn't mentioned last night's disclosure about Spencer. And as long as I lived, I would never reveal it.

Chapter 35

Fiona left after breakfast, leaving me to paint for a few hours. When I finally looked at my watch, I saw it was way past lunchtime. I made plans to meet Esther in the lobby for a walk over to Lindsay's Tea House.

Esther ordered a midafternoon treat of a Maid of Honour tartlet. She made a brief reference to last night's extravaganza and the five little tartlets out on the town. I settled for a good cupper of English breakfast tea and a salmon with cucumber sandwich.

"What a night," I said.

"Fiona is some hostess. The wine cellar alone got a good tweak last night."

"Fiona was too drunk to scout a toy boy."

Esther grunted. "I hope she's careful with her selections and her protection. She was too smashed to light her cigarette, much less do a rubber wrap on a stud's whacker."

"She told me once that she's careful. But I'm not the condom cop, so I stay out of it. She smokes and drinks too much. Risky behavior wouldn't amaze me."

"She enjoys the bucks and bounty of her success."

"She's trying to coerce me into putting all my new work in the exhibit."

"And?"

"I promised Bethany a painting. I'm working on it now. It's of both of us. And I would love to keep the one of Bethany with her smile."

"Fiona will end up agreeing with your decision. She'll get some concession from you. Maybe rush another one from you."

"Yes, but she'll have to wait. I'm working on the small portrait of Bethany and me first. Fiona probably expects me to stop painting the gift and complete some salable work."

"You could knock out a couple of foggy London landscapes in an hour," Esther said.

I was quiet for a long moment. "How can anyone have such intense feelings for two women at once?"

"We all may be a little disheveled in the romance department, but you've signed on for a lifetime of service. I'm not sure how life formed on this earth. But prebiotic chemistry aside, I'm relatively certain some pissed off women aliens dropped you on earth. They flew over and shoved you out of the capsule. That's it. These poor space alien women jaunted through interstellar space to ditch you. They brazened asteroids and space debris. And now we're stuck with you. How can you be in love with two women at once you ask? I've never been in love with less than several superb women on any given day."

"Several?"

"Several. I want to express my sexuality before I'm a simple cell remnant of life."

"At least all of our libidinal buttons are still in working order." My best response wasn't adequate. I grimaced, as Esther glared. "Do you think I should call Molly?"

"Danielle. What am I going to do with you? Carrie and Bethany have invited us to dinner tonight. Carrie claims Bethany is an excellent chef. Run yourself back to the hotel to paint while the light is still good. Then prepare for your date."

"Lighting. Awe-inspiring natural light." My mind raced with possibilities. "I was mentored by the Impressionists' paintings. Maybe I should allow even more light onto my canvas."

"So pull back the blinds to let the clouds above part and squeeze out sunshine. Do not call Molly. Don't be late tonight, and don't forget to do a trial run on how your buttons are operating."

"You must have invented being bitchy. Okay, I won't call Molly. I won't be late. And go check your own damned buttons." I took a final bite of the sandwich, finished the remaining tea, and stood. "I'm off to paint. Go bully someone else for a while."

"Berk," she uttered as I rushed through the doorway.

Back at my hotel suite, I doused the faces in my paintings with bright light, using every particle of sunlight.

The phone rang, interrupting my work. I picked up the receiver. Molly's voice greeted me.

"Molly, I'm surprised you called after leaving me behind at lunch."

"I couldn't leave things the way we left them. The way I left them. I want to apologize for my outburst. It's been an emotional time. Please forgive me."

"Of course. But I didn't understand why you left so quickly. Did I say anything wrong?"

"No. I did. I never should have told you what I did. It was wrong of me to have said what I said about my feelings for you. I apologize."

"If you meant it, it wasn't wrong."

"Our relationship is long past. It's too late. There are too many complications right now."

"You not only fell in love with a brilliant, beautiful woman and left me for her, you saw flaws in our relationship. I get that now. But nothing can desecrate the feeling of love I have for you. Will forever have."

"That's what I'm saying. I truly experienced the issues that surfaced. But you weren't at fault. Nothing was wrong with our love. I just believed there was. Your love for me was more than I deserved. You were being yourself. That's the *you* I fell in love with. You were fiercely honest about who you were. You were passionate about art. And I regret that I hurt you. I regret it more than anything I've ever regretted in my life."

"If we could care about one another as we did when we met thirty-eight years ago, do you think we could reunite?" I thought about what I wanted to say. "Molly, we might not have gotten it right before, but now we've had years to acquire wisdom. Our feelings are still there. Our love is there."

"Danielle, under other circumstances, we might have been able to regenerate a relationship."

"*Now* and *next* are what really matter in life."

"But 'now and next' aren't enough." Molly's words were soft, longing, and as tender as I recalled them before she would cry. "I really should go now."

"Molly, are you all right?"

"Yes. I only want you to be well. I want you to know I do love you. And the breakup wasn't your fault. I'm sorry for everything. For all the hurt."

"Can we meet again? We should at least see one another once more. While we're both in London. Catch a movie. Remember how we used to laugh, even at some of the badly acted, syrupy scenes? Please?"

"Danielle, keep those good memories near you. Let them be enough."

"We could make more good memories. I love you, Molly."

"I was blessed to have had your love once, twice would be more than I deserve. For now, I need to go on with my life. And I want you to go on with yours. I'm asking one thing of you. Please go on with your life without me and without thoughts of me being back in your life. Will you promise me?"

"As always, Molly, I want to do what makes you happy. I promise to try." I could say no more around the lump in my throat. I heard the click on the other end. Once again, I felt Molly's ineligibility. Although I was as perplexed as ever about her, I did know a final kiss-off when I got one.

If only we had the common sense to understand the bliss and the victory of love. And if only we could accept the residual elements of ruin and defeat.

Chapter 36

As I showered and got ready, I contemplated life. I found that no matter how one pleaded, begged, prodded, beseeched, hoped, or prayed for love, fortune in romance seemed to be an exclusive task of destiny.

Molly and I would not reconcile. Not because we didn't want it. There were, she explained, extenuating circumstances. I was out of options. I couldn't battle unknown limitations. I realized my hopelessness. In attempting to disseminate the fragile opulence and vileness life afforded us, I had only ended up more confused.

After I had showered and dressed, I rushed onto the sidewalk. Checking my watch, I saw I'd be late, even if I didn't take time to stop off for wine and flowers. I'd only be much later if I stopped. So I didn't, even though I knew Esther would scold me for being tardy and forgetting to bring a bottle of wine and sheaf of flowers.

"Sorry I'm late," I said as I stepped into the elegant entryway.

"Not to worry, luv." Bethany took my raincoat and hung it for me.

"Glad I brought plenty of wine," Esther said with great sarcasm. "Empty hands, I see."

"Oh, ignore her, Danielle," Carrie said. "We've got enough excellent wine to open a boozer. Or a very large pub. And it isn't plonk."

"Plonk?" I asked.

"Cheap wine," Bethany answered.

I kissed her cheek. "I didn't even bring any plonk."

"Esther is just being sarky to give you a little agro," Carrie said.

"You're correct." Esther winked in Carrie's direction. "Aggravating Danielle is my life's work."

I glared at Esther. "Let's not do agro tonight."

"Yes," Carrie agreed. "Esther, give it a rest."

Esther said, "I'm sorry you had such a lousy day, Danielle. Let's leave our troubles behind and partake in the wonderful feast prepared by Carrie and Bethany. Primarily Bethany."

A wondrous aroma drifted into the living room. "Smells delicious."

Esther turned to me. "And will be, I'm sure. But when we discuss the day, let's not purge our souls." Her eyes narrowed. I'm sure she was warning me not to talk about Molly. "Right?"

As we made our way to the table, I whispered to Esther, "You're becoming a cynic."

"A cynic is a failed romantic, and I'm certainly not that."

"How is Saturn tonight, by the way?"

"Close, high, bright, and with rings wide open. Just like the best women."

"And how are things going with Carrie?"

"She is a gem in a gravel pit."

When Carrie turned, I told her, "She complimented you."

"I hope to hell she's telling you that I'm in mint condition." Carrie pointed to the chairs. "If she has any expectations about what might happen when we go to bed, it would be a good idea to compliment me."

I could tell it would be a fun evening. There was the warmth of the women, their humor, and the pleasure of their company. The table was beautifully set, and a variety of appetizers lined the center. Bethany poured the wine, and we lifted our glasses.

"To sweet words and bed," Carrie toasted. "In fact, maybe just a little poetry and bed would be fine."

I nudged her. "You're going to wear Esther out."

Carrie waved off my comment. "She's got stamina enough, but I may be anemic."

Esther shook her head. "Generational warps are incredible."

We lifted our glasses of Chablis to toast. We continued with our quips and chatting throughout a wonderfully prepared dinner. We discovered Bethany was a gourmet chef. Carrie admitted her job was peeling the potatoes and stirring the pots.

We dined on superbly baked chicken with fluffy dumplings and vegetables. Dinner ended with luscious chocolate cheesecake, coffee, and a perfectly aged cognac.

I took a sip of my drink. "What a fun evening. I didn't know you were such a great cook, Bethany."

"I love cooking and baking. It relaxes me."

"Well, the meal was absolutely delectable. Excellent, like the chef."

"Bethany is excellent at everything," Esther said. "And it might be time for you to change horses, Danielle."

"I'm not sure I like that allegorical comparison," Bethany said.

Esther saw my displeasure with where she was taking the conversation. "Okay. So for now, let's just say it's a truly lovely night."

I awaited another quick jab or two. "And?"

"Let's pull back the curtains and gaze at the stars. I'm an astrobiologist, and I'm aware of the heavenly attributes. Always remember this, lovely women. Stars are free diamonds. We must always remember that stars are out during the day, too. We don't see them because of the sunlight."

"All stars have a rough go of it in foggy London," Carrie said. "Even the night stars have a long, hard slog here."

"You'll like this, Bethany," Esther told her. "In Canada and the upper North American states there was a raining down of precious metals." We looked at her in disbelief. "I swear it's true. Diamonds. During the last Ice Age, a comet shattered mainly over Canada. Nice about the diamonds falling, but it did kill off the animal and human population."

"Might this be theory or fact?" Carrie asked.

"Let's call it a categorical fact," Esther answered.

Bethany stated with complete seriousness, "I recall my family mentioning that time. They rushed off to England when a fragmented comet tossed all that bling at them."

We laughed, and Esther was silent a moment. "Let's have another spot of cognac," she said. "I have absolutely no chance of convincing you three of anything while you're sober."

"Half a glass for me," Bethany said. "I'd like to tuck in early."

As Bethany refilled our glasses, I thought about how much pure enjoyment the evening had held. Two couples, chatting, laughing, sharing a meal. Perfection. I felt exactly as I had so many years ago when I was part of a couple, rather than single.

Bethany asked if I might be ready for an early evening. She wanted me to hear a CD. I quickly agreed. She told me Tricia's second release had been cut only weeks before she died, and she wanted me to hear it.

We sat on the bed while she placed the CD carefully into the CD player's tray. I took the plastic jewel case from where she'd rested it on the nightstand. I gazed at the happy face in the photograph. Tricia was serene, yet she emitted a bright happiness. I was sure who had been the source of her peace and joy.

"Esther's right, Bethany. We've had unhappy endings. Each of us lingers in our past memories."

"Perhaps that's a first step toward realizing that lingering and living are two entirely different concepts. One is preferable."

As the first song played, Bethany leaned her head against my shoulder. I heard her soft sobs. I kissed her forehead when her tears began to soak into my blouse. My own were seeping from my eyes. I tried to comfort her by holding her tenderly. Then I drew her closer to me, and we joined in a tight embrace. I wondered if we held one another so near to preserve that very precious moment.

Chapter 37

My compulsion to be in my own home sometimes made my life difficult. Generally, sleeping at hotels or in other people's houses was gut-wrenching for me. Always, the first night away from my own home produced insomnia. But within the gentle embrace of Bethany's arms, I slept with ease. I felt the tranquility of her apartment that was reflective of her soul.

As I awakened, I recalled hearing the songs with Tricia's astounding voice. Her voice was gently controlled, and its passionate range resonated through my mind during the night.

I felt the similarity to my own quest through her magnificent voice. It seemed we rummaged through existence with our dreams intact. Painting, singing, acting, dancing, or writing became the sights and sounds, almost without human input. Could some spiritual emulsification occur from knowing the creativity of one another's art?

All I really knew was I'd set out to paint pictures, to download what I saw and felt into my brain and portray it on a canvas. I added my own specific experience. Music, voices, drama, and dance became part of my canvas. Perhaps the power of creativity actualized us. How else might we register life?

I heard Bethany in the kitchen and followed the sound of her rustling as she made coffee. Her morning hugs were always inviting and affectionate.

"You seem deep in thought," Bethany whispered in my ear as she embraced me. "I've made coffee. Hope it's the strength you like." She poured the brew and set the cup and pot down in front of me at the small breakfast nook.

I sipped. "Delicious. You're a wonderful chef and coffeemaker as well." I waited before continuing. "I was thinking about Tricia's lovely voice. Thank you for sharing it with me."

She took scones from the oven. "I enjoy sharing my past with you and finding out about yours. I'd love to sit for hours and excavate your history." She placed clotted cream and jam on the table. "You know, find the inside you."

"It's your vocation maybe? Digging up the dirt? I'm not able to properly vet you."

"First, let's get back to your wild life of yesteryear."

"Thankfully, my life has been too busy painting to have produced many X-rated stories. And absolutely no sequels."

"I've not been a template for playgirls either," she said. "Pretty tame stuff. In fact, if you want my history during the past several years, I haven't been emotionally or physically involved. Until you. You're someone with whom I can relate."

"Amazing how compatible we really are," I mused. "Our affair is delicate, comfortable, sweet, and honest."

She seemed to measure her response before speaking again. "Do you believe our affair might go beyond?"

"Beyond?"

"You seem to have come to terms with Molly being out of your life." She paused. "I'm sorry. I guess that was a presumptuous question. Forget it."

It took me several moments to realize the depth of her question. "I'm not an impulsive person. Are you asking if we might move our relationship up a notch?"

"Danielle, I could fall deeply in love with you. I know that's dangerous. I'm certainly not impulsive either. But if there's a chance this might not be just a vacation romance, it would be nice to consider."

"Yes." I quickly gulped a mouthful of coffee. My mind wanted to reject any thought of the possibility. "So many impediments exist to making any relationship work. Time's a great indicator. The older we get, the more unattainable the dream of a relationship becomes. We try to out-wait love. Yet even when I was young, I couldn't make a woman happy. You and I face so many obstacles and not only the set-in-our-ways problems. There are differences of culture and location. It would be complex."

"I see I'm the romantic here," she said. "Isn't it supposed to be the artist who is an idyllic, enamored romantic?"

"Well, for starters, we live a pond and half a continent away from one another. We belong to different circles of friends, home ties, and countries. Different cultures."

"As I've stated before, Danielle, Canadians are far more like Americans than we are like the English. And place is not my enemy. Place is where I love and am loved."

"When Molly and I met, she was going to college in my territory. I belonged there and didn't stray off from it. Initially, she planned to relocate permanently in Colorado. So place is important to me."

"I've always been a traveler at heart. My parents moved their entire large family from Canada to England and then back again."

"All my adult life I've been a homebody."

"I'm glad I've had the opportunity to travel the world. But as I grow older, I realize I'd like a home," Bethany said. "Where that place is doesn't matter as long as I'm happy there. All of my 'places' have been temporary. It was easy for me to pick up and move."

"You and I are different that way. It would seem foreign to me not to have a home base."

"With the airline, there's so much travel, home becomes little more than a rest stop. Tricia's studies, then later her performances, took her throughout the continent. We spent a year in Vienna, a year in Rome, and two years in Paris. Then we came back to London when her dying mother needed us. Luckily, I could easily obtain transfers with my airline. After Tricia's death, I stayed on in London. Now I'm here for my job."

"You've said you love your profession."

"I do, but it can be highly stressful. I started thinking about retirement last year when one of my fellow workers died of a stroke. He and I had started with the airline at the same time. We became friends, coming out to one another early on. Later he and his partner and Tricia and I were constant couples. When my friend died in his early fifties, it hit home how much tension and pressure our job entailed."

"I couldn't cope if I were to try your profession," I said.

"I'm not even sure if I *want* to cope with it any longer," she answered.

"Bethany, any decision you make would need to be carefully considered. For whatever reason. Above all, it should be your reason."

"It's important to consider all decisions carefully," she said. "But I'll never allow the fear of relocating to override the pursuit of love. Having lost love in such a permanent way, I'll never give up on love. I'm concerned that you'll continue to reject love because you no longer believe in it. That would be tragic, Danielle."

Chapter 38

We returned to my suite by noon where I painted and Bethany read. The day had been extraordinarily tranquil, productive, and enchanting. As evening approached, we thought a little exercise and fresh air before dinner would be wonderful.

We took a brisk walk. On our trek, we discovered a small neighborhood noodle shop. Blooms of fragrant spicy scents wafted from the doorway. The aroma was irresistible, and we immediately decided to make our meal a takeout. We ordered noodle and pork bowls and flavored tea. Aromatic seasonings, topped with slivers of candied ginger and almonds filled the noodle bowls. With the two sacks of oriental flavors, we jaunted back to the hotel.

When we reached the suite, the scent of noodles filled the room. We talked and laughed over our makeshift dinner, the seriousness of our earlier conversation now remote. I was disappointed she couldn't stay over, but she had an important early morning meeting to attend. She thought she'd feel more comfortable with a good night's sleep.

After Bethany left, I examined the portrait of the two of us. I had just started working on it when my room phone rang. I guessed she was calling to tell me she arrived home and to say goodnight.

That wasn't the case. I heard Samantha's hurried voice. "I'm sorry to bother you, but I thought you'd want to know…" She started sobbing.

"Samantha," I said with alarm, recognizing that she was hysterical. "Samantha, what is it?"

"Mother. She's gone."

"Gone? What do you mean 'gone'?"

For many moments there were sobs, and when she caught her breath, she began again. "She died this afternoon."

My mind couldn't take in the meaning of her words. The room seemed to grow smaller. I fell into a chair before my legs gave out. "I don't understand. What happened?"

"She had a cardiac arrest. We took this trip mainly to keep her mind from a surgery scheduled for when we got home. She's been suffering cardiac difficulties. She'd had two heart attacks in the past year alone. The upcoming operation was to alleviate some of the problems. The doctors believed it wasn't a solution to her weakened heart but would offer time. They agreed the vacation would do her good, and so we came. I shouldn't have even suggested it to her." She started crying again.

I struggled with my own emotions. "Samantha, I'm so sorry." I recalled that Molly's family had a medical history of cardiac afflictions. "She looked well."

"We all believed she would be fine. She believed she would be."

"I tried to convince her that we might make a new start." My words sounded like stones striking against a hard surface.

"She told me. She couldn't promise you anything because of her health."

"But I would have been there for her. She should have told me. I love her," I said, my voice trembling.

"She didn't say it exactly, but she implied that she didn't want you to go through her health problems with her and then lose her."

"But I would have been there..." I tried to stifle the whimper that caught in my throat. "Is there anything I can do?"

"No. We're leaving tomorrow afternoon. We'll take Mom's ashes back to California for services there. I'm calling not only to tell you that but also to tell you what a privilege it was to meet you. I know why my mother loved you so. And she did. She told me she had always dreamed of seeing you again. After seeing you in the market for the first time in all those years, she was so pleased. Just last night she mentioned you had always been able to peer into her soul. We were discussing your portraits of her. She was very proud of them."

"Paintings of Molly have always been the most special to me. I have one other at home. I'll send you a photo of it. It's titled *Twilight with Molly*. The painting has hung in my bedroom beside my bed for thirty years."

"Oh, Danielle. You loved her so deeply. I feel guilty about all of this."

"All of this?"

"I must make a confession. I found out you were showing here. Jeff and I chase our new finds. We're always aware of where they're showing. I had planned to take Mother with me on an acquisition search and naturally make it to your opening. We planned to reunite the two of you."

"All that trouble just because you felt guilty that she stayed with Pamela for your sake?" It wasn't adding up.

"That was only a small portion of the truth. I'm so terribly sorry, but our scheme was to get you back in her life. I know I've been deceitful, but Jeff and I believed if you were back in her life she would have something to fight for. Someone special. It might get her through the operation. So much of health requires a desire to live. We were desperate. I should have contacted you first. I hope you can understand."

"I do understand. You were trying to protect her. And I'm sure she fought to live for her family. Sometimes no matter how much you struggle, it isn't enough."

"She was able to see you again. That meant the world to her. I've had the opportunity to meet the love of her life and to get to know you as an artist. I want you to know that means the world to me."

It suddenly occurred to me they'd acquired a great many of my paintings. I wanted it to have been for the right reasons. "I hope this plan didn't include purchasing my work. I wouldn't want to think it might have drained your resources. I'm not a known commodity. The future of my work might be financially risky."

"Of course we were genuinely interested in your work as well. The reunion wouldn't have taken any purchases at all. We realized how magical your work truly is. It has already greatly appreciated financially. We've had multiple offers for the acquisitions we've purchased. Your work has become quite valued."

"I'm glad. I wouldn't have wanted to see you stuck with it."

"We both know better than that," she said. "Your art is Jeffery's magnificent find of the year. We treasure it and Mom treasured it. Jeff's of the opinion that you're just beginning. We have plans to purchase more of your work in Boston."

"You know about the Boston exhibit?"

"Jeff finds everything out about upcoming exhibits, it would seem. I hope that you might meet him and our sons. They'd also like to meet you. We're holding a service for Mom in a few weeks. If you think there might be a chance of coming to California, we'd love to have you stay with us. Mom often spoke of you to our sons."

"Of me?"

"Yes. Stories she told when they were small boys. She told them about your apartment patio garden. How you kept containers out on a little deck. How you would pat the herbs and their scent would lift. She loved the scented geraniums you grew. She also spoke of your painting flowers that looked like people's faces. Pansies and violets."

"I called them the—"

"People pansies. Yes. She told me those stories when I was a little girl, too. Whenever we passed a patch of pansies, we would do as you did. Name them. It was a great game for a small child."

I didn't try to stop the tears that streamed down my cheeks. I'd also named pansies and patted herbs with the children in my own family. "I'd like very much to attend the service. Please do let me know the details. I'll plan to be there. I'd love to meet your family. Molly loved you all so much. Please give your husband and sons my condolences. I'm so sorry."

"Thank you, Danielle. It's important that you believe me. She loved you with all her heart."

"I hope you know how much I love her. I've never really stopped believing in our love."

As we ended the call, I stood and replaced the receiver in its cradle. It dawned on me that all except love had now ended.

I now knew the reason behind Molly's decision to push me from her. The circumstances she spoke of were her failing health. She hadn't wanted us to get back together because she loved me too much to leave me again. And this leaving couldn't be helped.

One rarely reaches the age of sixty without having the impact of loss. Grief speaks with amazing fluency as years advance. The death of Molly seemed to deliver the most desolate words I had ever experienced. Suddenly, my legs gave out from under me, and I collapsed against the sofa's cushions in a heap. My sobs continued through the evening's thick cobalt night and into morning's vast eternity.

Chapter 39

It seemed even the undulating galaxy shook its fist at us. Our spin across the universe came down to time. When death occurred, the remembrance of love didn't end. We simply carried away with us what had been.

I liked to believe that an afterlife existed. Much of science seemed to concur. A reexamination of a lifetime is possible, yet one can never rewind it. The formula of life seemed simple. There was no magic elixir other than paying attention to life as it happened.

Perhaps the fortunate who prevailed learned that love actually does last as long as our remembrances. Just as we'd always believed. No matter how many times we faced discouragement, we came back to where we believed we'd last placed love.

A barrage of hard knocking at the door interrupted my thoughts. Esther's voice, although muted, kept rising. When I opened the door, she burst through. Like the wheeling panoply of the cosmos, she moved across the room. She flailed her arms, and her voice became shriller by the second.

"Damn it, Danielle, we're worried about you. You won't answer your phone. Bethany said when she left everything seemed fine. Then when you didn't call or accept calls, she thought you'd gone back to Molly." Her face was that of a demanding statue. "What's going on?"

I felt as though my life was chaos. Death made us remote, I thought as my mouth wobbled to get words to pass through my lips. "Samantha called. Molly died." With those words, sudden contempt filled my heart—Molly was again with Pamela.

Esther placed the sack she was carrying on the coffee table. I eased back against the sofa. She sat beside me, wrapped her arms around me, and allowed my tears to flow against her shoulder.

"How?" she asked after some length.

"Her heart. She was to have an operation when they returned. She'd had two episodes before. That's the reason she wouldn't encourage me. To spare me."

"I'm not sure what to say other than I'm sorry."

"I feel so empty inside, Esther. I remember Molly always said that her family, on both sides, had heart problems. When her grandmother died of cardiac difficulties, her parents told her not to attend the funeral. They didn't want her near the family because she was lesbian. It saddened her so."

Esther waited for a moment, then she asked, "Will you call Bethany?"

"Not now."

"Do you want me to call her? Like I said, she was afraid you'd gone to Molly. Or that you weren't well. She's concerned."

"Yes, if you wouldn't mind calling her. Please tell her I need a little time to myself right now."

Esther phoned Bethany and spoke out of earshot. She hung up and sat down again beside me.

"She said to tell you she's there if you need her. And she's very sorry. At least Molly didn't suffer."

"I believe we've both suffered for thirty years." The silence in the room seemed thick. I thought how my grandparents had handed down their wisdom to me, but none of it was of any help now. Death excluded sagacity. Sadness was never right side up. I felt so very alone.

Esther took a deep breath. "We lionize the people we lose. Maybe it's part of love's mystery. That makes the search deeper."

"I don't know why all this is happening."

"The rhythm of the stellar world is remarkable. We have the opportunity to select a cadence with it all, but we often opt against accepting. We continue to explore the reasons we believe to be correct, and the planet continues its route. That circling escapade."

I thought for a moment. "Maybe the rotation of earth is the only evidence of our existence. Death is a lifelong companion. It remains ready to act upon us at any time."

"We're all concerned over death's justification," Esther said. "After all, the body is home to us, and when that body collapses, home is gone. In the survivor's case, the home's neighbor is missing. Some believe that people become jaded to death when they're older. I don't believe it for a moment. Maybe, if anything, it's more difficult. Youth knows the rules, but age teaches exceptions."

"I seem to know nothing, Esther. I've always firmly believed in a creator. Right now, I'm not certain about a loving supreme being. The creator seems to be more of a henchman. The ultimate exterminator. To me, religion has always felt as if one is consulting with a boogeyman to connect to the higher boogeyman."

"I'm a scientist and not truly religious, as you know. But I've never doubted there is some type of beyond. Energy never ends. It only disperses or transforms. We approach our termination from birth. The same spirit, that energy that begins with us, has to go somewhere. Some scientists have tried to prove that immediately after death there is a miniscule, yet measurable, loss of weight. Their explanation is that this is the weight of the human soul leaving the body. There's no real proof, but I believe there is a beyond."

I sighed. "I was thinking, if there is this gigantic beyond, a heaven, then Molly has been reunited with Pamela. How sad is it that I'm jealous of a ghost?"

"From everything you've told me, I'd say Molly wouldn't be within a country or a heavenly mile of Pamela. She stayed with Pamela for Samantha's benefit. Molly said she was still in love with you. That says it all."

"And I still love her. When I felt a final rejection from her, I allowed myself to have feelings for Bethany."

"You always fight fate, Danielle. Maybe meeting Bethany was part of some grand plan. If not, maybe it was the best luck you've ever had. Accept it. She's a terrific woman. She makes you happy."

"I haven't done much in the way of making her happy, though. All I've talked about is Molly."

Esther held my gaze. "So why don't you crack open your heart enough to make room for Bethany?"

"Even now, I'm considering that as a transgression against my love for Molly."

"How is guilt connected to replacement love?"

I picked at my slacks for nonexistent lint. "Even if we knew, we probably couldn't pronounce it."

She chuckled slightly. "You know, there's a stellar family out there that is all crowded and in a violent neighborhood. Yet within the chaos, it seems normal. Sort of comparable to our existence down here on planet earth."

"That bit of minutia brightens my day."

"Oh, before I forget. Call Fiona. She's on your trail. She's getting fifteen percent to brighten your day. I'm only here to torment you with trivia."

"Mission accomplished," I replied dryly but with the hint of humor. Esther's mere presence had lifted my spirits.

"Danielle, you can't let this damage your health. You look very ragged around the edges. You need some food and sleep. Can I bring you anything?"

"No. If I get hungry, I'll order room service. But thank you. I'll sleep when I'm ready, so don't worry about me. Face it, I usually look disheveled."

"You're an artist. You're not supposed to look normal."

Then we hugged, and she left. I dialed up Fiona only to find her line was busy. After downing the remainder of my coffee, I redialed. Although I wasn't emotionally fortified to talk with anyone, Fiona would keep me out of the world's stormy spots for a few moments.

But her phone was, as the Brits say, still engaged.

Chapter 40

Fiona burst into my hotel suite. I hadn't bothered to lock up after Esther left.

Glancing up, I asked, "Why don't you come right on in? Don't bother knocking."

"It was fucking open! What's with your vanishing act crap?"

"I tried to call you, but your line was busy."

"I was talking with Esther. Oh, Danielle, I'm so sorry about Molly." She sat down in one of the armchairs. "I must have left a dozen calls trying to get hold of you."

"After I tried calling you earlier, I haven't wanted to talk. I'm not thrilled about it now."

"I hate being ignored." After silence, she wrestled around in her chair. "I apologize for barging in. But you obviously aren't working. You've gone into hiding. I'm stymied."

"I'm mourning," I said angrily. "I don't have anything to say. Fiona, this is a shock to me."

"Meanwhile, you could be working. Look," she said and waved her hand at the paintings, "you haven't touched the canvases. Why don't you paint it out?"

"Paint it out?" I asked incredulously.

"Think of the great art that's been produced when the artist is depressed. Grieving. Pick up a paintbrush. It would be good therapy. Great art might come of it. I'll order a few canvases to be delivered. Paint. Pick some subjects and paint."

"Subjects." Sometimes Fiona got on my last nerve.

She gave an enormous sigh. "Artists are mostly semiliterate. You're borderline, but just barely. Yes, paint now. You're finally coming into your own. Danielle, the art world is revisiting your work. Or maybe taking a first look at you. Last week, two international art magazines had articles about you. One said you're one of the finest contemporary realists in the world. That's major."

"Right now I'm the saddest artist in the world. Aren't you getting this, Fiona?"

"You've always been an emotional painter. So ratchet up your production. Tap into that powerful fervor of bereavement."

"I have no fervor." I stood, at the end of my patience. "Fiona, I'll paint when I'm damned well ready. Right now, I don't even feel ready to take the next breath. That's how flipping devastated I am."

"I'm trying to shake you back to reality. Approval in the art world is difficult. Accolades are rare. When you're the buzz, you'd better be there. I've witnessed your slow and steady climb. You've been in the vestibule. You're center stage now. That meteoric rise you've awaited for your entire career is here."

"I need a couple of days…"

"The hell you do. If I gave you a bouquet of roses, you'd find a fucking thorn and impale yourself on it." Her voice rose. "Until you die, it can always get worse. Molly wouldn't have wanted you to throw away everything you've worked to achieve."

"I'll get back to the easel when I'm ready."

"I've seen artists leave the easel for a little rest. Just a few days. Get over a bad bump or two. They get fucking lost. That is their few days. The rest of their life. They never return. I'm not going let you get lost," she yelled. "Do you hear me?"

My return shout was as cyclonic. "I need time. Either that or I'll leave London."

She was in my face like a smashing tempest. "That would break our contract. Don't let stupidity get the best of you. Fate is the shits. Sometimes you're the dog. Sometimes you're the hydrant. There's no passport to paradise, baby. Human suffering is basic. Life's storms are deep fucking drama."

I folded my arms across my chest. "Fiona, I know you're trying to help, but it isn't working. In fact, you're making it worse."

"I don't mind you moping. You artists are always moping. But you hit on tragedy, like death, and the wheels go out from under the cart. I can read it in your eyes, Danielle. You're ready to break. And damn it, I have no intention of watching you crumble in a slow out-the-door demise. It begins with a day, then a week. Soon you haven't produced for months. Then it's all over. I'm damned well not going to let you sink when you're finally on a roll."

"I need a rest."

Fiona wouldn't be deterred. "You need your art. I doubt if you've been away from your art for more than a day or two running in your entire adult life."

"Right now I don't really care."

"That's exactly what I was worried about and why I rushed over here. I see it in your eyes."

"I don't want you to worry. It's my life."

"Okay, you can continue to avoid the world, but it's going to cost you. You have always been autonomous, and we both know that's been expensive." She paused, then stood and walked to the door. "We're all here for you. We all love you. Whatever you need, you call me." After another hesitation, she added, "Go to an art museum."

"Cézanne said an art museum is a book in which we learn to read."

"Hot damn. See, you're not totally illiterate. Must be the Saph that saves you."

I smiled slightly. "Thanks. That may be the nicest thing you've ever said to me."

"So I'm still the Ladybugs Rock official mascot?"

"It's yours for life." I glanced away. "I'm sorry I can't paint right now. Sorrier than you are. Sorrier than your fifteen percent and my eighty-five percent together."

She gave me a sympathetic smile. "You do realize I don't care if I ever make another dime off of your work. I care about your work and about you. Fool."

Fiona left. Having always been impassioned by art, even during other adversity and loss, I'd felt the need to paint.

I picked up a brush and twirled its spindly handle. It felt foreign to my hand. I gripped it tightly. I tried to envision myself dipping it into a bright pillow of paint. I viewed the tubes of paint, the bouquet of brushes, and the canvas that needed attention.

With a sharp turn away from my painting station, I choked. Molly's name was on my lips. I whispered it to myself several times until it chained into my sobs.

Tears didn't feel cathartic, as they perhaps should have. I threw the brush down. I had nothing left inside me with which to create. A nightmare had replaced that part of my soul. I stepped over the paintbrush on my way to the bedroom, on my return to further sorrow.

Chapter 41

As I reclined in my bed, I realized I'd scarcely moved for nearly the entire day. From my fetal position, I continued staring across the room. Evening's twilight contrasted with the wall's darkening patterns. Traffic from below was screeching, wailing, and blaring with little cadence.

I ignored the pounding on my door until I couldn't stand it anymore. "Who is it?"

"Spencer. Spencer Murphy. Fiona's personal assistant. Miss Revere's assistant, Spencer."

I swung the door open. "Spencer?" I smiled in spite of my sorrow. "Your first name would have been enough to do the trick. You're the only Spencer I know."

He stepped inside my suite with four large canvases. "Fiona said to bring these by to you." He scrutinized my appearance. "You look like crap."

"Did she send you in as some kind of a comic-relief delivery man?"

"I'm not supposed to say, but I'm to report back to her on your condition. Also, can I bring you something to eat?"

"I have room service, but thank you for the offer."

"Wow, I love these pictures." Spencer examined the paintings of Bethany and the one of Bethany and me. "I've never seen one of your self-portraits."

"I haven't done many and certainly not for the past couple of decades."

"I'm sorry you're so sad. I hope I can always understand artists the way Fiona does. She's really worried about you."

"I promise I'm fine. And you do understand artists, Spence. I think you're terrific. If Fiona ever retires, I hope I'll be working with you."

He grinned, showing off his boyish good looks. "I'd like that. You elucidate the human emotion on canvas like no other."

"Is that what I do?" I asked with amusement.

"Fiona and I will always be there for you. You can count on us."

"I know that. Thanks, Spencer." I looked back at the packages of canvases he'd lugged up. "And thank you for the canvases. If you wouldn't mind hauling the two larger finished canvases back to the gallery, I would appreciate it."

"Anything for you, Danielle. Fiona will be pleased." He pulled the wrapping from the new canvases and carefully packaged my two larger paintings.

"Tell her I'm okay. I need a little time before I can begin elucidating human emotion again."

He blushed. "You know what I mean. I think you bring clarity to your art."

"At least you've made me smile. Maybe you'll become an art critic."

"I sort of am now," he said with enthusiasm and then sobered. "I'm sorry to hear about your friend."

"I'll be okay. Right now I just need some alone time."

"Fiona said you'd be as impregnable as a medieval fortification."

"Fiona's right." I walked him to the door. "Spence, I appreciate your coming up here. I like you immensely, and I think you'll make a great art critic, or a great art agent, or anything else you'd care to be."

"I think I'll stick with art agent. If I follow Fiona's lead, she'll see that I'm good at it."

I nodded in agreement.

After he left, I sat back a moment but not for long. Someone was again at the door. Certain that Spencer had forgotten something, I opened it quickly.

"Bethany." I stepped aside so she could enter.

"I'm sorry to intrude. I've been worried. Danielle, can I do anything?"

The moment was tense, and I had no idea how to make it warmer. Then she took me in her arms. It wasn't a sexual embrace, only one of gentle, tender friendship. I hugged her back, holding her tightly until I realized I was holding her too closely. I pulled away and began to sob. Again, she drew me close.

"Danielle, I'm here for you. As a lover, a friend—as your family. I know the sense of loss, and I know what you're going through."

"Thank you for coming. I'm sorry I didn't phone you. I've just been…"

"I know how difficult it is to be around others. Esther called. I rung up Fiona and she told me she'd seen you. I had to know you're okay. I hope you don't mind."

"No. Not at all."

"Look, I can leave." She motioned to the door. "I can call you later. Or if you need me, you can call."

"I appreciate your dropping by. I'm afraid I'm not good company right now."

"What about dinner? Would you like to go out for something to eat? We can grab a quick dinner and then walk, if you like. It would be good for you to get out. We don't need to talk. I only want to be near you."

"I don't think I can eat right now."

"Well, I'll leave you then. But I hope you'll at least order something to eat."

Her eyes held a compassion that mingled with the pain of remembrance.

I relented. "Have a seat. I'll shower and get on some fresh clothing. Then we can go out. Do you mind waiting?"

Without a moment's hesitation, she said, "I'd wait forever. Like you would have waited forever for Molly, and I would have waited for Tricia."

I was well aware of what she meant. Fate had reduced our number. We were only two now.

Chapter 42

Lindsay's Tea House seemed strange, as if I'd never been there before. Bethany watched as I slowly sipped tea. She had ordered tea and Cornish pasties for us. I found the food bland, with no taste and flavor. I continued to pick at mine. The usually delicious tea tasted stale. Even sounds were muted, and colors seemed dull.

After our meal, we walked through London's center for what seemed like many miles. Bethany seemed to know the affection of silence, as well as the benevolence of having someone near. Boxy black cabs whirled the roundabouts. Sights blurred. Only a smile from Bethany brought me back into the soul of the moment.

"I haven't had the desire to paint since Samantha's call. That's never happened to me before. Ever. There were times when I didn't want to paint. Yet I felt the desire, regardless. Even if I wasn't actually painting, my mind was planning a work. Sketching. But not now."

"You'll begin again," she said with utter certainty.

"What if I can't?"

"You've been shifted into a new dimension of love. You'll paint again."

"I don't know, Bethany."

"Of course you will. You have to paint."

"I don't recognize this feeling inside," I said, my voice shaky.

As we approached the Marshall, she kissed my cheek. "I think you need to be alone tonight. I'd love to hold you in my arms, but I'm not sure that's what you need most right now. I'll make a suggestion you may or may not understand. Have a talk with Molly. Talk out loud and visualize her across from you. Tell her you'll always keep her in your heart. And you will."

I thought about it, and it somehow made sense. "Thank you, Bethany. You've been wonderful."

"Tomorrow afternoon, are you free?"

"Aren't you working?"

"I requested the day off."

"But why would you want to be around my sadness?"

"No one is allowed to grieve when on a picnic. I have somewhere special to show you."

I couldn't help but smile at her kindness. "Noon?"

"I'll pick you up in front of your hotel." She hailed a cab and then turned back to me. "Danielle, there are a thousand shades of night's heartbreak. In the darkness, it's easy to fall. Artists can't work without luminosity."

I leaned near to kiss her cheek. "Can I bring anything to the picnic?"

"Only your sketchpad and desire to sketch. I'll provide the nosh and models."

I waved at her and walked toward the hotel lobby. I took one more look at her taxi pulling away. She had lifted my heart.

As I walked through the lobby, I heard Esther calling my name.

"I'm glad to see you out and about, Danielle."

"Bethany came by. We went out for a quick dinner. I got half a pastie down. Then we trudged the city streets awhile. I bet you're probably leaving to see Carrie."

"Right." She tugged on my shirtsleeve. "Come on, I have time for a glass of wine at the bar."

"I'm really not in the mood."

"Then make it a half glass. It might help you sleep tonight. You look like you could use the sleep. Why did Bethany leave?"

"She believes I need my space. I didn't ask her to leave."

"She's a remarkable woman. Come on, one wine to catch me up."

"Okay. One glass and then I'm going up to my room. I doubt if I'll sleep, but I'm going to try. I wish I still wanted to paint. That might help me. But I can't even look at a paintbrush."

We sat in a booth. I caught a glimpse of myself on a panel mirror lining the inside wall. It stunned me for a moment. My reddened eyes were puffy and dark. Creviced lines crossed my face. I appeared to have aged years overnight.

Esther ordered for both of us.

"Are you going to mention the fact that you still don't want to paint to Fiona?" she asked.

"I'm sure she knows. I have other things on my mind." I sipped a glass of excellent cab. "Tastes nice. I haven't been able to experience flavor."

"You could use several of those. So did Bethany understand?"

"Yes. Why wouldn't she? She's experienced what I feel."

"You can take lessons from a woman of class and expertise in the matter of loss. Hell, Bethany lived with the woman for twenty years. Right up until the time her lover died."

"Does that mean because there was an interlude between the years Molly and I were together that I don't love her as much? I shouldn't grieve?" I snapped.

"I'm not using a damned scorecard on time, Danielle. Don't be so touchy. I'm not saying you weren't in love with Molly. So what now?"

"What do you mean what now? I finish up my contract with the gallery, and I go home. I'll be sad for a long, long time. You remember that song from years ago by Dory Previn? I think it was titled 'Going Home—Mythical Kings and Iguanas.' It talks about going home being a low and lonely ride. That's how this trip will be. A very low and lonely ride. I'll be saying goodbye to two of the best women I've ever shared love with."

Esther looked at me in disbelief. "Let's take your statements one at a time. First, I remember the song. Great song. Second, one of the best women you've ever been with has died, sadly. And you wouldn't have been going home with her anyway. That was the way she wanted it. If she hadn't wanted it that way, you would have been together years ago. And third, the other best woman is falling in love with you. Which means she might return stateside if you'd ask her."

"You truly believe Bethany is falling in love with me?"

"I realize you wouldn't recognize a love palpitation from a kettledrum. The passion carnival keeps right on passing you by and passing you by. Berk!"

"When we return home, are you going to stop calling me a berk?"

"Maybe yes, maybe no. I haven't decided." She glanced down at her watch. "Speaking of passion, I'd better push off."

"Thanks for brightening my evening, Esther. You little sunbeam."

She hugged my shoulders. "Try and get some rest. If you need me, call. I'll be there."

"I know." It was something I counted on.

Chapter 43

In my attempt to sleep, memories swam through my mind. Although my loss seemed foreign, it seemed not to be morbidly so. Perhaps death was only as temporary as life itself. We invested ourselves with others and they with us. Prayers seemed inadequate, yet admirable. I prayed to have a moment with Molly. I implored deities, saints, and angels for just another touch. Just another moment.

The reigning divinity ignored me. Molly would not return. My own beliefs were that religion had a very checkered past. But faith was a different matter. Faith could be scripted on our hearts. Of course, I thought myself intelligent enough to believe something awaited us after we died. It could be named anything. Heaven. Why not? It had a pleasant sound.

My faith came in part because humanity was of a spirit that amazed me. Our recognition of beauty and creativity astounded me. Each time I took my liner brush, my trusty dagger striper, to sign a canvas, I felt a tinge of fraudulence. Had an aesthetic embodiment forged within my existence manufactured the work? How fortunate I was to be able to create. But now, my desire to do so had evaporated.

Finally, at four-thirty in the morning I glanced at the clock. I sat up. I began to talk to Molly, as Bethany had suggested. My words were halting and hushed. I was half-embarrassed to be saying my thoughts out loud.

"Molly," I said, "my sorrow is compounded by my own failure to win back your love. Right now, there's no discursive rhetoric aimed at a creator that would take you from me. Nor is there anger because you've left me behind once again. From the moment we met, I've loved you. Years ago, when a plane emptied, I realized you weren't there. My appointment with you and your beautiful smile wasn't meant to be. But my love for you has remained as crisp as the moment Esther introduced us.

"You confessed you still loved me. You didn't have the confidence in my love to know I would stand by you in spite of your health problems. I would have. Maybe it was too complicated, just as it was three decades ago.

"Perhaps you were correct in leaving me. But I'll always hear your laughter, feel your embrace, and taste your kiss. Always see your smile.

"No matter the diversion, somehow our love has remained. That's a credit not only to each of us but to love itself. How strong those feelings have persisted over the years of our parting. After the last thirty years of my life, I'm still in love with you. And always will be."

I held my head in my hands. Too many seasons had passed where I, and I alone, had willingly relinquished my pleasure. Because I'd feared losing love again, I hadn't allowed the sharing of my home and hearth. I hadn't had the wisdom required to know the truth. Fear was never a safe haven.

And what of my current inability to paint? I had a sliver of anxiety but also the conviction that when I was ready my barrier would collapse. When it imploded, perhaps I would be even freer in the realm of my art.

The creative spirit was forever infused with that panic of losing one's ability. Yet apprehension further diminished the creative process. So, for now, I'd look longingly at my brushes and my tubes of paint. I'd resist pessimism. The empty canvases Fiona sent were stacked against the wall and awaited my brush. For me, blank canvases were always lonely.

I got out of bed and walked to where the canvases leaned against the wall. I bent down and picked up a paintbrush that had fallen. Carefully, I replaced it in my wooden artist's case. Where it belonged. Where I would find it when I next needed it. Then I returned to bed.

When morning arrived, I'd go to the gallery then meet Bethany for our picnic lunch. She mentioned an excursion to somewhere special. I had no doubt that it would be. She also had mentioned models. Maybe she would invite Esther and Carrie along. I needed to bring my sketchpad and pencils and a watercolor set to capture proper pigmentation.

I would always be grateful to Bethany. She'd taken on the cause of repairing my sorrow. I felt comforted that many blessings surrounded me. My eyes fluttered closed, weighed down by exhaustion. Thankfully, I drifted toward what I hoped would be a peaceful sleep.

Chapter 44

"According to Esther, you're dining alfresco with that adorable Bethany?" Fiona's questions began the instant I entered the gallery. "Yummy edibles this noon."

I gestured at my art supplies. "I'll try to do a little pleine-air painting with watercolors. Draw a little. How's the show going?"

She led me through the gallery, pointing out the various paintings that had sold. "I'm not sure how it could be better. Success is a great reason to return to your easel." She pushed her designer glasses slightly down the ridge of her nose and looked at me pointedly over the rims. "Don't you think?"

"Yes, Fiona," I answered dutifully.

Continuing to another painting, she pointed. "This one goes to Germany. Who would have thought the Germans like contemporary realism?"

"Let's not exclude anyone. There are some extraordinarily fine German artists and art experts."

"Well, Rome loves you. Italy adores class and elegance. Always has and always will. A museum there purchased the one of the garden…"

"*Sunflowers and Sunshine Mixing.* I painted it several years ago."

"Italy approves of your daffy and dumb era. Back when you were a one-date woman. Unlike now when you've actually had multiple dates with Bethany. She's a saint. I hope you appreciate that."

"I can tell you've recently had a gabfest with Esther." She didn't try to deny it. "Back then I was just cautious. I didn't want my love life to get out of hand."

"For all we know, you don't have more than half a sex hormone in your entire body. That brings us back to a picnic hamper. An afternoon in the great outdoors is exactly what you need to get your artistic drive zooming again. Add a lovely woman, and it can't hurt your sex drive."

"You've got sex drive enough for both of us." I declined to talk about my love life. Fiona had no such limit, so I thought I'd goad her. "Speaking of which, how are you scoring?"

"This city is bursting with young studs. I love it. And I'm going to Paris and Germany next. Consider the possibilities. What an absolute festival. I'll only be in Europe a couple weeks before I return to New York. Back to the sanity of mass confusion. I'll miss you and your friends. But I'll see you again in Boston. Think you'll have a Boston show ready for me?"

"Yes. I'll dig out some of the pictures I've done in the past—whatever's left over from your raiding pictures for this show. I'll photograph and send photos. Let me know what you want for Boston. Add to that, we'll have whatever I can produce in the next few months."

"Might want to consider storing your paintings in a secured place from now on. Get an alarm system set up. Your personal collection is damned valuable. As for your new work—just do it. Danielle, you've never been a prissy diva. Let's not start that business in your golden years. You aren't cut out to be a prima donna."

"No? Should I take that as an insult?" I joked.

"Money and fame are diseases. You exude an innocence, a simplicity. Don't let fame corrupt you. I've seen artists devoured and exploited by celebrity and money."

"Your admonition is noted. I'll be careful."

"And it wouldn't hurt to have someone along on your journey. Someone who loves you and has business acumen. You're dismal with finances."

"How have you managed alone all of these years, Fiona?"

"I'm smarter than most everyone else. All those fools out there are clueless next to me." Her expression reflected a pride in her statement, not merely an explanation. "And I'm more heartless than anyone else."

"You keep in touch with your inner bitch, and I'll stay as sweet as I am."

"It's good to see you up and about. I was worried about your productivity. Any movement on the paint-splattering front?"

"I promise I'll get back to it. I've been resting up."

"Think of Boston and make it a fucking brief intermission. Take the afternoon and have fun. Then grab your brushes."

"I plan on it."

"You do realize shutting down isn't an option, don't you?"

"Don't worry. I've never shut down." I meant my words to bolster myself, as well as Fiona. "I'll paint again."

"We need a celebration before you Saphs leave for the hinterland. A party."

Knowing Fiona's world revolved around festivals, I agreed. "How about a pub crawl with Ladybugs Rock before we leave?"

"Let's consider closing night after the finishing ceremony. Meanwhile, between your picnics, do pick up a brush."

"I will." I left the gallery. I needed a walk to clear my mind. Accolades, fortunes, all the sublime goals became less important without love.

When I was very young, my mother once mentioned something while she was telling me about the birds and the bees. The conversation stumbled. Her eyes were glittered with drugs, and her ramblings were often unintelligible.

I'd asked what love was supposed to feel like. She had touched my face. Then she answered that love felt like a smile. A smile was an aphrodisiac, she'd said. I had needed to look up the word. Then it made sense.

Within two blocks, I'd arrived back in front of my hotel. Waiting was a cab with Bethany, and her face brightened when she saw me. She pushed a basket aside so I could slide in.

I took her hand and squeezed it gently. "Sorry you had to wait a few minutes."

"I think we've been over that. I'm prepared to wait much longer. Forever if I have to."

Chapter 45

I had squeezed a 7x10 spiral-bound sketchpad, a metal tin containing a dozen graphite drawing pencils, and a set of watercolors with brushes into my oversized handbag. I felt some fear about delving into my art again.

The cab driver drove us to a lovely park. Bright with autumn's floral color, it looked lush and inviting. A few people were milling, playing, and snuggling. I followed behind Bethany as we trekked to a small space surrounded by bushes as a wall of privacy. A tree had been planted in the middle of the area as if it were an altar. Bethany set the hamper down.

"This is absolutely amazing," I said. "How did you find it?"

"Tricia and I met in this park. We'd been walking our Yorkies. We spoke about the dogs. I think they call it 'gaydar' rather than radar. At any rate, we began seeing one another. Fell in love. Then moved in together."

"Yorkies?"

"We always had at least one Yorkie. Our last died three years after Tricia, and I didn't have the heart to get another."

"I'm glad you're a dog lover. I somehow trust animal lovers more."

"I didn't bring the subject up before because I knew you miss little Clover. I'd like to one day get another Yorkie. When I retire, I shall."

I didn't say it but wished I had. Clover would welcome a cute little scampering Yorkie sister.

"This was our place of retreat. I'm sure that by night it's probably a favorite snog spot," she said.

"Almost without a doubt. It should be a place for lovers. It's beautiful."

She removed a blanket from the hamper and quickly shut the lid. "I have a surprise lunch for us. No peeking." After spreading the blanket on the ground, she motioned for me to sit. Then she pulled out a fancy tablecloth and began to assemble the picnic.

I reclined on the soft blanket. "So you came here often?"

"We did. I haven't been here since Tricia died. I even walked our little Yorkie, Gidget, in another park. The loveliness of this spot deserves sharing, but I never knew anyone special enough to show it to."

"Thank you," I said softly as our eyes met.

From the hamper she pulled a cooled bottle of wine and an opener. "Will you do the honors while I set the table?"

I worked on opening and pouring the wine while she placed four plates on the cloth. She took out the silverware and set all four place settings. Then she spread out an alfresco delight.

The small platters held poached salmon and cucumber sandwiches, cold beef brisket sandwiches, artichoke and sausage quiche in small pastry shells, crab-stuffed mushroom caps, spinach-and-cheese-stuffed caps, and miniature champagne grapes. She told me dessert would be crepes with almond macaroon crumbs soaked in Kahlua.

"This looks wonderful, Bethany. What a feast. Did you invite Esther and Carrie?" I pointed to the two extra services.

"No. Only two models for you to draw." Her eyes sparkled with mirth. She reached inside the hamper and pulled out two stuffed toys. They were fluffy bison, and she rested them against the empty plates. "They won't eat much, but they're our guests. As well as your models."

I burst out laughing. "Where did you get these?"

"Finding them was rather difficult. I tried toy stores, but when I said bison or buffalo, the clerks led me to the mastodons. I nearly gave up. Finally, I called a pilot friend and told her of my dilemma. She was doing a turn from New York and called one of the crew members boarding there. The famous toy store FAO Swartz has everything. Here they are. Happily enough, they escaped the usual animal quarantine."

"They're absolutely precious. I can't believe you went to all that trouble."

"No trouble. I remember you told me about sketching bison while you were in Kansas. Well, these aren't real, but they'll be very still, well-behaved models for you. They might even jumpstart your desire to create."

"I brought my supplies to sketch you."

"I'm not meant to be the model today. Only a friend to be with you, Danielle."

"And a lover?"

"If a lover is what you'd like."

I lowered my head. "There's what I'd like, barring difficulties. And there are realities."

Bethany tilted my chin up with her fingertips. "In my work, I learned early that if I were to survive, I must resolve difficulties quickly and confidently. Tell me what you'd like to have happen to our relationship and what difficulties you foresee."

I pondered as I ate. "I'm not sure. I know I want to return home. Back to my territory, my dog, my garden, all the things that make my life work. My bohemian habits of art. It would be nice if you were with me, but that shouldn't happen."

"Shouldn't?" she asked with a hopeful tone. "Is it inconceivable to believe it could happen?"

"Your life is here, as I've said before. Leaving would be such a major risk. I wouldn't want to be responsible for your unhappiness. I'm difficult to live with. I'm exhausting. I'm driven." I twisted the napkin in my lap as I spoke.

Bethany stilled my fidgeting with a touch. "I know you, Danielle. I know you from the sensitivity with which you paint. The enormous agony you're in from losing a past lover. I know you from the friend who flew across an ocean to be with you. A woman you work with who has a deep and abiding respect for you. And mostly I know you from your gentle nature. A nature that loves for decades, against all hope."

"Maybe if you visited me when you take your next vacation, you'd be able to see how I live. Where I live. Will you visit me?"

She squeezed my hand. "Of course. If I'm willing to march off into the sunset with you at this very moment, I'm certainly more than happy to visit you. And more than willing."

"If you still feel this way after a little pause…"

"I'm pretty sure a pause, as you say, isn't going to change how I feel. I'm not certain how you feel. You've been purposely noncommittal."

"Not so purposely. I've explained about Molly. I thought it best that I sort myself out before telling you how I feel." I hesitated. "Bethany, I've been falling in love with you for some time."

She leaned in, and when our lips met, I felt her softness and warmth. She cupped my face in her hands. Her thumb passed over my lips. When our eyes met, she said. "And I've been falling in love with you. Now, are you planning on immortalizing those bison on paper? Or are you just going to sit there and allow them to pretend to graze?"

Chapter 46

I sketched the stuffed bison and colored in hues and lighting. Although they were only about eight inches long and five or six inches tall, they fit beautifully in front of their plates. In a few sketches, I placed Bethany alongside the bison. I also took some photos with my phone to refer to when painting them. I was confident that when I actually did face an empty canvas, excitement would return.

After I closed the cover of the sketchpad and packed it away, we strolled along the park's pathways. I carried the hamper while Bethany carried the bison. Perhaps I would paint my remembrances of live bison and somehow superimpose the two stuffed toys.

When we returned to the hotel, Bethany gave me a fantastic backrub. Afterwards, she handed me a brush and pointed to my easel. She'd make phone calls and read a book she'd brought with her, and I was to finish the painting of us. Maybe begin a new one.

I sat before the canvas showing the two of us. Bethany's smile made me thrill all over again. I highlighted our faces with brightness. Finally, the picture was completed.

I set it aside and automatically reached for a larger canvas. I selected a photo of Bethany hugging the two bison near her face. In the background, the picnic basket rested on the lush burgundy blanket. Verdant foliage and blotches of sunshine surrounded the scene.

Feverishly, I began under-painting and slathered paint where the canvas itself seemed to be craving it. Without my usual tonal sketch, I dabbed the places requiring life. There would be very little shadowing or slight shading. I wanted her resplendence to show as brightly as possible. I wanted an explosion of life.

I felt Bethany's arm around my shoulder. "You've started a new painting."

"You inspired me not only to finish our painting but to begin a new one."

She kissed my temple. "I have so many questions. I used to pester Tricia with questions about her art. I hope you don't mind."

"Not at all. I'm glad you're interested," I said as I continued my work.

"How do you decide on brushes, colors, and all?"

"For some unknown reason, each decision is nearly without my conscious selection. Each brush seems correct. Each color exact. It's humbling when I think about it. The symmetry falls into place from what was the confusion in my mind. I'm certain it begins with experience. Suddenly, I reach for the correct implement and use the right technique. A rainbow of colors finds their home on the canvas."

"Amazing. Even the bison are taking on character of their own. And you paint me very much as I feel I am."

"How could I fail to paint you with less beauty than you have?"

She gave me a quick kiss. "When you were a child, did you recognize that you wanted to be an artist?"

"I think so. It occupied and entertained me, and I seemed less alone. I felt a sense of abandonment because of my parents leaving when I was young. My maternal grandparents became primary custodians, so I shouldn't have been lonely."

"You never talk about your parents."

"For many years I considered that I never measured up in their eyes. Or they wouldn't have left. Thus, a low self-esteem. With the exception of my art."

"I'm sure being addicts didn't allow them to see goodness."

"I know you're right. My grandparents certainly helped my art vocation. They made up sketching games. Awards were cookies, small toys, and decorative stickers. They're responsible for the beginnings of my love of art."

"I think I would have liked them immensely."

"Yes. And they would have loved you." I closed my eyes as I pictured them. "They trained me so completely that I impressed my teachers. I remember in kindergarten, the teacher's assignment was to draw an apple like the example on the side of our paper. I refused to draw. The teacher asked why I wasn't doing what she requested. I told her the picture, a circle with a line on top, didn't look like an apple. She told me to draw what I thought an apple looked like. I drew the apple with shading, definition, and depth, and it looked like an apple. When I handed it to her, she was dumbfounded."

"Look where you are now."

"I've got a monstrous compulsion to create," I said jokingly.

"Thankfully. I'll let you get back to it." She squeezed my shoulder and returned to the bedroom.

I considered our conversation as I worked on the painting. Where I was now, I thought. I'd never had illusions of grandeur. Still, I had to have believed in myself, for I received no accolades early on. After forty years, a reward had appeared on the horizon.

The morning arrived quickly. I placed my brush down and wiped my hands on a splattered cloth. The vast majority of the painting was in place and reliably accurate.

Looking into the bedroom where Bethany slept peacefully, I leaned against the doorjamb. I watched her sleep. I felt an overwhelming desire to touch her and hold her. Not wanting to disturb her, I silently yearned for her touch in return. Her body lifted slightly in small waves of breath.

After several remarkable minutes of studying her while she slept, I felt wonderment. She knew my feelings for Molly. She tolerated my inconsistencies. She was a remarkable woman to have stayed valiantly at my side, enduring my self-absorption. With an intrinsic dignity, she had allowed me to gush about another woman, cry over that woman, and profess my love of that woman. She accepted my every design flaw. Even the fact that I seemed consumed by art.

Through it all, she hadn't abandoned me.

Chapter 47

Bethany had left early and gone to her apartment so she could get ready for work. I had made it to bed for a couple of hours then returned to what had been lonely, empty canvases. They were filling quickly. Almost simultaneously.

My previously choked-off ability to paint had expired. It had converted to a painting frenzy. Inside, I felt an agitation that swirled with multiple concepts, a restless necessity to compose art. Something had reinvigorated me completely.

I finished the painting of Bethany and my self-portrait, and I had nearly finished the one of Bethany with the bison. I titled it *Noonday Bison Picnic with Bethany*. I had also begun another one from the picnic but with the bison only. They sat before their place-setting. I'd call it *Invited Guests*. The background would show off the marvelous portion of Bethany's park.

Another was a brief sketch of Fiona, Esther, Bethany, Carrie, and me, titled *Ladybugs Rock London*. I would work from photos taken when we celebrated at The Scripted Banquet. A waiter had kindly taken a group photo of the five of us in our finery and festivity. My paints would memorialize our toasting at the Ladybugs Rock party.

The last canvas contained only swaths of paint that created skeletal-thin wash outlines. It was of Molly as she looked back at me for the final time. She was entering the limousine and had turned. I hadn't named the painting. As I was placing outlines of my intentions, I considered calling it *Perpetual Smile*. For her final smile would forever be with me. It was one of pathos, of love, and certainly of a profound farewell.

Seldom in my past had I jumped from work to work. Usually I found it an irritant when necessity forced me to work on two paintings at once. Not now. Now I found it exhilarating to throw myself into the newness of each work.

I hadn't fully envisioned the unfinished paintings before me. But as I greeted each canvas, they revealed themselves to me. Amazed at my prolific work, I pressed on until late afternoon. I felt tired, aching to rest my eyes and cramping hand.

I called Esther's room and was glad she answered. "Too early for a midday snack?"

"Not going to wait for dinner with Bethany?"

"Been painting all day so I forgot to have lunch," I said. "How about a snack? Maybe a tea. You can do pastry, and I'll order a half sandwich and soup. That will tide me over until dinner."

"Fine."

Within fifteen minutes, we were at the teahouse, orders delivered, and chatting. We began, as usual, with her report about new data from NASA'S Chandra X-ray Observatory. Hydrogen gases, which they named "blobs" years ago, were brightly glowing optical light. These blobs, formed around young distant galaxies, were the source of immense energy. Not unlike Carrie's youth, Esther joked. At any rate, she said, the source of the blob energy emanated from super massive black holes. Another mystery of the universe solved, she told me.

"Whoop-de-do," I commented dryly.

"This is important stuff." She could barely contain her enthusiasm. "Needless to say, it tells us more about the original formations of galaxies. In this case, they believe blobs might be leftovers."

"I know the galaxies are tangible. But the heavens all seem intangible to me. Did you talk with Bethany this morning?"

"She arrived, and I was awake. Very early. Carrie was sleeping in, bless her."

"Carrie's finding it difficult to keep up with you?"

"Damn right."

"Are you going to miss her when we return to Colorado?"

"Of course. But she'll visit. And I'll visit her. I need to give her a chance to recharge her batteries. Are you going to miss Bethany?"

"A great deal. I spent most of last night painting. She patiently read or slept. She doesn't expect to be entertained. She quietly attends to her own realm and allows me to paint. Actually, she insists on my painting."

"She's got it all. Adorable. Available. And she encourages your painting. What else could you possibly want, Danielle?"

"I would agree if we had met somewhere near Colorado's central region. But we didn't."

"It's just a puddle jump from Denver to London. If you invite her to join you, you can give domesticity a shot. If it works, fine. If she wants to return to London, she jumps on a plane and back she comes. Don't let a good thing get away."

"Esther, if it's a good thing, taking it slowly won't matter."

"Get the trial run over first. Then you won't be stretching it over the months. Invite her to stay with you now until the two of you figure out what is next. Come on, I introduced you to Molly, and it lasted for several years. At our age, several years could be a quick 'until death do us part.' Look at how quickly you lost Molly."

"Molly was special. When we met, we knew immediately we belonged together." I thought a moment about all we'd shared during our years. Little things like our tiny terrace garden. Molly loved spring flowers. I held images in my mind of the multicolored primrose that made her smile. She had once told me that the primrose was sweet, but only the golden-colored flower had a fragrance.

People were also of varied types. But only certain ones are meant for love. If lovers didn't get it right, an affair flamed out. How, I wondered, had my mind transcribed flowers into women?

Esther sighed heavily. "Bethany is special. There's an old saying I really like. 'There are more ways of getting to the top of a tree than sitting on an acorn.'"

"I'm not a quick-decision kinda gal. I'm not even a past-tense hootchie."

"Right now you're a broom-riding kinda gal. Is it because you're too particular? You don't think Bethany is good enough?"

"Not at all. If anything, she's too good for me. I don't want anyone hurt. Bethany lost someone she loved. I lost someone I loved. We're vulnerable. And she's a lovely human being. I wouldn't want her to give up everything she has here to follow me. She might be disappointed in life there. Maybe disappointed by life with me."

"That could certainly happen," Esther said with honesty. "I wouldn't want to think of a lifetime with you."

"Are you just being bitchy, or is it true? I'm that bad, right?"

"Not all the time. But Danielle, you're in another world. Being involved with astronomy, I'm very much in other worlds as well. But you stumble around unconnected entirely. Look at yourself." She began to itemize my fashion flaws.

I took note of her very stylish blaze-blue angora tunic with decorative stitching. Her denims were pencil-legged and tucked into ruched boots. I wore a stretched-out red T-shirt with sand-colored overblouse and nondesigner jeans.

I fumbled for an excuse. "Remember, I've been painting all day."

"I swear, as long as you can fog a mirror, you're going to look dismal."

We both chuckled at the same time.

I returned to the subject at hand. "Esther, I do care deeply about Bethany, but I don't want anyone hurt. She's had enough pain and loss."

"Pain and loss are part of the challenges of love, Danielle. They hang directly above. Not all of life is validated with a guarantee."

"Validity may be nothing more than self-approval. I've thought about that many times before. It seems everything ends in sadness." I turned my head to examine the collection of teapots they had on shelves and closed my burning eyes to rest them.

"Life shows torture at times, and at other times, tenderness. But you have to ignore thoughts that it might be negative," Esther said. "You've gone into a funk since the moment you saw Molly. Bethany has cheered you. What the hell else can you expect from life?"

"Okay, so I want masterpieces in a world of trash. Maybe I'm not up to creating that world for someone else."

"The Danielle I knew lived masterpieces. You could see jewels in light beams. Now you act as though you're confronted by some supernatural dejection. If you want to get so damned philosophical about it, then fine. But remember, to find true happiness, you sometimes trudge through mistakes, accidents, and great losses. Get a grip before I'm very much older. I'm nearly out of pep talks."

"Sorry to have such an exclusionary life."

"Death is a terribly hard bench. But you don't have to sit on it forever."

"I love Molly so much." Tears filled my eyes. "I need to get over this feeling before I can give love totally again. Bethany deserves that."

"Come on, Danielle, do you think Bethany is over it with Tricia? She isn't, and you will never be over Molly either. Grieve and get on with it." She brushed her hands together. "That's my free course from the University of Potpourri. Take it or leave it. I'm tired of listening to you moan."

"You're tired of listening to me?" I asked, irritated. "I promise you I'm tired of being me. I've been on a damned roller coaster since I arrived here. I have every right to be confused about my emotions." My words tumbled out raw and angry. Tears rolled down my cheeks. I wiped them furiously. "Don't you understand? It's all going too quickly." I took a deep breath. "Well?" I nearly shouted.

"I'm not sure when you became a fussy boots. That's Carrie's saying. Be that as it may, you have become one. And I can't shake you back to reality."

"What the hell do you know about reality?"

"I know the concentration of neon allows scientists to determine the time a tiny grain of sand has spent in interstellar space. That's my kind of reality."

In amazement, my jaw dropped. "And I'm coming to you for my advice to the lovelorn. Someone fresh from a Mars science laboratory. What the hell do you know about true romance?"

She started laughing. "I'll tell you what I know about romance," she said, sputtering through gulps for air. "Carrie asked me this morning if I Twitter. I said only if someone touches my G-spot. She thinks I'm a hoot. She says I'm barking nuts."

"I didn't even think you knew what a G-spot *is*."

"I do. It's part of the Constellation Erogenous."

While giggling, I stood. "Esther, our dates are probably waiting for us. And Carrie is probably waiting for the Constellation Erogenous."

By the time we pulled up to the hotel, Bethany and Carrie had arrived. The four of us decided on a walk and a late dinner at the hotel's dining room. Our trek offered witticisms and was a diversion from thoughts that troubled me.

After dinner, Esther and Carrie departed for Esther's room.

Bethany glanced my way. "Would you like the evening alone? I know you'd like to paint, and I think I'm sensing conflict in you."

"I'd like you to come up. Spend the evening with me. Yes, I'd like to paint, if you wouldn't mind. But you're right. I'm experiencing some conflict. You're very observant."

"I need to be, in my line of work. Remember?"

As the elevator lifted, she took my hand. "Would you like to talk about it?"

"I want you to know how I'm feeling. I'm so confused about my emotions. I really don't want either of us to get hurt."

"That's why you're holding back? Why the words aren't being said?"

"I suppose."

"I'll give you a backrub and then you should paint. There's total honesty in your work. The great illusion of living is that justice saves you. But life isn't just. Fate isn't at all equitable. I felt guilt each time I was happy. It was as if I went into Tricia's grave with her. Then it occurred to me she wouldn't have wanted that. She wouldn't have wanted me to linger without hope of happiness. I had been doing exactly that for years. Before I met you, I accepted those wasted years. Perhaps I was only waiting for you."

"You also said time is short and fleeting. I don't want you to wait for me. It isn't fair. The things we can make equitable, we should."

"Why don't you let me decide what's fair, luv?"

Chapter 48

In the morning after Bethany left for work, I meandered over to the gallery. Only a few days remained until the closing of my exhibit. Then I would fly back to my life in Colorado. I would enjoy returning to my family, friends, and Clover.

With these thoughts of home came the memories of small and precious portions of my life. I recalled the scent of the autumn ground as I turned my garden for the final time before winter's snow blanketed it. I knew the feel of the doorknob as I entered my small studio. The studio was at the side of my home, and I could mentally see the stepping-stones. Massive windows on all sides, along with two skylights, captured Colorado's brightness.

"I've been calling you," Fiona said when I entered. "The gallery has decided to host a huge closing party on your final night. Huge. Not a fiddling, diddling little event. An all-inclusive affair. Patrons, art critics, media, and so on. I've been working with Max on the promotion. Large e-mail message campaign, daily newspaper adverts, all the bells and whistles. They estimated the gathering will be triple the opening attendance. We'll need Roxie to ship a dozen of your paintings. Can she do that today?"

I glanced at my watch. "It's the middle of the night in Colorado. But yes, I'll phone. Roxie's always willing to help."

"Get hold of her and give her the directives. She shouldn't mind getting out of bed for art's sake. Probably needs to let the dogs take a leak anyway. One of the three ought to need a piss. Tell her I can have a twenty-four-hour-shipping company crate them and ship them immediately. Roxie may miss a few hours sleep, but she'll be handsomely rewarded, I assure you."

"She's a student, so a few extra bucks will come in handy."

"Danielle, she's been such a great help. I was thinking more about paying off her college loan or some damned thing. Give her a grant. Always a good tax deduction."

"Wow, Fiona. You amaze me. A benefactor of the arts."

"Friends are hard to come by. Tell her a dozen or more."

"Okay. A dozen it is. I'll have her clean out a closet."

"As soon as my European exhibits are complete, I want to come out there to Colorado to see exactly what you've got hidden away. With relative certainty, I believe you've stashed away some great work. Your remaining paintings need to be accurately categorized and photographed. We'll want an entire array, including early work for Boston. We plan to have that catalogue of your work become an art piece in itself. Best printer in the United States. We'll need all available work included."

"I'd like to do the selecting. Some work isn't really ready."

"You say some of your work is terrible, and actually it's superb. I'm afraid you'll try to be your own critic. You won't shoot photos of all your work. I must come to Colorado and scrounge."

"Can't fool me. Any excuse to come to Colorado. You're a good Ladybugs Rock mascot. Love that Colorado."

"You are my very favorite Saph, but you really get on my nerves sometimes, Danielle. Now, as to what you have in your current inventory. At your hotel room."

"I have *Bethany's Smile, Arrival of Hope, Together,* and *Noonday Bison Picnic* completed. There are three in various stages of completion: *Invited Guests, Ladybugs Rock London,* and *Perpetual Smile.* I've promised the one of Bethany and me, *Together,* to Bethany."

"Did it occur to you to give her flowers and candy? Nothing like handing over a painting worth thousands when a nice bundle of roses would do."

"She's not just any woman, Fiona. She deserves roses, of course. I haven't even sent those. She's been an enormous help, as well as my model and muse."

"I'll send Spencer over to pick up the three completed works when you're ready. Ones you haven't given away, that is. Now then, get your bum over to the hotel and paint your heart out. Load those brushes. We need stock. Once again, we're nearly sold out."

"I always paint my heart out," I said a little too curtly. "Not because I can make more sales. Because I do."

"Well, keep doing. I do live for your making more sales. That's my job. About Friday night after the show. I'll book a lavish dinner at The Scripted Banquet."

"We'll love that."

"Go to the hotel and call when you've completed each painting. I'll get the staff here to frame them as soon as they arrive. If you need any more blank canvases, just holler."

"Will do. I'll call Roxie before I go on a little excursion this morning. After which I'll sit down and paint."

"Excursion?"

"Something I need to do. I want to go to the open-air market again. Afterwards, I'll have an early lunch at a certain restaurant before I get back to painting."

"Places you saw Molly. Am I right?" Fiona asked gently.

I nodded. "I want to paint one final picture of Molly, and I'd like to add some things."

"It's pretty much all emotional with you, isn't it?"

"I've never done assembly-line art, and I won't ever do stamp-out art. You know that, Fiona."

"You're beginning to sound like a counterculture bitch."

"That description will look dandy in my fancy-dancy Boston promotional materials. Feel free to use it in our shiny new catalogue. Counterculture bitch paints."

"Go paint, silly. Don't let your paints dry out. Your work isn't done."

After the call to Roxie, I considered what a wonderful surprise it would be for her not to have to pay off student loans for the next twenty years. She had indeed reported that all three of the dogs needed to be let out for their potty break.

I took a brisk walk that helped clear my head. I first stopped at an elegant jewelry shop I'd passed by several times. I ordered five gold pins with ladybugs on the decorated side. On the backs, I had four of them engraved with "Ladybugs Rock Member" and individual names. On the other, "Ladybugs Rock Mascot" and Fiona's name. The manager assured me they'd be ready prior to the closing evening of my art show.

I continued on to the market. Through an open-air market's buzz and swirl of motion, I searched for the stall where Molly looked at the book. I remembered mostly watching her with indifference toward what she was holding. When I approached the stall, I examined the various large books with predominantly white and black covers.

"Excuse me, sir." I called the stall keeper over. "I don't suppose you recall an American woman here a little over a week ago." I described Molly and expected a negative response.

"Ducky, I do remember just such a woman. Classy. Looking at an art book, she was. I say that my brother likes to draw. She tells me she had a friend in her past who paints. Anyway, an art book."

"Do you recall which one? And do you still have it?" I tried to temper my excitement.

He pawed through several stacks of books on the opposite counter. He pulled one from the bottom and handed it to me. "This, 'en. I remember. Thought I would flog it off to her, but in the end, she said no. Then she says too many memories."

I swallowed hard. The book was the biography of my favorite artist, Cecilia Beaux. I thumbed through a few pages. I wondered if Molly had viewed the same paintings I had. She had held it to her breast, nearly embracing it.

"I'll take it," I said. I pulled out my money and handed him a twenty-pound note. "Perhaps she put it back so that I might have it."

"Chance would be a fine thing." He handed me coins and a note. "You stumped up too much lolly, ducky."

"Please, keep the change. Your good memory was a great help."

I left that stall and made my way to the next. There I searched out the small teacup set that Molly had examined. After finding it and purchasing it, I took a cab to Fav's Restaurant where I'd met Molly both times.

I requested the table where we had sat the last time I was with her. I ordered as I was being seated. I selected the exact salad, tea, and wine that Molly and I had when we met.

I called Roxie again to ask whether she'd had any problems shipping those additional paintings. She told me no, and the shipping company had been in touch. They would be there in a couple of hours. Roxie would call Fiona after the shipment was crated and on its way. Roxie said she assumed Fiona stayed awake all night running her business. I chuckled, stating it was probably not all night and probably not all business.

I also suggested that Roxie get some of her own artwork together. I told her Fiona would be coming to Colorado and would tell her exactly how terrific her art was. Knowing Fiona, she would assist Roxie in any way she could. The key was that Roxie's art deserved attention.

With phone still in hand, I ordered a dozen yellow roses delivered to Bethany's office. I had neglected her dreadfully. I knew better. My grandparents always taught us never to neglect treasures. They had taught their children that as well. But I forever questioned why the others, my aunts and uncles, had learned it, and my mother hadn't. There were two possibilities. Perhaps she had never learned it. Or perhaps she had and didn't consider my brother and me as treasures. Even after decades, I questioned both incoming love and outgoing love.

The waiter brought a lush salad while I was examining the book I'd purchased. Although many artists had made distinct impressions on me, Cecilia Beaux had the most influence on my work. Naturally, a confluence of artists lent to my style and technique. But I'd been smitten with Beaux's work since first seeing it all those many years ago. Molly hadn't forgotten. I wondered, had she actually put the book back thinking I somehow might find it? Probably not, but I had.

I replaced it in my shopping bag and carefully took out the little cup and saucer. Standing only about two inches high, the cup had elegantly inscribed flourishes in delft blue. Blue was Molly's favorite color. This was her favorite restaurant in London. Carefully I placed the little teacup down on its saucer. Gazing at the teapot on the table, I smiled and poured a spot of tea into the miniature cup. I toasted, saying in my mind, "For you, Molly. I'll forever love you." Tears formed in my eyes as I sipped.

Chapter 49

For the next three days, I painted relentlessly. Having told Bethany that, per Fiona, I was under extreme duress to paint, I gave her the option to stay with me at the hotel while I painted. The option was hardly a good one for someone in a newly formed romance. She elected to stay, informing me I needed someone to wash my brushes. She also joked that I needed a handler-slash-keeper.

Between watching me work and being ignored, Bethany more than proved her dedication. She spent her nonworking time at my side. What I failed to tell her was that looking across the room and seeing her smile actually fortified my massive resolve to complete the final three paintings. She did, as promised, clean my brushes. She also ordered food for us and rubbed my sometimes-aching shoulders.

I hadn't the words to tell her how she inspired me to continue. When she thanked me for the roses, I failed to mention she deserved flowers every day. Being with me, understanding me, and loving me couldn't be easy. A quickly whispered "thanks" when she poured tea and brought it to me seemed only barely gracious. As I finished *Ladybugs Rock London*, I hoped she could see the gratitude in my eyes.

As hours and days dwindled, I was working on *Perpetual Smile*. It was beginning to get the exact look Molly gave me as she turned back while getting into the limousine. I had superimposed a tote bag that hung from Molly's shoulder. The small cup and saucer peeked out from it. In her arm was the book she'd perused. They seemed not only appropriate but also necessary. I made a mental note to send the little tea set to Samantha and to tell her the story about Molly's cosseting it at the market.

By Friday midafternoon, I had completed *Perpetual Smile* to my satisfaction. It was my final painting to be included in the show. I called the gallery to have the canvases picked up. The gallery had already selected the frames. The grand finale, after the show's closing, would be the Ladybugs Rock party.

Bethany had gone back to her apartment to get ready. She said she would meet me at the gallery at seven. Fiona had called several times to verify and set prices. Her price list included a few that were in the gallery, a dozen sent from Colorado a couple of days earlier, and the works I had produced within the last week.

The final time she called, she was doing the tally and realized I'd completed a total of ten pictures during the two weeks I'd been in London.

"Maybe you should think of relocating," she said with a taunting lilt to her voice.

"This has been an extraordinary time in my life. I've never been the world's most prolific painter. I'm certain there's no way I can keep up this pace."

"Picasso did."

"I probably won't. So don't bet the farm on it."

"Well, it's wonderful, Danielle. I'm thrilled. And I'm personally purchasing the *Ladybugs Rock England* painting. I've never been a model before."

"Maybe some of the nightmarish harridans painted by that German artist are meant to be you."

"Oh, fuck you," she said as casually as if she were asking me to tea. "You're such a character."

I held the phone back and looked disbelievingly at it. "I'm the character?"

"I'm not character material. Bitch, yes. Character, no."

"You haven't told me if you like your image in *Ladybugs Rock England*."

"I do. I wouldn't buy it if I didn't like it. In fact, if you didn't make me look damned good, the painting would be exhibiting in South Dirt Road, Colorado."

"Where?" I asked.

"Precisely. Enough said. I'm paying full price, too. I didn't off-price it."

"That was good of you. What was the price?"

"Two-hundred grand."

"Do I have to make change?" Would I ever get used to the seemingly excessive price tags on my work?

"I took my fifteen percent off the top. Don't worry, I'll make it back if I ever want to sell it. And then some."

"If? You'd consider selling it?"

"You're right. I'll probably have it off the frame and tucked in my casket with me. Until then, I'm putting it in my main living room in my Manhattan penthouse. Not everyone is a fucking Ladybugs Rock mascot. Which reminds me, I booked The Scripted Banquet for our party."

"Nothing but the best for your Saph buddies."

"Don't be late."

"Fiona, I wouldn't dream of it."

I hung up. Because I was in fact running late, I called the jewelers and asked that they deliver the five gold ladybug pins to the hotel. The manager assured me he'd checked the engravings, and the order was exactly to my specification. I jumped in the shower, dressed, and nibbled on a salad I'd ordered. The gold pins arrived, and the manager was right. They looked terrific.

Esther was ready and would drop by my room so we could walk together to the gallery. When she arrived, she gushed over my newest outfit, a pant and jacket set finely tailored in powder blue. She modeled a new apricot-colored, elbow-sleeved cardigan. Matching slacks along with nutmeg accessories gave her a look of perfect autumn style.

She pointed to my shoes. "You could have used a little more of a stacked-heel, but I truly love the outfit. Flattering."

"You like it because I didn't pick it out. Bethany shopped for me yesterday while I put the finishing touches on one of the paintings. She has style and class. I'd have bought some dowdy duds that would never have met with your approval."

"This exceeds expectations. With Bethany around, there's hope that your frump stage may be a thing of the past. You look wonderful."

"Thanks, you look wonderful, too. But then you usually do." I suddenly stopped. "You haven't mentioned my relationship with Bethany. You aren't working on me tonight?"

"Nope. Talked with her earlier. She thinks you're right. You wore her down with your complete indifference and probably all the crap about still loving Molly."

"She also probably got fed up babysitting me while I painted. See, women don't want to be left behind by someone so compulsive about art."

"You're right, Danielle. Someone else will snap her up. Now that she knows she can fall in love again, she'll find someone who cares about her."

I felt a sudden stabbing to my heart. "She didn't talk with me about this."

"There's no reason to. You've made your position very clear."

"I don't want her doing anything that commits to my life. She was talking about giving up her job, her home, and everything."

"Why shouldn't she? She's eligible for a handsome retirement. She has savings, company stock, nearly free airline service. More than enough money to provide for her upkeep wherever she wants to live. Health care, security, pension, everything she needs. I'm certain she knows the words to our national anthem. And Canada's. And England's. She's flexible with the world."

"Money isn't a problem. I could provide for her, and I would."

"With the recent surge in your income, you might feel as though her stash can't compare to yours. You might suspect that she hasn't paid the price of being by your side when things were slim picking. Well, consider this. She spent two decades of her life backing a singer who was just on the edge of becoming a great opera star. Bethany didn't waver. She paid the price to the arts. She's an honest human being."

"I know she's not after my money or notoriety, Esther. I've never believed she was."

"Of course not. When you met her two weeks ago, her bank account was undoubtedly far more substantial than yours. Your retirement fund was nonexistent, bank account slim pickings. If you recall, you were hard-pressed to scrape enough together to get your poor old car's radiator fixed last month. You were happy to get fifteen grand on a sale in Albuquerque. That was the state of your fortune when she met you. She didn't set out to profit from your sudden, meteoritic rise in capital. Or celebrity."

"That's not it at all. I don't care what she has or doesn't have. I'm falling in love with her. But I'm frightened..." I started crying. "Oh, hell, my makeup's going to run."

"It can use a brushup anyway. Danielle, what are you really so terrified about?"

"Being left behind," I finally confessed. I went to the dresser mirror and spread a quick layer of makeup around my eyes. "I know it isn't rational, but I expect everyone to run out on me now."

She took me in her arms. "The only running Bethany does is when she's in training. She would never run from you. The question is, will you be there for her."

I grabbed my handbag, stuffed the jeweler's sack inside, and turned back to Esther. "Until I'm sure, I won't consider anything permanent."

"Nothing in life is permanent. You should know that by now. Let's go. Fiona will flay your bum if we're late."

We took the elevator down and walked out onto the street. "What does Bethany see in me?"

"I haven't got a clue as to what any woman would see in you," she said dramatically. "You're an abysmal disappointment to me. Buzzards have been circling your sex life for years. Not only have you hidden out, but women weren't exactly stampeding to you. Finally, you meet the perfect woman, and you disconnect. You're a damned black hole of neediness. You're this accretion disk that exhausts people. Especially women. Particularly me."

"Sorry for burdening your life," I said sarcastically.

"Danielle, you're burdening your own life. Repeatedly, you've told me your grandfather's saying about tough times. That if you take a hit, get back on your feet, make a fist at life, and then go on."

"I remember. I'd nearly forgotten."

"Listen, I want an answer. Are you in love with her?"

"I've told you. I do love her. I'm just scared."

"Sweet cakes, you better put on those big girl panties and grow up. For whatever reason, she loves you. She doesn't need you or your fortune."

"I do care for her."

"You are the most insecure ingrate I've ever met. Care for her? Days have dwindled down to almost the time of our departure while you sit on your pity pot. Now we're down to a day. Our plane leaves tomorrow morning, and you've run her off."

"It's better if she leaves me now than it would be later after we lived together."

"It isn't like you, Danielle. You're being cruel. One of my exes used to say that it's nice to be important but more important to be nice."

"Was that because you weren't being nice?"

She glared at me. "You are best in small doses."

"And you're bitchy in large doses!" I reached for the gallery's door handle. We entered, and I studied the crowded room. The final closing party Fiona and Max had planned with patrons, art critics, and media, was in full swing. "I don't see Bethany."

"She's probably come to her senses and is doing something incredibly important with her life. Like watching BBC." Her dour expression changed. "Ah, but I see my sweet little crumpet."

Esther walked toward Carrie. I went back outside to fill my lungs with air. I'd never experienced claustrophobia before. I never knew how uncomfortable it was to be alone in a throng of people. Emotions were an extension of us. We were all balled up in our own hemisphere, and we struggled. If not dashing toward a cluster of fellow human beings, we were making attempts to extricate ourselves from society. Not much of it was rational. In two weeks, I had spent the most irrational, profoundly painful, and upliftingly joyous moments of my life.

Outside I breathed deeply. I glanced at the gallery front with fancy scripted placards resting on easels that announced my work. My offering to humanity. Me. Well, that was another question. I may well have been affiliated with those canvases that were smeared with paint and my heart. But me?

Touching the large placard, I felt the inked ridges of my name. Maybe an important part of life was the self-discovery of knowing we might one day find our true selves. Locating the *me* in each of us was revelatory. As important, was finding the others in *me*. I suddenly balled my hand into a fist, raised it up, and gave it a couple of whirls.

Chapter 50

Upon reentering the gallery, I spied Fiona.

"You're actually on time," she said as she took my arm.

She introduced me to what seemed like hundreds of people. I maintained a degree of pleasantry. I glanced in each direction as we walked. Pieces of conversations penetrated my mind. One critic told me I caught emotional flashes in my paintings that he'd never seen before. Another said my work resonated.

When finally alone with Fiona a moment, I asked, "What the hell are they talking about?"

"You. Unlike the people who know you, they think you're terrific."

"You've been talking with Esther again, haven't you?"

"Yes. To quote her, you're impossible. Carrie is more generous. She says you're causing everyone a great deal of agro by being a sarky bitch."

"Have you seen Bethany?"

"I've seen her. Just not tonight. But I don't think you've ever really seen her, Danielle. Funny, because you paint her beautiful soul with such authenticity. Within *Bethany's Smile*, it seems apparent you understand her integrity and love for you." She shrugged. "Guess not. I've always maintained you're a crazy Saph. Now more than ever."

"Have we sold any paintings?" I tried changing the subject to Fiona's favorite topic.

"Amazingly, almost all of the new ones are gone. Samantha phoned earlier and purchased *Perpetual Smile* and three of your earlier paintings: one of the herbs growing in pots on a balcony terrace; a scene of snow with cross-country skiers; and another of a little boy seated on his tricycle. Said it reminded her of her younger son."

"I've never seen her younger son. The child I painted is my neighbor. He's in high school now."

"She saw it on the gallery's Internet page. Loved it. By the way, she said to tell you good luck with the show. She also said to tell you she'll be in contact later in the week, after you've returned to Colorado."

"I owe Samantha and her husband a great deal. I'd like to do a formal painting of Samantha and her family. Before you ask, yes, without charge. Maybe she could phone photo me a picture of them all together. I could take the painting to them when I attend Molly's service."

"They haven't set a date?"

"I'm thinking that's probably what she wanted to talk with me about." Again, I pivoted around. "What else sold?"

"All of Bethany's portraits sold, and some fool bought the one of those stupid bison."

"Who purchased them?"

"I haven't a clue. Probably a Buffalo Bill descendent. Max informed me when I got here that they'd sold. Investors are buying anything with an O'Hara signature, even ridiculous toy bison."

"They aren't ridiculous." I searched the gallery again. "I wonder what's keeping Bethany."

"I'm guessing what's keeping Bethany away is a crazy Saph artist. I mostly use the word 'fool' as a habit. But in your case, I truly mean it. You are a fool. You've treated her dreadfully. Esther's right."

"I knew Esther had a say in this."

"It's not her fault you're pitching love away with both hands. Esther keeps you stabilized. I couldn't have handled you the past couple of weeks without her. I'm going to pick up her hotel tab. That woman needs to be put on the payroll to keep you in line."

"None of this has been easy for me to cope with, Fiona."

"I know you almost as well as you know yourself. I know you from your art. You're happy when Bethany's with you. You're productive. In my case, I know what's right for me." She scanned the room. "See that adorable Italian over there?" I followed her gaze. "He writes for one of the London dailies. He is *so* right for me. He's here with that scraggy woman over by the wine bar. But he's taking me to dinner tomorrow night."

I squinted to get a better look. "Good Lord, he can't be over twenty-five."

She smacked my shoulder. "You're way off. He's twenty-seven. Slightly young for me. But look at that body."

"You are one fired up Ladybugs Rock mascot. Or maybe you'll start a chapter in New York. Call it Cougars Rock."

"I'm hoping the Italian won't give me time enough for social groups." She grinned at me and then in his direction. "It certainly doesn't hurt his cause that he thinks you're the new messiah of portraiture, and he does know who Cecilia Beaux is."

"Imagine a critic actually knowing the name of a well-hidden portraitist."

"Imagine an intelligent art critic with incredible abs." Fiona fanned her face. "And those Italians live up to their legacy. He told me I'm very cool."

"You are, Fiona. You've taken me from anonymity in the art world to this. In my eyes, that makes you totally cool." I looked at my watch. "Only an hour more to go and we can hightail it over to The Scripted Banquet. Have a little Ladybugs Rock festival."

For the next hour, between chats with patrons and critics, I scoured the room for Bethany. I wondered if she hadn't arrived because it was over between us. I examined my cell phone. Calls from everyone except Bethany. I'd already left her a half-dozen messages.

"Got a limousine waiting," Fiona said as we exited. "I'm not trusting a Bentley in Carrie's hands again."

Once we arrived and entered The Scripted Banquet, I resumed my search for Bethany. Maybe she had relented and would at least see me to say goodbye. That seemed not to be the case. As wine was served, I glanced over at the empty chair where Bethany should've been.

My heart sank.

Halfway through the first glass of wine, I looked up. Bethany was making her way toward the table.

She kissed my cheek. "Sorry. Forgive me for missing your show's closing. We had a red alert emergency. I was called in, and obviously I couldn't contact you." Tears welled in her eyes. "For over twenty-five years, I've been living my professional life for the airline. I've missed so many of the parts of life I would've liked to have experienced. This one was so important, and it was beyond my control. Forgive me?"

I couldn't keep the smile off my face. "It's okay, Bethany. I was worried that you were upset with me."

"No. I'm upset with myself right now. It's time I stop living my life around my job. It shouldn't be that way. I wanted so to be here with you." She straightened her hair. "I must look a wreck."

"You look wonderful."

Her eyes were somber. "You'll hear about it in the news. We had a terrorist threat. Things were extremely tense."

Esther's eyes opened wide. "We're flying out of here in the morning, taking a British Airways 777 out of Heathrow. Was the threat a 777?"

"It was international," Bethany said. "But now is the safest time to travel. After an incident, security really tightens up. Tomorrow when you board, they'll probably do a strip search."

We laughed uproariously. I waited until I could catch my breath. "Come on, Esther, you might like it."

Carrie poured Bethany some wine. We lifted our glasses. "Ladybugs Rock, forever!" we said together.

Throughout the evening, we chanted our motto. Other patrons often joined in. As dinner ended, I took the engraved ladybug pins from my handbag. After ceremoniously pinning them on each member's blouse, I raised my glass for a final toast of the evening. "To the London Sisterhood of Ladybugs Rock."

Bethany's smile was her first uncomplicated smile of the night. She'd been visibly tense.

"You're safe now," I whispered.

"Perhaps." Her eyes dimmed slightly. "But unforeseen crisis is always around. From the Jetway, to the tarmac, and in the air. Some humans are evil."

"Most humans aren't." I took her hand in mine and kissed her fingertips.

After dinner, we left. Fiona was somewhat blitzed. When the limousine arrived at her hotel, she told me I was probably not a complete fool. She wished us a good, safe return trip to Colorado. I was to keep a bleeping paintbrush in hand until Boston. I promised I'd be diligent in producing more paintings.

As the limo driver dropped off Carrie and Esther at Carrie's, Esther told me she would take a cab to the airport in the morning and meet me at the check-in desk.

I hugged Carrie goodbye. She whispered in my ear, "You must keep one thing in mind. Bethany can move anywhere she wants, anytime she wants. If she wants to up sticks and move, she can. You and Bethany belong together. That's it, really."

The trip to the Marshall inched on until we arrived in my suite. Carrie's words echoed. I wondered if that really was it. Bethany appeared glum, but no more than I. She'd slipped one of the tiny bison into my handbag. I missed her already.

As we slid beneath the covers, her warmth enticed me. Within her embrace, I understood that this was really it. I moved away from her.

"What's wrong?" she asked.

"Bethany, you know I have feelings for you. Sometimes loving someone means you need to give them time to consider. You need to consider what our being together would cost you."

"We've been over this. I'm willing to take the chance." Her face reflected the pain of rejection. "It's evident that you aren't. You've dealt with so much, and in so little time, Danielle. I can't blame you for wanting..." She hesitated. "For needing a time-out."

My hand swiped across my eyes. They burned from executing the many miniscule brushstrokes over the past two weeks and from the multitude of tears I'd shed. "I'm sorry for what I've put you through. You deserve better."

She closed her eyes. It reminded me of the final curtain dropping on a play. When she opened them again, she sighed. "You could be right, but I don't believe you are. I love you more than you'll ever know."

I started to speak and stopped as I gathered my thoughts. "Bethany, I've never known a more special woman than you."

Those words were all I was willing to give at that moment, but we both knew I hadn't said enough.

Chapter 51

Esther and I boarded easily without the strip search. We took our first-class seats that Fiona had upgraded. We began to chat. Esther was ecstatic. Beyond the flight upgrade, Fiona had picked up her hotel bill.

Then Esther immediately zeroed in on last night. "How did it go with Bethany?"

"A very warm and gentle night. Difficult to say goodbye this morning."

"You're so lucky. Don't you realize most of us don't even meet one good, tenderhearted woman who's compatible? You've had two women fall in love with you."

"One left me," I reminded her.

"But Molly continued to love you, and there were extenuating circumstances. That leaves one who still loves you."

"I know where this conversation is going, Esther. I realize I'm taking a chance in not making a commitment now. I asked Bethany to visit in a couple of weeks."

"Listen to yourself. Do you think you might want to take the chance on love again?"

"Not at someone else's expense." I opened my shoulder bag and saw the toy stuffed bison. I wondered if Bethany might be looking at hers.

"Oh, then by all means, be an altruistic jerk. Give up the woman you love because you don't want to inconvenience her. Great plan, Danielle."

I looked out onto the tarmac. "After saying goodbye to her earlier this morning, I'll admit, I might have made a big mistake. I can't stop thinking about her. Wishing she were here with me. Love makes all parting sad."

"Not loving makes the world sad. You are such a pillock."

"Is that Carrie's latest name for me?"

"Mine and hers. She calls Fiona a sweet rum-bucket."

I said with humor, "Fiona does put it away. I believe she drank two bottles of wine. And they were of an extremely expensive vintage. Hope she'll be okay for her big date tonight."

"She's shameless. Needless to say, we had a hilarious time. Once Bethany arrived, it all seemed complete."

"How was your parting with Carrie?"

"Hot and heavy. She'll be visiting Colorado next month. I'll be heading back to England the following month. The month after that, she has a couple of comp cruise tickets, and she's invited me."

"You're going to have a heavy travel schedule."

"And Bethany will be making at least one transatlantic."

"Maybe she'll decide my lifestyle isn't for her."

"She's certainly not a mediocre human being. That reminds me of the Principle of Mediocrity."

"Mediocrity has its own principle?" I asked with disbelief.

Esther straightened in her seat as if preparing to launch into a lecture. "The Principle of Mediocrity suggests that life on earth isn't exceptional at all. There's a good possibility that life is likely to be found on many other planets. There's also the Anthropic Principle that believes the fundamental laws of the universe work to make life possible. Random chance. Like meeting people you really care about. I introduced you to two extraordinary women—Molly and Bethany—and you fell in love with them. Or are you even in love with Bethany?"

I hesitated only slightly. "Yes, I am, but I also love my home. I can't wait to get back there and to see little Clover."

"Clover will be excited to see you. Sadie and Aggie will be ecstatic to see me."

"I'm sure Bethany will love Clover, too. She always had Yorkshire Terriers up until the final one died a few years ago." I thought about the day I comforted her when she told me about her dogs.

"You keep bringing up Bethany's name. I take it you miss her already? I knew you would. Admit it, you miss her." Esther nudged me.

"Yes, I miss her. I'm taking a huge chance in leaving her behind, even for a couple of weeks. But she's got her job and her home to think about."

"You must realize she's totally burnt out on her job. Who wouldn't be? Who needs to live that 'hair-on-fire' existence? Even if you aren't in the picture, she's going to be leaving her job. She talked with Carrie about going on a leave of absence. LOAs are for six months. You know, if she didn't like Colorado, she could always return to London and the airlines. Carrie said she'd always have a home with her. Bethany is a more adventuresome person than you are. I'm astounded you interest her at all. Or that you interest any woman of substance for that matter."

"Esther, I'm feeling beat up enough without your help. You're right about the LOA. I know I made a mistake. I should have just helped her pack." My resolve was crumbling. "I was wrong. I didn't even tell her I loved her before I left."

"Is that how you truly feel? You are the most skittish human being alive."

"Random chance," I repeated what Esther had said earlier. "That's my life of complete mediocrity. You're right. I never take chances because I'm frightened. If I had my wish, Bethany would be with me right now. We each took a bison." I again examined the small stuffed bison that jutted from my bag. "They shouldn't be parted. They're a matching set."

"Call her and tell her that."

It suddenly dawned on me that everyone was right. If she didn't want to be with me, she would make her own decision. "Maybe she can take a flight out tomorrow. I'll invite her." I fumbled with my cell phone.

Esther smirked with satisfaction.

While I punched up her number on my telephone contact list, I watched the final passengers boarding. Soon I'd be flying away from the woman I loved. When she answered, I rushed on with what I wanted to say.

"Bethany, I've made a terrible mistake. Forgive me. I realize now that I want you with me. I love you."

"I was beginning to think my wait might be forever," she said. "But it was worth the wait to hear your words."

"I know this sounds crazy, but is there any chance you can board a plane tomorrow or the next day? As soon as you can? I can't wait to show you my Colorado."

From my periphery, I saw Esther moving to the inside seat. I looked down the aisle. There Bethany stood folding her cell phone.

"And I can't wait to see *our* Colorado through your eyes, Danielle. My LOA began today." She examined her wristwatch. "Officially, an hour ago. I'm free."

Standing, I hugged her tightly as I blinked back tears. "This is one of the best moments in my life." I moved to the next seat and motioned for Bethany to sit.

"Mine as well."

"What if I hadn't called you?" I asked.

"I'd have taken the airline's quickest turn out of Denver. Even if I had to sit on a jump seat for the return trip across the pond."

"But you would have come to visit me in Colorado?"

"Of course."

As she sat down and buckled up, I couldn't take my gaze from her. This was a moment of enchantment. I took her hand. "I do love you so."

Esther suddenly piped in, saying, "I just thought of something. If Bethany's here, who's watching out for bad guys?"

"We're well-covered," Bethany told her.

"You knew about this, Esther?"

"Naturally. I'm always a shuttle ride ahead of you. I told Bethany you would regret your decision. That at least by mid ocean, you would be wishing you'd taken a chance. We didn't even get off the ground, and you recognized your mistake. So I congratulate you."

"Thanks," I said as I glowered mockingly at her. I turned back to Bethany and mouthed the words, "I love you."

Bethany laughed as she squeezed my hand. "Yes, finally the words. And although it must be obvious by now, I'm also in love with you."

As the plane began its ascent, I felt exhilaration. The plane continued to climb, and I felt love's radiant elevation. I was going home. And I was sitting between two Ladybugs. One was my dear friend; the other was the woman with whom I'd fallen in love.

Part training, part diligence, Bethany began her checklist. "Can't wait to meet your family and friends. I'll need names and descriptions so I can keep everyone in order. But first, I want to meet Clover. I'll definitely know her without so much as an introduction."

"Clover will be thrilled to know you get the truly important things first. She appreciates proper prioritization."

"Unlike you. You seemed to have left the most important thing until last."

"Bethany, I promise you it's the last time you won't be first in my life. That's my first plan."

"What do you have in mind for the second, luv?"

"It looks like a Yorkie will be joining our household," I said with a chuckle. "We can expect the pitter patter of extremely tiny paws."

Epilogue

Nearly a month after I arrived back in Colorado, I boarded a private jet for Palo Alto, California. It was still very early when we landed. Samantha and Jeffery had insisted that they send their private jet to bring me to Molly's service. They were aware I didn't like being away from my home. According to the flight schedule, I would be returned home before Denver's sunset.

When I arrived at the Wesleys' luxurious beachside home, I immediately understood the beauty Molly loved about California. I also experienced the love everyone felt for Molly. Before the outdoor garden services began, I looked out at the crowd of her family and friends who knew and loved her.

A giant wall of flowers and floral sprays lined the area. The family understood fully the unconventional plant arrangement I'd chosen. I had sent a huge decorative container of pansies and assorted scented geraniums. Samantha and Jeff's sons constantly patted the geraniums' sprigs with precision, just as Molly had done decades ago. Lifting from the greenery was the redolence of Molly's favorite plant. The boys giggled as they bent and sniffed. I overheard them naming the pansies.

Samantha commented that Molly would have loved it. Even more, Molly would have loved a woman's comment I overheard. She said the plant was the most exotic she'd ever seen. Molly and I would have had an outrageous laugh at that.

My eyes suddenly became teary as I stared at the shiny silver funeral urn containing Molly's ashes. On either side were the many paintings I'd done of her. Lining the ultra-luxurious terrace, they stretched for many yards. From paintings of her in her youth to the final painting, her beauty was evident. Samantha told me that Molly loved this place most of all.

The ocean roared in the background as a small orchestral group played ABBA's "I Have a Dream."

"It was her favorite," Samantha said. "But you know that."

"It came out after she left. Or rather as she was leaving." But I knew it was Molly's favorite. I just knew.

"I'm so pleased you can be here, Danielle. Thank you for the painting of the family. We all treasure it as well as the tiny teacup and saucer. The teacup set does have meaning. I had a similar set when I was a child. Mom and I had tea parties." Her eyes glistened in the sun. "Gingersnaps and herbal mint tea. Mom lavishly fixed my small table with a snack feast. How we loved those parties."

"She was always wonderful with children. Everyone, actually."

"Yes, everyone. You're settling back in Colorado?"

"Early days, but I'm very happy." Happier than I'd been for thirty years, or thought I would ever be again, I admitted to myself. Part of the delight was witnessing the joy and love Bethany was experiencing. Both a jubilant Clover and our new little Gidgie-Two provided her with much contentment. Family and friends, of course, loved her.

Since Bethany's arrival, the house had become more than my studio with a structure attached. She had made it a home where love transformed each room into light, laughter, and warmth. I was no longer an unabridged soul. A mirthful exuberance heightened my senses. I'd gone from living for art to living with art, and with Bethany.

"I'm so glad to hear that." Samantha put her arm around my shoulder. "I know it would have pleased Mom to know you're happy."

I was also of the opinion my newfound love was what Molly had wanted for me. She had once told me that the truest gift of love was the way it made a person feel about themselves. Molly's philosophy was accurate. I was no longer weighed down by concerns of being inadequate; love had made me someone's champion.

Samantha interrupted my musings. "How is your painting coming along for the Boston exhibit?"

"Bethany insists that I paint. Fiona is pleased with my production, so all is on point."

"Bethany's good for you, Danielle. She's doing the art world a great service by encouraging you."

"Which reminds me, Bethany and I would like to invite your family to stay with us. Maybe visit for a skiing trip. Bethany has fallen in love with Colorado. She's investing some of her retirement funds to purchase a place in Aspen. Somewhere we can go to unwind. Anyway, we'd love you all to join us. It would be great fun to get your boys interested in snowshoeing and cross-country skiing."

She laughed. "I'd like to redirect them from snowboarding. We'd enjoy getting to know both you and Bethany better. Although our lives are extremely full, I miss Mom, and you enrich my memories of her. Maybe it was some serendipitous good fortune we met. First of the year good?"

"It's wonderful. Just let me know when you can make it, and we'll put up signs restricting all snowboarding. It will be a rule of the mountain." I somehow knew we would all become very close. Love spills over. "I haven't officially met your sons yet."

She looked puzzled. "Sorry, I thought Jeffery had introduced you earlier." She motioned for the boys, and they quickly arrived at our side. "This is your grandmother's friend from Colorado," she told them. "Danielle, I'd like you to meet our son Daniel and our younger son, Jeffery Junior, or as we call him, JJ."

I extended my hand. "JJ, and Daniel."

Suddenly, the realization hit me. I surveyed Samantha's face.

She nodded. "Mom named the boys. Daniel is your namesake. She loved you more than you can ever imagine."

That wasn't true at all. Something inside me had always imagined. Indeed, for many decades I had imagined. I had long ago envisioned love. Tenaciously, Molly and I had held onto our love. A love in our hearts that was indestructible.

There might have been many explanations and excuses. But we both had believed in love. Not just the everyday love, for that had eluded our lives. But beyond was a consequential, extravagant love that transcended the moments of our time and bound us to one another's dreams. Certainly, Molly never left my life, no matter where she was. In spite of it all, she and I lived love's most precious and unceasing excursion. Perhaps it would forever be our destination. Eternal love had filled our souls faster than life emptied them.

Simply put, I do believe in angels. Yes, I shall forever believe in love.

Author Kieran York

About the Author

Kieran York has authored both Sapphic fiction and poetry. Her lesbian mystery series *Timber City Masks* and *Crystal Mountain Veils,* featuring Royce Madison, were written and published in the mid – 1990s. She also wrote a collection of lesbian short fiction entitled *Sugar With Spice* – published in 1989.

In 2012, York's book, *Appointment with a Smile,* was published and was a 2013 Lambda Literary Society Award Finalist in the romance category. Her next novel, *Careful Flowers,* was released in 2013, followed by two releases in 2014 – *Earthen Trinkets* and *Night Without Time,* published by Scarlet Clover Publishers. Forthcoming is *Touring Kelly's Poem* and *Loitering on the Frontier*

York was also a contributor in *Sappho's Corner Poetry Series – Wet Violet, Volume 2; Roses Read, Volume 3;* and *Delectable Daisies, Volume 4.*

In 2014, her volume of poetry, *Blushing Aspen,* was published as the Sappho's Corner Solo Poets book of poetry, and won The Rainbow Award Honorable Mention for poetry.

Previously, during the seventies and eighties, Kieran worked as a reporter and reviewer for both newspapers and magazines, and was a newspaper publisher for three years. She also wrote and performed songs with a woman's band. She has been guest lecturer and panel member at various events, including Rocky Mountain Book Exhibition, Colorado Musicians Series, Sisters in Crime Mystery Writers, and Mystery Writers of America, Inc. She is a member of Lambda Literary Society, and Golden Crown Literary Society.

She has written for *Journal of Mystery Readers International.* In addition, she has given numerous campus and coffeehouse poetry readings, as well as taught poetry and creative writing workshops.

She graduated from a Kansas university and attended Mexico's University of the Americas her junior year. She has done graduate work at the University of Colorado.

Kieran lives in the Rocky Mountain foothills of Colorado with her schnauzer, Clover. She enjoys gardening, music, literature, and art. She considers her valuables to include Clover and other family and friends, her library, her antique typewriter collection, her guitar, and her garden.

Additional information is available on her websites: www.scarletcloverpublishers.com and she has a blog – Embellish Your Smile at http://kieranyork.com.

FORTHCOMING IN 2015......

Touring Kelly's Poems

Touring Kelly's Poem takes place in 1963. A small-town Kansas student travels to Mexico City to search. 'Search' is the keyword for her year of finding herself within the constant grip of adventure. It is two books in one – a very large read.

Kelly Benjamin is turning twenty when a skiing accident redirects her life. With humor, and with the pathos known to youth, Kelly wants one thing most – to be a poet. Her new roommates are: a 'proper' fellow student, a wild European prostitute, and a lesbian archeology student. That should have been enough excitement for her.

Then she met the beguiling Doctora. Now that was enough excitement for anyone.

Loitering on the Frontier

Things were different in the gay and lesbian world of the mid-sixties. Olivia Kirby had just moved to Denver, Colorado. She entered the shabby lesbian bar, where she witnessed the commission of a crime. From then on, she was endangered – she was hunted. Terrified, she hid out - and hoped.

Hatred and bigotry are always dangerous. On the way to saving herself – she fell in love.

Human beings reside within the heart of time. We are born inside a slot of actuality. Our soul lights up at the time and place where we become our own.

If love is the art of shelter, maybe we can all become more cognizant of taking care of one another – sheltering one another.

OTHER PUBLISHED TITLES BY KIERAN YORK

Fiction:

Sugar With Spice
Publisher: Banned Books (November 1989)

Timber City Masks
Publisher: Third Side Press, 1st Edition (May 1993)
Publisher: Scarlet Clover Publishers, 2nd Edition, (November 2014)

Crystal Mountain Veils
Publisher: Third Side Press, 1st Edition (April 1995)
Publisher: Scarlet Clover Publishers, 2nd Edition, (January 2015)

Appointment with a Smile
Publisher: Blue Feather Books, 1st Edition (March 2012)
Publisher: Scarlet Clover Publishers, 2nd Edition (January 2015)

Careful Flowers
Publisher: Blue Feather Books, 1st Edition (October 2013)
Publisher: Scarlet Clover Publishers, 2nd Edition (January 2015)

Earthen Trinkets
Publisher: Scarlet Clover Publishers, (September 2014)

Night Without Time
Publisher: Scarlet Clover Publishers, (November 2014)

Touring Kelly's Poem
Publisher: Scarlet Clover Publishers, (forthcoming 2015)

Loitering on the Frontier
Publisher: Scarlet Clover Publishers, (forthcoming 2015)

Poetry:
Blushing Aspen
Publisher: UltraVioletLove Publishing, (May 2014)

www.ingramcontent.com/pod-product-compliance
Lightning Source LLC
Chambersburg PA
CBHW071006280626
47160CB00015B/1418